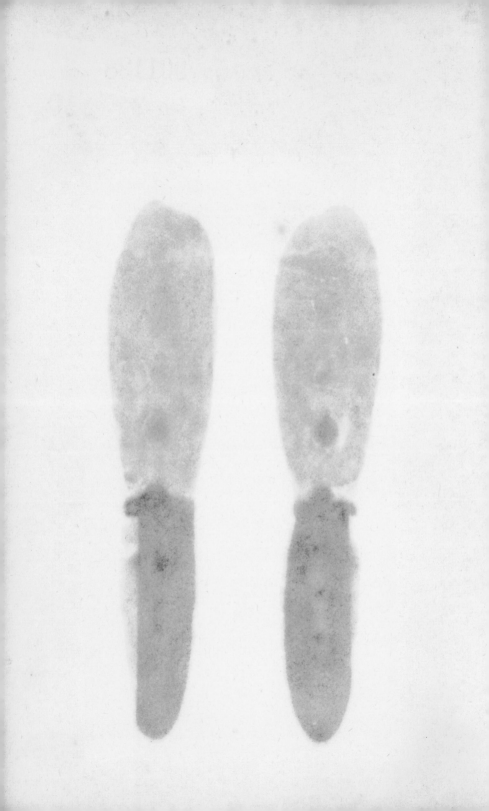

MUSIC WHEN
SWEET VOICES DIE

MUSIC WHEN SWEET VOICES DIE

by

Chelsea Quinn Yarbro

G. P. Putnam's Sons · New York

Copyright © 1979 by Chelsea Quinn Yarbro

All rights reserved. This book, or parts thereof, must
not be reproduced in any form without permission.
Published simultaneously in Canada by Longman Canada Limited,
Toronto.

Library of Congress Cataloging in Publication Data

Yarbro, Chelsea Quinn, 1942-
    Music when sweet voices die.

    I. Title.
PZ4.Y25Mu   [PS3575.A7]   813'.5'4   78-13324

SBN: 399-12004-1

PRINTED IN THE UNITED STATES OF AMERICA

—

for
The San Francisco Opera Company
with a quarter century of love

ACKNOWLEDGMENTS

The writer wishes to thank the following persons for their time, their encouragement and their generosity in sharing knowledge and expertise:

Mr. Frederick D. Gottfried, attorney-at-law

Ms. Wendy Rose, distinguished Indian poet and artist

The staff of the Magic Cellar, particularly Cedric and Jan Clute and magicians Paul Svengari and Arthur Murata

Ms. Sylvia M. Mollick, astrological consultant

Ms. Barbara Clifford, super with the San Francisco Opera

Mo. Robert and Mrs. Anneke Sayre

MUSIC WHEN
SWEET VOICES DIE

PROLOGUE

Wednesday
October 27, 1976

Gui-Adam Feuier knew he should not mix music and heroin. His eyes ached, and he lifted one elegant hand to his sweating brow. Only twelve minutes to go, then another ten for curtain calls. He groaned. Behind him, the scene change was under way, Venice disappearing into the fly gallery, giving way to Luther's Tavern once more. He sank heavily onto the chair at center stage, facing away from the audience, his arms on the back of the chair, his head pressed against the angle of his elbow.

From his vantage point in the pit, Maestro Richard Tey silently cursed Feuier. He would have to work around the tenor once again. With a gesture of his left hand, he brought out the bass sonority of Offenbach's music. By now, he had developed a fatalistic attitude about Feuier; he was not surprised that the tenor was ignoring him, the prompter, and the television monitors at either side of the stage. He turned his attention to the scene change and the final ritard of the "Barcarole."

He was feeling worse, if that was possible. Feuier bit into his hand and forced himself to breathe deeply. His senses were escaping him, and nausea surged through him. No good. No good. He sagged as his dizziness grew.

The stage manager checked the clock on his right, then glanced at his clipboard. The cues were running well tonight, everything smooth, everything right on tempo. He murmured a light cue into the pencil-thin microphone near his lips. The opera would be over by eleven-forty. Then it would be time for a drink and a long, hot bath.

The scene change was nearly complete. Where the groundrow of the Venetian skyline had been, there was now an ornately German tavern wall, and the sensuous, blue-tinged light had faded to a ruddy amber. The chorus, once again in their German students' costumes, gathered around Feuier, and a few of them exchanged exasperated glances. It was an awkward moment because, as usual, Feuier was not where he was supposed to be. The men had grown used to compensating for the unpredictable French tenor; they moved farther down-stage.
Jocelynne Hendricks, looking wonderfully boyish as Nicklausse, walked casually to Feuier's side, making her ironic toast to all Hoffmann's mistresses. For an instant, her eyes met Maestro Tey's, and she gave a fatalistic, almost imperceptible shrug.

Tory Ian Malcomb glared down at a slice of the stage from what was very likely the worst seat in the house. He had been General Manager of the opera somewhat less than six months, and he hated to see his pet production ruined by Feuier. This center-stage rebellion was typical of Feuier's behavior, and as Malcomb ground his teeth, he searched his mind for an excuse to fire the volatile French tenor. Crossing his arms, he waited to see what new outrage Feuier had planned for the end of this third performance of *Les Contes d'Hoffmann*.

When the musical bridge was through, Richard Tey looked up, his blue eyes crackling with energy. He motioned to the chorus, then waited for Feuier to make his response. When nothing happened, he beetled his brows and pointed to Jocelynne Hendricks, forcefully indicating that she should take the short phrase.

When she had sung the few words, the chorus came in too loudly, as if embarrassed by Feuier's latest display. As the tone changed, Feuier stirred, and his head lolled to one side. Jocelynne looked at him, and in that moment felt the stirrings of alarm. Her eyes flicked to Richard Tey, filled with meaning, and then to Tory Ian Malcomb in his inconvenient box. The men's chorus saw this, and a kind of apprehension made them falter in their singing.

Apparently the audience sensed something as well, for the rustling of whispers sighed around the cream-and-gilt Opera House like a low wind passing through trees. There was an extra tension in the air now.

In the prompter's box, Graeham Kelly looked up from the score again and felt his body go cold. He could see Gui-Adam Feuier's feet less than three yards away, and he could tell from their position that something was dreadfully wrong. Making a sudden decision, he lurched from the prompter's box, stumbling through the semidarkness to the stairs that would take him backstage.

Maestro Richard Tey had heard the prompter leave the box, and he felt his first real twinge of worry. He automatically cued Jocelynne to take Feuier's next short phrase, but he knew she could not do the one after, which was not only more extended, but was so clearly Hoffmann's music that the audience would be aware in an instant that there was trouble on the stage. Fixing Jocelynne in his bright stare, he mouthed, "What's wrong?"

He could sense that someone was touching him, but by now Gui-Adam was past caring. His body ached intolerably, and if it had not taken more strength than he had, he would have driven the people near him away by force and screamed. He remembered that he ought to be singing, but through the agony that possessed him, he was unable to think clearly. He tried to move in his chair, but even that little motion caught hold of him. The chair tipped over, and he fell to the stage, thrashing feebly. It was strange, he thought as he died. Heroin had never done that to him before.

The men of the chorus stopped, strangling on the rowdy words they had been singing. Jocelynne stepped back, her face gone white under her makeup. Out of the corner of her eye, she could see Tory Ian Malcomb as he bolted from his box, and then, as she turned, she glimpsed the horror on the stage manager's face. The noise in the house caught her attention, and she tried to see beyond the lights to the more than three thousand people gathered in the darkness.

Then, suddenly, Richard Tey's clenched fists were high in the air, like a rider lifting the head of a falling horse. He got the attention of the musicians and singers and cut them off cleanly as the curtain fell, shutting off the terrible sight on the stage.

A roar like the sea spread through the house. Consternation was reflected in every face, and panic threatened to erupt. Some of the audience were on their feet, and at least one woman was sobbing hysterically when the heavy gold curtains parted and Tory Ian Malcomb walked onto the apron.

"Ladies! Gentlemen! Please! If I may have your attention!" His damaged voice might not be able to sing, but it was still deep, resonant, and penetrating. He waited for silence with the calm authority that was enhanced by his great height: nearly six-and-a-half feet.

The tempest of voices became a buzz, then straggled away into nothing. Malcomb remained silent for a few moments longer, then said, "Thank you. Thank you very much. As I am sure you all realize, Mr. Feuier has suffered an unfortunate accident. For his sake as much as your own, I must ask you to leave the Opera House now. Please do not linger or wait in your seats. If you are parked on Van Ness, Franklin, or Grove, or in the lot across the street, I must ask you to wait in your cars until any emergency vehicle that might be required has come." He knew that there was already a call in for an ambulance. "Please do not ask the ushers for information. They know no more than any of you."

The muttering began again, and Malcomb raised his voice just enough to quiet it. "If there is anything seriously wrong, rest assured that the news media will make all information available to you as soon as possible." He said this with the cold certainty that he would have to deal with reporters within the next twenty minutes.

In the orchestra pit, Richard Tey said softly to his musicians, "No one is to leave until Malcomb gives us the signal. Do you understand?" He saw an uneasy acceptance in most faces. He singled out the most obviously upset of the players. "That includes you, Cranston," he warned the first bassoonist.

Tory Ian Malcomb was almost finished. "There is no need at all to rush. Leave by the nearest exit. The house staff will be on hand to help you if you require assistance. Let me thank you now for the consideration you've shown to Mr. Feuier." He looked over the restless house. "Those of you who are physicians and who have left your seat numbers with the box office, please stay where you are. If we need your assistance, one of the ushers will come for you." He took a deep breath. "We will be doing Rossini's *La Donna del Lago* on Friday night, as scheduled. We very much appreciate your cooperation, and on behalf of the entire company, I thank you." He kept his position on the apron until he saw the beginning of a fairly orderly departure. Then he stepped back through the curtains.

To one side of the stage, the chorus waited, saying little among themselves. The women, most of whom were out of costume now, stood with the men, and for one insane moment, Malcomb wondered if they would react to this death with the same music that had greeted Schlemil's death onstage.

He looked anxiously around for the rest of the cast. There was Elise Baumtretter, all rigged out as Stella, only the sequins on her face showing that she had not finished changing from the Giulietta makeup. Her huge eyes were horrified, and Malcomb knew that her torrential weeping was not far off.

Jocelynne Hendricks had disappeared, and it took Malcomb a moment to find her in the backstage shadows, in the protective, massive embrace of Domenico Solechiaro. Idly Malcomb wondered why Solechiaro was still in the building; his costume fitting had been finished more than an hour before.

On the other side of the stage, Cort Nørrehavn had come down from the baritone's stage-left dressing room. He was in between the characters of Dapertutto and Lindorf, long trousers contrasting oddly with his

Napoleonic embroidered velvet coat. Under his heavy makeup, his face was pasty with shock. "Good God," he said to no one in particular as he turned away, aghast. "How? How?"

"Mr. Malcomb," said a voice at his elbow. Tory Ian Malcomb looked into the frightened face of the prompter. "I checked him over," Graeham Kelly said, his hands moving nervously. "No mistake. He's dead." He stopped. "Should I get a doctor, do you think?"

Suddenly it was very still on the Opera House stage. "I saw Bob Curtis in the house," Malcomb said softly. "He's still in his seat. Left side, orchestra, row D. Someone bring him back here. And call the cops. Call the cops, then call the papers." There was little emotion in his voice, or in his face. Slowly he crossed the stage to the huddled figure of Gui-Adam Feuier. It occurred to him that this might well become one of those famous moments in opera, and that those who had been in the audience might take a perverse pride in having seen Feuier die.

As he stared down at the dead man, Tory Ian Malcomb did not know whether he should cry or laugh.

October 29
through
November 8,
1976

Friday, October 29

Charlie Moon had almost finished lugging the last of his book boxes into the hall when the phone rang. He swore as the box thudded to the floor. The phone rang again.

"Oh, all right," Charlie growled, abandoning the box to thread his way down the hall that had been made perilously narrow with more boxes. At last, he reached the phone stand at the head of the stairs and snatched the receiver from its cradle on the fourth ring. "Yes? This is Charles Moon."

"Your office said I'd find you there, Charlie," said the familiar, indomitable voice of Elizabeth Kendrie. "I'm glad I caught you before the moving van came."

"Good morning, Elizabeth," Charlie said, hoping vainly that this was a social call. "What can I do for you?"

She did not answer at once, and Charlie knew from long experience that this boded ill. "Well, if you have some time free this evening," she said with uncharacteristic reluctance, "I'd appreciate it if you'd have dinner with me . . ."

"I'm sorry, Elizabeth," Charlie cut in, secretly relieved that he had an excuse. "I'd love to come to dinner with you, but Morgan Studevant has already promised . . ."

"You may bring her, too, of course. This is business, Charlie. It's important."

Now, that imperious manner was more like the Elizabeth Kendrie Charlie knew. He was about to interrupt, but she went on. "I've taken the liberty of speaking to Ms. Studevant. She said that she'd be delighted to eat here."

"Elizabeth," Charlie began, knowing that it was a losing battle. "Look, Elizabeth, the moving van will be here in half an hour. I'm going to be moving all afternoon. I'm going to be awful company when all this is through."

"Then you'll be glad for a quiet meal and some stimulating conversation." She paused again, then said in quite another voice, "It *is* important, Charlie. I wouldn't ask you otherwise. I would value any advice you can give me."

Charlie sighed and sank down on the packing crate near the door. "What is it, Elizabeth?"

"You'll come?"

"If Morgan's willing," he capitulated. "Now, stop all this evasion and tell me what's wrong."

On the other end of the line, Elizabeth took a deep breath, marshaling her arguments. "You recall that Mr. Kendrie established a grant for the opera, a grant which I have continued?"

"Yes?" Cold foreboding gathered under his belt. "If this is about that death a couple nights ago . . ."

"It's not what you think," Elizabeth snapped. "Hear me out, Charlie. You will recall that the conditions of the grant are that the money be used to pay for major international singers. You may say that I am paying the salaries of about twenty percent of the singers in the company, in rough figures."

In his mind, Charlie reviewed the terms of the grant, and had to agree that the substantial figure would pay quite a few singers. "And what has that to do with the matter?"

"The problem, Charlie," Elizabeth said, not answering his question directly, "is that most of the singers involved in this unfortunate business are foreign. They don't know American law, let alone California law,. and they don't know what they ought to say and what they ought not to say, and most of them have never had to deal with a matter as serious as this."

"What do you want me to do, Elizabeth?" Charlie asked as he rubbed his eyes with his free hand.

"Now, you needn't feel apprehensive," she said brightly. Charlie began to drum his fingers on the side of the nearest carton. "I don't expect you to devote a lot of time to this. I know you have more important things to do. But I do want you to explain the situation to the people involved. Let them know what their rights are and what might be expected of them. Most of them have never been near a police investigation, and they may make things difficult for themselves and one another without being aware of it."

Charlie had begun to nod, a slight, sardonic smile pulling at his mouth. "The guy who died was unpopular, you say?"

"Well," Elizabeth said, as if it explained everything, "he was a tenor, you see. Not that *all* tenors are like Mr. Feuier. He did have a reputation for being difficult." It was rare for Elizabeth to be so tactful, and Charlie called her on it.

"A bastard, you say?"

She gave in. "Blue-ribbon. Arrogant, high-handed, egotistical, overindulged, vain, and with the morals of a mink!"

"I see," Charlie sighed. No wonder Elizabeth was worried about what the singers might say. "Was this well known?"

"Not publicly, but there were rumors, some of them most unpleasant. Gui-Adam Feuier did not go out of his way to be conciliating."

Charlie hesitated, knowing in his bones that he did not want to be involved with a case that threatened to blow itself apart with scandal. "All right, Elizabeth. You can tell me the rest at dinner. And you can tell me what the devil you expect me to do about it. What time did you say you wanted us there?"

"Seven will be fine. We dine at seven-thirty. There's no need to dress." She sounded very relieved. "I appreciate this, Charlie. There are four attorneys retained by the opera, but none of them are the least bit familiar with this kind of situation. They negotiate contracts and set up terms of grants and trusts and funding, and every now and then, they come down on someone for abusing the company. I don't think any of them have been inside a criminal court in all their legal lives. You, on the other hand, know more about trials than your two partners combined."

"You're piling it on rather thick, Elizabeth," he warned her as he rose, ready to break the connection. "At seven, then."

"There is one more thing," Elizabeth cut in, obviously very uncomfortable. "I don't know how some of the singers may feel about Indians."

Charlie managed a rather tired chuckle. "I'll find out, Elizabeth. You can bet on that."

"They're mostly Europeans, Charlie." There was an unfamiliar pleading in the old woman's voice.

"Then they might not notice. Probably they'll think I'm Russian, or," he added, recalling a time when just this error had been made, "Chinese."

"I don't want you to be . . . offended." Elizabeth stopped, waiting.

"Don't worry about it. If they make too many comments, I'll put a feather in my hair, or show up in a loincloth and war paint." He wished that he could think about such difficulties without the acute discomfort that still bothered him.

"Thank you, Charlie. You're very kind. And I won't say anything more, because I know how embarrassed you get. I'll see you and Ms. Studevant this evening around seven."

"I'm looking forward to it," he said, more stiffly than he knew.

Elizabeth cracked out a laugh. "Charles Spotted Moon, you are the *worst* liar. See you at seven."

As he hung up and prepared to get back to his moving, Charlie wondered, rather wistfully, if he would ever have the last word with the formidable Elizabeth Kendrie.

After the movers had unloaded the van and gone, Charlie felt himself grow cold with doubts. Did he really want to own this house, any house? He felt a stranger here, alien in these large, well-proportioned rooms. He got up from the sofa and moved it experimentally, first against the wall, then under the window. It looked wrong in both places. Charlie sighed and wandered into the dining room, where the high windows were letting in the last of the sun. It was a big room, wainscoted in redwood and painted an ivory color above. Charlie touched the beautiful wood, grateful that no one had painted over the lovingly waxed panels. In the middle of the room, his round oak table squatted under a load of boxes. It looked very small to him here, and he reminded himself that he would have to order new leaves for it.

The kitchen looked catastrophic, and so did the breakfast nook beyond it. Charlie shrugged and turned instead down the hall toward the stairs that led to the three bedrooms above. As he climbed, he asked himself again why he had wanted to buy a three-bedroom house, and found, as he always did, that he had no answer for himself. He went into the middle bedroom, the one he had chosen for his own, the one that faced toward the greenery of Golden Gate Park, less than three houses away. He turned on the light and flinched as he saw the green-striped wallpaper. That would have to go. He knew he couldn't stand to look at it more than a few days. His big mattress sagged against the wall, and Charlie welcomed the effort it took to put his bed into place.

He was in the large front bedroom, which would serve as his study, when there was a loud, unfamiliar sound. It took him a moment to realize that it was the doorbell.

Setting his correspondence file aside, Charlie called out, "Coming!" to the darkened house as he went uncertainly down the stairs to the front door.

"Good," Morgan Studevant said as Charlie opened the door. "I was afraid I'd have to try breaking and entering next." She hesitated, her head tilted to one side. "May I come in, Charlie?"

Awkwardly Charlie stood aside and held the door for her. "I didn't know it was so late," he said rather lamely as he felt for the light switch. He found it at last, and the hall leaped into brightness.

Morgan nodded as she pulled off her coat. Charlie had learned long ago not to offer her assistance, and all he did now was open the door of the small coat closet. "Do you want to hang that up?"

"No, thanks."

"Then throw it over the sofa, if you like. Would you be interested in a tour?"

"That would be fine." Morgan followed him into the living room as she spoke and waited while Charlie searched for a socket to plug in the lamp. When there was light, she nodded approvingly. "It's a handsome room. The fireplace is great. I like natural stone. Do you think you'll use it much?"

"I might," he said as he entered the dining room. "And we can agree that the redwood wainscoting is superb."

She nodded noncommittally. "But you've got to do something about that chandelier. It won't do at all." She looked at the stacks of cartons around the room. "Would you like some help unpacking all this? I've got some time free on Sunday."

Even though he wanted her help, Charlie said, "If you'd like to, that's fine. I can use all the help I can get. But you don't have to, Morgan."

She was already poking her head into the kitchen. "I have to be in court Monday morning, but it's a simple matter, and there isn't that much to prepare now. The District Attorney's office, I am reliably informed, will not seriously oppose a motion for dismissal."

"Oh?" Charlie's professional interest was piqued. "What case is this?"

"I don't think you know much about it. The client's a part-time prostitute. They arrested her but not her client, she was not informed of her rights or the charge against her at the time of her arrest, and with the new Consenting Adults Law, none of Cronin's staff has a prayer of winning the case. Besides, she did not solicit the act, but was approached by an undercover officer, who propositioned *her,* as she came out of a hotel room where she had been taking care of business, and that could be construed as entrapment."

"Do you know who her client was just before she was arrested?" Charlie asked as he switched on the kitchen lights.

"I do. That was what made the officer approach her in the first place. And my, my, my, it would cause a great many red faces if the client was exposed." She smiled grimly. "And Winslow knows that I'll make damn sure her client's name comes out if he insists on a trial. He's handling the prosecution."

"Winslow's not exactly the star of the DA's staff," Charlie said dryly, picturing the pale-eyed, plodding attorney.

Morgan turned to him after giving the kitchen a critical appraisal. "Not too bad. The stove arrangement is good, and at least there's room enough to cook in."

Charlie shrugged. "I don't do all that much cooking. But I do like the kitchen. The breakfast nook is nice, too. Windows on two sides, and you get a view of the backyard."

This did not particularly interest Morgan. "Is Rufus out there?"

"No, he's at a kennel. I'm picking him up Sunday, after I get some of this under control. I don't want him to be any more upset than he has to be. Moving is always hard on dogs."

"I guess." In general, Morgan did not like dogs, but in the year and a half she had known Charlie, she had learned to tolerate Rufus. "What else is there?"

"Well, there's a garage underneath, and there's some storage space down there as well. There's three bedrooms and a sun porch upstairs. If you'd like to take a look . . . ?"

"Do you want to show me? Or would you rather wait until Sunday?" She had pulled off her driving gloves, and now she shoved them into the pocket of her suit jacket. "It's a pleasant house, Charlie. I hope you're happy here." She caught a startled expression on his face. "You weren't happy at your flat, were you? You didn't like Twenty-seventh Avenue."

He regarded her evenly. "I didn't know it showed."

"It didn't." Her response was almost too quick. "It's just that I noticed you were . . . subdued there." She turned away from him and made a show of looking at her watch. "We'd better leave soon. Elizabeth won't want us to be late."

"All right," Charlie said, but made no move to go.

She tossed her coffee-brown hair and returned his gaze. "You can be a real bastard, Charlie, do you know that?"

"I believe you've mentioned it once or twice." He broke the tension between them. "Okay. I'll get my coat."

He joined her at the front door a few minutes later, somewhat neatened. "I hope Elizabeth isn't being formal tonight," he said as he corrected the roll of his turtleneck sweater.

"That's obvious." She was pulling on her coat when she stopped. "I should have told you earlier. There was a call for you this afternoon, and I took it."

"Who called?"

"Sandy Halsford. She's having trouble with her ex-husband again. He's threatened to take their kids, or something of the sort. I told her to call the police and get someone to stay with her. She was pretty frightened."

Charlie felt a flicker of annoyance at Morgan. "Why didn't you say something earlier?" He was worried about Sandy Halsford and had urged her more than once to get out of the Bay Area until her divorce was final. "Is she okay?"

"I think so. Look, I was working on an interrogatory all afternoon. It slipped my mind. Besides, she has a court order prohibiting her ex-husband from calling her or seeing her, doesn't she? You told me that it had been granted. The cops will act on that if she calls them." She stopped in the middle of putting on her gloves. "Charlie, I feel shitty for forgetting her. I know I should have told you when I got here. Don't be mad at me. I'm mad enough for both of us."

That admission touched Charlie. He knew how much it cost Morgan to say it. "I won't be mad. Word of an Ojibwa."

It was as if she hadn't heard him. "Your car or mine?"

"How about yours?" Charlie asked. "What did Bret threaten to do this time? Was Sandy specific?"

"She said he was going to send some of his friends over to beat her up, and then he'd take the children. That's one of the reasons I suggested she get someone to stay with her. He sounds just crazy enough to try a stunt like that." She paused on the steps while Charlie pulled the door closed and tested it.

"It feels strange," he said quietly. "I don't believe it yet. My house."

Morgan pulled her keys from her large tailored purse. "You'll get used to it. I'm parked near the end of the block." She pointed to the low shape of her racing-green MGB.

"Bret Halsford is a dangerous man. I wish I could get Sandy to believe that. She knows he's desperate, but she refuses to admit that he's completely capable of doing what he threatens to do. I think he'd welcome the excuse to harm her." Charlie had fallen into step beside Morgan.

Her face tightened. "Bret Halsford isn't unique, and you know it. The courts still resist the idea of protecting women, I mean really protecting them, instead of making them powerless and saying that's protection. How many times have you seen a wife-beater get off with his wrists slapped? And what about rape? What the victim goes through is a disgrace. You know that a lot of cops still think that a woman is just being vindictive or hysterical when she asks for protection from her husband, even her ex-husband. The new divorce law isn't as fair as it's cracked up to be, not for housewives. Wives' rights are a joke. A bad, bad joke." She pulled her car door open so roughly that the hinges cracked in protest.

"Hey, Morgan, remember me? I agree with you."

She paid him no attention. "God, when I think what gets done to women, what we have to take . . ." She rounded on Charlie as he got into the passenger seat.

"Remember that woman last year? I think her name was Chappin. The one whose husband deserted her. Do you remember everything we went through? And she still didn't get one-third of what the court ordered she be paid. And it wasn't just because her husband had been converted and had given all his worldly goods to God, it was because she was a wife, and that made her unentitled to a living wage." Pausing to twist the key savagely, she glared at Charlie as the motor leaped to life.

"I remember, Morgan. But let me remind you, for what it's worth, that if there were no injustice in the world, you and I would be out of work."

"Is that all it means to you?" she demanded, regretting the words as soon as they were out. "No. I know you better than that. I didn't mean it, Charlie."

He looked away from her. "Okay."

"It's so hard, Charlie," she said softly, and eased the car into gear.

Elizabeth Kendrie's magnificent home on Clement Street looked exactly like what it was: an English Tudor manor house, the extravagant present from her late husband.

"I love this place," Morgan said as Charlie walked with her up the curving path to the broad porch. There were occasional tall brass lampposts with bright lights guiding the visitors along the flagstones.

Charlie nodded as he rang the bell and waited while the sonorous peal sounded deep within the house.

"Good evening, Mr. Moon, Ms. Studevant," Henry Tsukamoto said as he opened the door. He had been Elizabeth's houseboy for more than twenty years and was filled as much with her dignity as his own, which was considerable. "You're expected."

"Thank you, Henry. If you'll tell me where we can find Mrs. Kendrie . . ."

"Indeed." He stood aside to admit Charlie and Morgan to the house. "Mrs. Kendrie and Mr. Malcomb are in the lanai. If you like, I would be pleased to show you there . . ."

This was more than Charlie could stand. "Thank you, Henry, but I know the way. I wouldn't want to trouble you, since you probably have dinner to attend to."

Henry bowed very slightly, very majestically. "It is no trouble, Mr. Moon." He closed the door behind them and waited patiently to take Charlie's and Morgan's coats. When they had handed these to him, he preceded them down the long hall to the lanai, which had been added to the house a dozen years ago. It was a long room, beautifully proportioned. By choice, it was the room where Elizabeth served cocktails and where, against the huge sliding-glass doors, she kept her impressive collection of houseplants.

"Mrs. Kendrie, Mr. Moon and Ms. Studevant have arrived," Henry announced, then withdrew most properly, as if from the presence of a duchess.

Elizabeth beamed at Charlie and Morgan as she crossed the lanai, her determined, stiff-legged walk making her seem even more formidable than she was. "Charlie. Ms. Studevant. I'm delighted to see you." She turned her head to someone in the large rattan chair behind them. "Ty, do get up. You must meet these good friends." Elizabeth motioned to Charlie to come nearer.

It was rare that Charlie, who was moderately tall, ever felt dwarfed, but the man who unfolded from the chair had that effect. Deep-chested, broad-shouldered, standing six-feet-five in bare feet, Elizabeth's guest made the others shrink in comparison.

Elizabeth was not intimidated. She reached to take the stranger's arm, saying, "Charlie, this is Tory Ian Malcomb. Ty, this is the attorney I've been telling you about, Charles Moon."

Malcomb engulfed Charlie's hand in his. "I'm very glad
to meet you, Mr. Moon. And very, very grateful."

Charlie frowned but responded automatically. "I'm
pleased to meet you."

Morgan, who had been regarding Malcomb with a
slight, knowing smile, accepted Elizabeth's introduction
with amusement, and as she clasped Malcomb's hand,
said, "I want to tell you how much I enjoyed the *Vespri*. I
liked it better than anything else so far this season.
Harness and Wixell were magnificent. And the sets were
incredible. It was completely amazing. When Scotto sang
that terribly difficult aria in the last act, I wanted to shout
for joy."

There was a slight trace of sadness in Malcomb's
response. "I'm honored to have you say so. It was a
remarkably successful production, but I found it somewhat painful. I agree with you about Schoen's sets, Ms.
Studevant. Next season he'll do both the *Don Carlo* and
the *Pelléas et Mélisande*." Then, as if compelled, he said, "I
found the *Vespri* painful because Procida was the last role
I sang before the fire, when smoke damaged my voice."

Curiosity and annoyance warred in Charlie. "Vespers?
Procida?"

"*I Vespri Siciliani*. It's a highly romanticized account of
the legendary founding of the Mafia. It was the second
opera this season," Morgan explained. She smiled up at
Malcomb. "You're doing some very exciting things with
the company. I'm really looking forward to next season."

"Malcomb!" Charlie said in sudden recognition. "You're
that Malcomb." Charlie glared at his hostess. "Elizabeth,
this was a dirty trick, even for you."

Elizabeth chose to ignore this outburst, saying, "Ty, of
course, is the new General Manager of the opera. He was
a singer, as I gather you understood from his reference to
the unfortunate end of his career. I thought you might
get along better if you met away from the Opera House.

So, when you agreed to come to dinner, I asked Ty if he could join us." She handed Charlie a glass of white wine. It was Mondavi Fumé Blanc, which she knew was one of Charlie's favorites. "I was sure," she went on blithely, "that since you're going to help out with this Feuier business, that you'd be anxious to meet the man in charge."

"I see." Charlie nodded. He put his wine down untasted.

It was Ty Malcomb who saved the situation. Looking down at Charlie, he said, "I'm sorry, Mr. Moon. I thought you knew I'd be here. Elizabeth didn't tell me you had any reservations about the job. I assumed the matter was settled. If you'd prefer not to be involved, I certainly understand."

Perversely, now that he had the opportunity to refuse the case, Charlie relented. He admitted to himself that he ought to have known Elizabeth would pull something like this. "There's no problem," he said as he glanced significantly at Elizabeth. "I wasn't prepared." He picked up the wineglass and took a taste, smiling in spite of his irritation. Elizabeth gave the most subtle of bribes, he thought. "I'm afraid you might not want me on the case, though, if there is a case. I'm quite ignorant about opera. In fact, I don't particularly like it. You'll have to make allowances for that."

"I'll be happy to." Ty Malcomb nodded toward Morgan. "But from the sound of it, Ms. Studevant can help you out." Then, in spite of himself, he let himself be pulled away from the matter at hand. "Tell me," he said to Morgan. "What else have you seen this season? Did you get to *Merry Mount?*"

Morgan had just picked up the vermouth that Elizabeth had given her, but she put it aside to answer. "Yes, I did, the Wednesday performance. I'm not sure I liked it."

Ty lowered himself into the chair once more. "Well, it's part of the Bicentennial Celebration, after all. An American opera by an American composer, with Puritans and Cavaliers in a New England setting, all very appropriate. It was that or *Baby Doe*."

To Charlie's surprise, Morgan laughed. "And it's not nearly so appropriate, is it?" She sat down opposite Ty Malcomb and smiled enthusiastically. "I loved the *Gioconda*, but who doesn't like Pavarotti? And I think that Tey did a spectacular job on *Rake's Progress*. Stravinsky is so spiky the work falls apart without a good conductor."

"And *Hoffmann*? Have you seen that?" There was real pain in Ty's voice now.

"I saw the second performance, a week ago," Morgan admitted, flushing without reason. "I was sorry about what happened. I didn't like Feuier much—he always shrieks so on the top—but it's really a beautiful production . . ." She faltered and looked inquiringly at Charlie.

"That's the man who died?" Charlie caught confirming nods. "Do you know anything more about his death than what was on the news?"

Before Ty could answer, Elizabeth cut in. "You must be very frank with Charlie. I have been. If you wish to speak nothing but good of the dead, I will tell Charlie right now that he needn't bother dealing with you or the singers. I know how clannish you can be, but this is no time for it." She picked up a tray of canapés and offered the lot to Ty Malcomb.

With rare diplomacy, Morgan took the tray and set it aside. Elizabeth gave one curt nod. "Good girl. You're right, of course."

Ty was staring at his drink abstractedly, not seeing the liquid that swirled in the glass. "No, I don't know much more. We haven't got autopsy results yet. And we're under a lot of pressure. This kind of thing is rotten for an opera company, not just for the death, that goes without saying. It's the sensation around the death that can be disastrous." He put his drink down and looked squarely at

Charlie. "We do need help, Mr. Moon. Quiet help. Tactful help. I've got to protect my company."

"You mean that you want me to do this as privately as possible." As he said it, Charlie realized he still did not know what he was expected to do.

"Very privately. Please." Ty reached for his glass and changed his mind. "Elizabeth assures me of your discretion. And, Christ, we have to have someone who's discreet."

Morgan almost spoke, but Charlie stopped her. "You have my word, personally and professionally, that I will act as confidentially as I can, within the limits of the law. I can't do any better than that." As he said this, he studied Ty Malcomb's face and liked what he saw.

"I'm not asking for more, Mr. Moon. Please try to understand." Malcomb leaned forward. "I've got this season to finish, the next season to prepare, and I'm knee-deep in that already. Spring Opera is coming up fast, and I've got some of the jumpiest talent you're ever going to see . . . Opera is worse than a small town when it comes to rumors and scandal and gossip. I've had five phone calls from singers wanting to replace Feuier, one just ten minutes after the body was in the ambulance." He began to roll a bit of bread between his finger and thumb. "We're very vulnerable, Mr. Moon. It takes very little to destroy us."

Charlie nodded. "Go on."

"I can't have these people exposed to all the publicity, all the furor that's growing out of this death. I went through something like this myself once, and I promise you, it can be disastrous. This case is explosive, because Feuier was monumentally unpopular with his colleagues. And you know how much the news media loves a mess like that. We're talking about the European press as well as the American." Malcomb dropped the bread pellet onto the tray with the canapés. "I have to see that the company is not harmed any more than is absolutely necessary."

Henry Tsukamoto appeared in the door, prepared to announce dinner. Only Elizabeth saw him, and she motioned him away with an impatient flick of her hand.

"From what? From a few unkind remarks in print?" Charlie sipped his wine and wished that he did not feel so damned awkward. "From what you say, your people must be used to it."

"There's more to it than that." Ty looked up; he saw the sternness in Charlie's flinty eyes.

"If there's more to it, Mr. Malcomb, don't you think you'd better tell me about it? Obviously you're worried that one of your company might, in some way, be responsible for Feuier's death. That's it, isn't it? You're afraid that someone in your opera company let Feuier die. Okay. Would you like to tell me something about that? Who didn't like him? Who had a grudge against him?" He took a canapé and glanced at Morgan. "If I overlook something, will you tell me? I don't know anything about these people."

"I'll tell you," she assured him, and turned her concentration on Ty Malcomb.

Elizabeth sighed and retired to the other side of the room, where she busied herself with misting several large ferns which were moist already.

"Now, I've heard," Charlie said evenly, beginning to feel in control of this awkward conversation at last, "that Feuier was a difficult man. Is there anyone who worked with him who had reason to dislike him? Beyond normal professional rivalry, that is."

"Dislike him?" Ty Malcomb laughed. "Everyone disliked him. Well," he amended after a moment, "not everyone, but most of us. Some more than others, and with good cause."

"You're being evasive, Mr. Malcomb," Charlie warned

him. "Can you give me some examples? And some reasons?"

It was Morgan who answered the question. "What about Cort Nørrehavn? I remember maybe a year ago there was a rumor that Feuier was involved with his wife."

"Yes, he was. Before she died. That was about, oh, eighteen months since." Ty put his glass down and clasped his hands in front of him. "I hated asking Cort to work with Feuier."

"Then why did you?" Charlie did his best to disguise his bafflement. Only the frown that flicked his brows betrayed him.

"*Hoffmann* is a special pet of mine, and having Cort in the baritone lead is really important to me. When I asked him about it, I didn't realize Feuier was going to be Hoffmann. When I did learn about it from my predecessor, I gave Cort the option of canceling. But he said that he'd given his word. Cort's a very honorable, a very moral man." He looked away, then met Charlie's eyes, and there was guilt in Malcomb's face. "This is my first season as General Manager, and everything except *Hoffmann* and *Manon Lescaut* was set up before I took over. It's very important to me that these two go well, even more than the rest of the season. And a *Hoffmann* with Feuier and without Nørrehavn would have been a disaster. Maybe it was wrong, but when Cort said that he'd stay on, I jumped at the chance."

Charlie studied Ty Malcomb's unhappy face. "And?" he prodded.

Ty looked down at the backs of his huge hands. "I don't know. It wasn't a very cheerful cast, but it was that or a terrible *Hoffmann*."

"Why?" Charlie felt his curiosity take over. He set his wine aside and leaned forward in his chair. "Why hire Feuier in the first place if you knew there'd be trouble?"

"Because it's who Brodie wanted, that's why." Malcomb

spoke with asperity, then explained. "Opera costs a lot of money, Mr. Moon. We have soloists, *comprimari,* chorus, supers, designers, directors, orchestra conductors, stage crew, makeup crew, costume crew, prop crew, sound crew, lighting crew, prompters, house staff, and maintenance personnel to pay. To say nothing of the front office and the cost of things like programs, advertising, publicity . . ."

Again Morgan interrupted. "I was upset when I had to buy a program this year. I don't like the tacky thing you hand out, and I don't like the lack of information on all the people and the whole season. I felt cheated."

Ty shook his head. "Costs. I don't like it, either. But the expense of those slick programs was out of sight."

Elizabeth had stopped misting her plants, but said nothing as she came nearer her guests.

"Mr. Moon . . ."

Charlie relented. "If I may call you Ty, you can call me Charlie. If I'm going to get involved in this mare's nest of yours, we might as well be able to talk to each other without formality. You were saying about costs and why you hired Feuier . . ."

Ty looked anxiously at Elizabeth, but she offered him no help. He rubbed his eyes. "Think of it this way: a whole symphony piled on top of a large-cast historical play, and throw in a few extras, like occasional ballet dancers and the scarcity of top singers, and you'll get some idea of the complexities of what we're dealing with. Even the horrendous price we have to charge for tickets doesn't begin to pay the bills. So, like a lot of other businesses, we need backers, angels. Like Elizabeth. We wouldn't have half the international talent we attract if it weren't for her and people like her. Well, one of these angels is a fruit grower in the San Joaquin Valley, named Sal Brodie. Every other season, he picks up the cost of a new production, usually a French opera. Of course, he has some favorite singers,

and it is understood that those singers will be part of the
production he pays for. We're already negotiating for a *Le
Cid* in seventy-eight, and Sal has indicated that he's
interested, and has told us the singers he'd like to hear. So
what can we do?" He looked at Elizabeth. "Thank God
you're not like that."

"Brodie liked Feuier?" Charlie asked sharply.

"Like is hardly the word. He's a rabid fan. Opera buffs
tend to be that way."

"And the condition for the production was Feuier?"
Charlie frowned. "Couldn't you negotiate with Brodie?"

"Maybe, if I'd been General Manager last season. But by
the time I came in, it was settled, and besides, Carerras
and Burrows were busy elsewhere, and time was tight.
Feuier had been signed and would have kicked up one
hell of a row if we'd tried to back out. It seemed like a
good compromise at the time, in spite of the difficulties."

"I see. I'm sorry." To his own surprise, Charlie realized
that he meant it.

"Well, we've got another tenor lined up for Tuesday
night. In a way, the production is saved. I hear that tickets
are going at high prices from the scalpers." He reached
for his glass quite suddenly and drained it.

Morgan gave Charlie a quick, meaningful look. He
acknowledged it with a curt nod and said to Elizabeth,
"When will dinner be served? I've been moving all day,
and I'm famished."

"Any time you like," she answered quickly, but with
strong disapproval in her tone.

"I'd be grateful for a meal."

Visible relief washed over Ty Malcomb. "Sounds great.
I'm kind of hungry myself." He rose from the chair, and
once again Charlie was aware of Ty's imposing height.

"Very well. I'll tell Henry to begin serving immediately."
Elizabeth had marched up to Ty, and though she was little
more than five feet tall, she managed to take command of

her gigantic guest. "You may escort me, Ty, since I know that Charlie will want to compare notes with Ms. Studevant en route to the dining room." Imperiously she held out her arm.

Charlie felt the last remnant of annoyance slip away, and he chuckled. "You'd better do as she says, Ty." He added, as an afterthought, waving Ty back to his chair. "She's right; I do want a couple of words alone with Morgan. But there is one thing you can tell me now, and then we'll leave it alone for a bit. Do you know anyone in particular who might want to see Feuier dead? I mean, other than Nørrehavn, if he's a possibility."

Tory Ian Malcomb closed his eyes and nodded. "All right. Other than Nørrehavn." He sighed. "I don't know if the feelings were strong enough to want Feuier dead, necessarily, but there are a few who hated his guts. Jocelynne Hendricks, who's singing Nicklausse. Unless I read it wrong, their affair was over, and I think she may be very angry about it. Maybe not even angry. Perhaps contemptuous is a better word. Then there's Domenico Solechiaro . . ."

"Who's that?"

"A professional rival. He sings pretty much the same roles that Feuier . . . sang. And he does them much better. He's younger, too, in his mid-thirties. Feuier hated him. He pulled a couple of unfunny pranks on Nico. I don't think it was enough to make Nico want to see him dead, but there was enmity there."

Charlie interrupted him again. "What kind of pranks?"

Ty explained reluctantly. "Oh, paying people to go to Nico's concerts and read newspapers in front-row seats. Sending Nico bouquets of lilacs, which Nico's terribly allergic to. That kind of thing. But it wouldn't be enough to make Nico want to to . . ." He stopped.

"To what?" Charlie asked. "Kill him?"

Morgan shook her head in distress.

"Wait a minute," Charlie said. "There are a few things

you should understand. First, from what I've heard, there is absolutely no hard evidence that Feuier's death was anything more than misadventure. You shouldn't bandy words about like kill so easily. It creates precisely the climate you're trying to avoid." Charlie leaned forward, his flinty eyes intent on Ty Malcomb, measuring his reaction. "Look. No one knows yet how Feuier died. For all we know, it was natural causes. All the law knows is that he dropped dead on stage, the reason for it still unknown."

"But there are many people who hated Feuier," Ty said, quite unhappy. "I know some of them would kill him if they had the chance."

"No," Charlie corrected him quickly. "No, you have heard them say it, perhaps. Saying and doing are two different things. And knowledge, Ty, is not proof." He saw the uncertainty in Ty's face and tried to explain. "There's a difference between knowledge and proof. Suppose, for example, you know that a person has recently got a new color TV. You know that he did not pay for it, and, from circumstances, you assume that the TV is stolen property. Then you hear that a friend a couple blocks away recently had such a TV stolen. In your heart, you're sure that the guy with the new color TV took it from your friend. You may, in fact, be wrong. Perhaps it was a gift or a legacy. Unless you can show that the serial number on that TV—or establish some verifiable identification—is the same as the one on your friend's, all you have is supposition. As a lawyer, I could pull your argument to shreds in three quick questions. And I would. Because that is how the law works. It works on provable facts, not on guesses—even good guesses. So don't, please, talk publicly about what you know unless you can prove it."

Ty considered Charlie. "That could mean that guilty people go free."

"Yes, it could. Sometimes it does. But if the guilt cannot

be proven in law, under the test of the law, then it must be rejected. Otherwise, we're back to Star Chamber techniques." Charlie shifted to a more relaxed position. "In Scots law, there's a third verdict for exactly the circumstances I've told you about. It's called 'Not Proven,' which is sometimes facetiously described as 'not guilty but don't do it again.' We don't have that in our law, and so the evidence—evidence, Ty, not circumstances or supposition—must meet the test of convincing beyond a reasonable doubt. There are times I wish we had the 'Not Proven' verdict."

"You think it might turn out that way with Feuier?"

"It might, but that would mean narrowing the matter down to one suspect. From what you've said, that might be rather hard to do. Unless," Charlie added with an ironic smile, "you think it was a conspiracy."

"No," Ty said, partly amused and partly horrified. "I don't think that."

"Then don't use words like 'kill.' It's possible that if you establish the climate of suspicion this whole thing could turn into a circus."

"All right." Ty had straightened somewhat, put off by Charlie's emphatic tone. "It's just that with someone like Feuier, killing feels justified."

Charlie's voice was sharp. "Killing is never justified. Not the way you mean. In the eyes of the law, there's no excuse. Murder settles nothing. It cures nothing." He stopped, and added with a wide smile, "Though there is an old Oriental proverb that says there is very little trouble that cannot be solved quickly by a suicide, a large bag of gold, or pushing a hated rival over a precipice at night."

This had the effect Charlie had hoped for. Everyone laughed quietly.

"Okay. Is there anyone else who didn't get along with Feuier?"

"It's a long list. I'll give you a breakdown on it if you like."

Charlie was not prepared to deal with lists of names and personality sketches. "Later. But does anyone working with him come to mind, other than the man you mentioned?"

Ty thought about it and shrugged. "Well, Richard Tey doesn't like him."

"Richard Tey?"

Morgan explained. "He's the conductor of *Hoffmann* and *Rake's Progress.*"

"The conductor." Charlie tried to smile at Elizabeth. "You've really got me into something. I'm going to need a little time to sort this all out. And I gather we don't have much time."

"No," Elizabeth agreed. "That's why I wanted you to work with Ty on this."

Ty was staring down into his empty glass. "How do you know, then, when there really is a crime?"

"Well, anyone with knowledge of a crime is obliged to report it," Charlie said easily. "Knowledge, that is, not supposition. Knowledge, such as witnessing the commission, hearing it firsthand, or coming upon evidence." He regarded Ty with a certain compassion. "If you have any doubts, ask me. Tell me everything, no matter how farfetched. I'll listen. It's my job."

"Very well." Ty stretched, as if waking from an unpleasant dream. "I'll keep that in mind."

Charlie accepted this but said, "Is there anyone else you think might have reason to want Feuier dead who had access to him on Wednesday night?"

In a strained voice, Ty said, "Yes. There's me."

Traffic on Geary was light, and Morgan drove fairly fast. There was just enough moisture in the air that she needed to turn the windshield wipers on. Against the *whick* of these and the rush of the tires, her silence was very noticeable.

"I hope we get some real rain soon, but I doubt it," Charlie said when they had gone almost a mile without a word exchanged between them.

"It's supposed to rain next week."

He shrugged. "That storm last month helped a little." He watched the set line of her jaw, seeing the severity of her mouth in contrast to the clean lines of her profile and the sweep of her soft brown hair that just brushed her collar.

She made no comment, and Charlie tried to accept her silence, but at last, he said, "I wish you'd tell me what you think."

They had swung onto Seventh Avenue when Morgan finally spoke. "I know what Ty was talking about."

"When?" He could tell that she had broken into her own thoughts, and was not certain that she heard him.

"He said that he didn't like Feuier. That was because of that fire in Buenos Aires. There was a lot of unrest there about imported singers, and one of the insurgent groups set fire to the opera house. Feuier wasn't on stage and got out of the opera house without harm, and he said that there was no way for him to give warning to the other singers. Ty was onstage and suffered very serious smoke inhalation. He hasn't been able to sing since."

"Come on. If his voice is lost, how come he speaks like that?" Charlie admired the effortless resonance of Ty Malcomb's voice, thinking it reminded him of some of the best British actors he had seen.

"His singing voice is lost. Not his speaking voice, that's pretty much the same as it was, but there's a world of difference between speaking and singing. I read an interview he gave shortly after the fire. It was one of the saddest things I've ever read."

"It's in the next block," Charlie reminded her as they

went through the third intersection.

"I know." She shifted into second gear and pushed her turn signal. "Poor Ty. I can't imagine what it would be like to lose a gift like that."

"What about the other people he mentioned? What do you know about them?"

She shruggged as she turned her MGB's nose into the driveway behind Charlie's Volvo. "About as much as any buff knows. Solechiaro's right on the edge of being a very big star. He started a little late. He's only been singing about eight years. From what I've read about him, he's a delight. His singing's magnificent. Very lyric, but he can do some spectacular bel canto things when he wants to. He did a recital album recently, all Rossini and Bellini. It's very impressive!"

"And the others?" Charlie waited while she decided to turn off the motor. "Come in, why don't you, and fill me in on these people. I need to know more about them."

"There are plenty of sources," Morgan said, suddenly very reserved. "I'll give you some material."

"Look, Morgan, I've seen exactly two operas in my life, and I don't remember much about them except that the sets were the darkest things I've ever seen in a theater. It was like watching a show in a cave." He opened the door and got out of the car. "Morgan, please."

"I don't know. It's pretty late."

"It's Friday. You can sleep tomorrow." He felt the mist gather on his face and turn clammy.

"I've got aikido class at ten." She was about to turn the key, and then changed her mind. She snapped off the lights. "I don't know," she said again. She was still, then got out of the car, pulling up the velvet collar of her coat as she did.

"Thank you." He was already heading up the steps, fumbling in his pocket for the unfamiliar keys. By the time he had opened the door, she had come up beside him. Holding the door open, he stood aside for her to enter.

She gave him an irritated sniff, then stepped into the hallway, which was lit by a sliver of brightness from the kitchen.

Charlie pulled the door closed as he came inside. "The living room's about the best place. The couch is there, and I've plugged in a couple of lamps." He found his way, somewhat uncertainly, to the nearest table, and felt for the lamp there, turning it on as he looked toward Morgan.

She had pulled off her coat and draped it over the nearest stack of cartons. "Elizabeth is worried, isn't she?" she said as she went to the sofa.

"Small wonder."

"So's Ty. What a rotten thing to happen." Absentmindedly she began to fiddle with the catch on her purse.

"Would you like some coffee or tea?" Charlie had turned up the thermostat, but it would be some little while before the room was warm.

"Tea would be nice." She said this scowling. "But I can't stay too long."

"I know. Aikido in the morning at ten. Will Earl Grey do?" He waited in the dining room archway while she made up her mind, and at her nod, almost bolted for the kitchen.

He was back shortly with a tray holding a teapot, a milk jug, and a small glass of sugar cubes. He cleared a space in the mess on the coffee table and put the tray down. "Help yourself just as soon as I get the cups." He went back to the kitchen and got the cups and saucers. "I've got a bigger tray somewhere, but I can't find it."

"It's still very elegant," Morgan allowed.

"This is the Canadian part of me. We don't take tea lightly, not even at tribal councils." He pulled up one of the packing boxes and sat opposite her.

Morgan nodded, but her eyes were far away. "I saw

Feuier last year in *Carmen*. He had a lot of flash, a very bravura style, but he was a pretty sloppy singer, and in spite of being handsome, he didn't have very much talent. I found him pretty disappointing."

"Disappointing? How?"

"I remember thinking that he sounded strained. His top notes were really bad—thin and squeezed out. I wonder what was wrong."

Charlie paused in pouring his own tea. "Did something have to be wrong? Maybe it was just an off night. Maybe he had a cold, or dinner didn't agree with him."

Morgan shook her head. "It was more than that. This wasn't anything new for him, just more of it, and more noticeable. He had been getting worse for some time."

"Did he know it? Maybe he decided to go out with everyone watching. If that's what happened, it would make it a lot easier for everyone." He stirred his tea and studied Morgan's face.

"Christ, that sounds ghoulish." She looked at the empty walls. "Are you going to hang that portrait of Lois in here?"

"No." Charlie put his cup down more sharply than he had intended. "No, I sent it back to her father. I had a call from him day before yesterday thanking me. He told me that her little girl is doing very well. Janos is delighted. Lois is thrilled." As he said this, he felt he had lost the rancor he felt for Janos Zylis. "Lois and I have been divorced close to five years now. That's longer than we were married. She's happy with Janos. I think it's time I let her go, really let her go."

With her disastrous acuity Morgan asked, "That's the reason you moved, isn't it?" She couldn't meet his eyes.

"One of the reasons." He stood up. "Let me pour you some more tea."

She made a gesture of refusal. "No. I do have to go. It's awfully late, and it's still going to take me twenty minutes to get home." She had risen and stood now somewhat awkwardly, her purse on the sofa, her coat by the door. "Thanks for the tea, Charlie."

"Any time," he said lightly, reminding himself that thanks came easily to Morgan, and that for her there was no obligation in the word. It had taken him more than half his lifetime to learn that the rituals of thanks that made such demands on him were not shared by his non-Indian friends.

"It's a nice house."

"I'm glad you like it." He reached for her coat and rather slowly handed it to her. "Do you want some help?"

"I can manage." She tugged her coat on, picked up her purse, then went quickly to the door. "I'll let myself out." And before Charlie could object, she had pulled the door open and closed it sharply behind her.

Charlie stood still, listening to the sound of her MGB as she drove away. When the street was silent again, he gathered the cups onto the tray with the tea things and went to the kitchen to wash up.

Saturday, October 30

Sandy Halsford gestured helplessly around the high-ceilinged room. "But what can I do, Charlie?" she asked. "The landlord won't install new locks, and I can't afford to have it done until my next paycheck, and there's a rule against keeping dogs." She pressed her fingers against her eyes, and Charlie saw that her ragged nails had been bitten to the quick. "I'm sorry. I'm frightened. I shouldn't have said that."

Charlie shook his head. "You've got to protect yourself, Sandy." What he said next was strictly against the policy of Ogilvie, Tallant & Moon, but he neither considered that nor cared. "If you can't afford it, I'll lend you the money or hire it done for you."

"I can't afford that, either, Charlie."

"No strings, Sandy. Just an investment in a client. This isn't just a messy divorce case; it touches on the kidnapping charges as well. A lot depends on you." His smile was rueful. "I don't want Bret breaking in here some night. He has threatened to, hasn't he?"

Sandy Halsford tried to laugh and failed. "Among other things. He makes those threats when he's feeling charitable. Other times, he's a lot worse." She looked around the room again, at the faded and cracking paint, at the crumbling plaster decorations on the ceiling. The whole building sagged with the weight of neglect. At one time, near the turn of the century, it had been an elegant home. It had survived both earthquake and fire, but what that double disaster could not do, time and abuse were accomplishing now. The building creaked and groaned at night, there were several varieties of insects living in the walls, and the plumbing had reached a stage of unreliability that was neither ignorable nor funny. "Shit, Charlie, look at this place. I've got the kids in the other room today. Lisa from downstairs is keeping an eye on them. But I can't do this all the time. They should be able to go outside to play and not be afraid that their father will try to kidnap them. Really, it's too hard on them."

"And on you, Sandy?" he asked. He did not need an answer. Sandy Halsford had lost more than twenty pounds in the last six weeks. Her clothes hung on her, and her face had that gaunt, tight look he had sometimes seen on the faces of prisoners.

"I don't know. I have to hang on."

"What about friends? Is there anywhere you can go until your court date?"

She shook her head. "No. I've got to keep this job. I don't want to go on welfare unless there's no other choice. If I lose this job, I *will* have to get welfare. Mr. Brendan says he's willing to keep me on, in spite of the phone calls Bret makes to the office. But I don't know how much longer he'll feel that way. Thursday afternoon, Bret called Mr. Brendan and said that he'd plant a bomb in the building. You know how many machines we've got in the shop, and Bret could hook a bomb up to any one of them. Every time I think of that big blueprinter, the fifty-two-inch press, I get dizzy. That much iron blown around the shop . . ."

"You should have told me about that earlier," Charlie said brusquely. "This happened on Thursday, you say?"

She nodded. "Carling, the manager, thinks that Mr. Brendan should fire me. He said so. He was talking to some of the men in the shop, saying it wasn't worth getting the presses busted up for a crazy broad. He told me I ought to let Bret get a little and he wouldn't be so troublesome." Her breath was unsteady, and she clutched her elbows with bony fingers.

"I see." Charlie turned from the sealed fireplace, which offered no heat and no decoration, walking to the window. Across the street were four more abused Victorians and three cheaply made apartment houses, indicating more plainly than the faces of the people in the street that this block was succumbing to the same mysterious disease that had created slums within two blocks. Five more years and this building, too, would be rotten with it.

"I can't afford to move, either, if that's your next question." She tried to smooth the wrinkles from the cheap cover she had put over the daybed that served as a couch. "I wrote to my mother, as you suggested, but it didn't do any good. She sent me a long letter full of chapter and verse, and two pamphlets on the role of a wife in marriage according to her particularly fundamentalist pastor. She won't even take the kids for a little while."

Charlie touched the glass of the window. "You're too accessible here." He looked out through the distorting ripples, thinking that the world, from this place, seemed drowned. "I don't want to alarm you, Sandy, or make it worse for you, but I hope you realize that Bret means what he says." He looked down at her, at her lank hair, at her old blouse carefully darned at the collar. The room was chilly, but rather than turn on the heat, Sandy had pulled an old cardigan over her shoulders. "You can't take much more of this."

"Then maybe I ought to forget the whole thing, as my mother says. I'll go back to Bret and those thugs he calls his revolutionary comrades. At least when we were together, we ate regularly, and the rent was paid." Quite suddenly she started to cry, the sound gasping, as much in shame as in despair.

Charlie went to her side, putting his hand on her shoulder. "Sandy, Sandy." Her name sounded inane, but it had an effect. In a few moments, she had wiped her hands over her eyes and regained control of herself.

"I suppose you think I'm being stupid," she said, more sullenly than she had intended.

"Stubborn, yes; stupid, no. I think you still don't realize how much Bret wants to hurt you."

"But Charlie," she objected reasonably, "those are his children in the other room. We were married for almost nine years. He can't mean it . . ." She looked up at him. "I keep forgetting how much he's changed. I mean, he was always ultraliberal, but I never thought he'd turn revolutionary. It wasn't until after that time he was arrested in the demonstration at Cal and he was beat up . . ." She lost herself in the tangle of her thoughts. "He was always saying that this is a good system but that it needs to be prodded. He's doing very strange things with very strange people now. I can't reach him anymore." She was confused and frightened, but determined not to give way to her fear.

Charlie spoke gently, respecting her spirit. "You forget. If it weren't for you, the cops would still be in the dark about that kidnapping his bunch was planning. You're dangerous to him now. You're threatening his cause." He sat down on the cushion beside the useless fireplace. "Listen to me, Sandy. You must not let him win. You've got to protect your children, and you can't do that if you don't protect yourself. If you're in the hospital, you can't harm Bret, and he will take the kids. He wants them. He wants to make them part of his world . . ."

"His fantasy," Sandy corrected bitterly.

"Yes, his fantasy. But to him, it's real. You're the irrational one, and he must stop you or admit that he's wrong." He did not tell her his fear that Bret might be capable of killing her to get their children. "I want you to promise me that you'll start making inquiries for places to stay outside San Francisco. You said that you've got a cousin up in Eureka?" He paused long enough for her to nod. "Write to him and ask if you can stay for a while. If you feel you need money for that, tell me. I'll see that you have it. If you want, I'll write a letter for you explaining the situation."

"How will you explain a man about to get his PhD in political science who suddenly throws it all over for a group of extremist self-proclaimed revolutionaries who think that the SLA was too moderate?"

"I'll find a way," Charlie promised her. "I won't scare your cousin, but he should know how serious the trouble is. When we're ready to go to trial, I'll have you flown back. But I can't have you staying here. Do you understand that?"

"Jerry doesn't like to get involved in sordid matters," she said rather bitterly. "I asked him once."

"Ask him again." Charlie drummed his fingers on the frayed tatami mats which served in place of rugs. "Your divorce will be final in March, Sandy. The trial won't get under way until April at the very earliest, and if I know Masters there will be a few more delays. Surely you can stay up in Eureka for four months, until the divorce is final."

Sandy twisted her fingers. "I don't know, Charlie. I can ask him again, if you think it'll do any good. But I've got to stay on the job at least until December first. I can't walk out on Mr. Brendan. He's been good to me, and with the holiday season coming up, we've got a lot of specialty print orders, and I always process those for him. If I tell him I have to leave, he'll want me to train a replacement. And," she added, rather guiltily, "I need the money, Charlie. Rats skinned his knee last week, and I had to take him to the doctor. He had three stitches."

"How is he now? Okay?" Charlie liked Sandy's seven-year-old son, Gavin, whose preoccupation with his pets had earned him his nickname.

"Sure. He's fine. The cut is healing up great. Charlie, you can't imagine how a kid can bleed. I wrapped a towel around his leg to take him to the doctor, and the thing was soaked when we got to the hospital. The driver almost didn't let us on the bus when he saw the towel. Rats was shocky for a day or two, but he's over that and getting fretful staying indoors." She looked at the wall as if it might provide an escape. "Heather was as scared as I was, but Rats took the whole thing in stride."

As he got to his feet, Charlie said, "I want you to mail that letter on Monday. I want you to check with me every morning before ten. If I'm out of the office, talk to my associate, Morgan Studevant. You've got my home number, and use it if you need it. Call me any time if anything bothers you. If you can't reach me, the office has an answering service. I'll leave your name with them so that you can find me in an emergency. Bret shouldn't be trifled with." As if it were an afterthought, he said, "What's your cousin's name again, the one in Eureka?"

"Jerry."

"Jerry what? I can't send a letter to Jerry something-or-other."

"Jerry . . . Gerard Gustavsen." She waited while Charlie wrote this down. "Twenty-seven Horizon Point. Eureka, California. I don't remember the zip."

"I'll have the secretary look it up. We've got zip code

directories at the office. I'll put a letter in the mail on Monday or Tuesday, and I want you to do the same thing."

She shrugged, but her apathy was her defense against her relentless fear. "If you want to. I still think it's a waste of time."

"It might be. But I've got to try."

"After nine years of marriage," she said, and there was still disbelief in the words, "you'd think this couldn't happen."

"You didn't believe it about the drugs at first, Sandy," Charlie reminded her. "I'm glad you had sense enough to ask Tim Haskell for my number. If you'd tried to handle this alone . . ." He stopped, recalling what his friend Frank Shirer of the San Francisco Police homicide division had told him about Bret Halsford's contacts and their methods.

Sandy had risen from the daybed, and she walked toward the door. "I thought I knew him. You know, after so many years and the kids, I never thought I could be so wrong about Bret. But when he brought Daisy to the house . . ." She shuddered at the memory of the young albino black man who carried three knives and had lovingly described how he used those knives.

"There are cops looking for Daisy. And for Bret." He studied her. "A lot of murders take place within families. And Bret is in a great deal of trouble. Cronin wants to make that drug charge stick, and what Horatio Cronin wants he does his damnedest to get. And in this case, I'm delighted to help him."

Standing in the door, Sandy seemed to shrink into herself. "Bret's out on bail pending trial on that first charge. Isn't there any way to put him back in jail until the trial?"

"I'll see what I can do. But I think you'd be better off in Eureka."

Sandy refused to look at Charlie. "I'll write to Jerry. And I will call you if there's anything wrong. What the hell."

"Good. And if you can't reach me, talk to Morgan." He'd pulled on his jacket and begun the walk down two flights of stairs.

"I've got to get back to the kids." She made a motion with her hands, gave Charlie a fleeting, deprecating smile, and closed the door.

In the end, Charlie had to park more than six blocks away from the Opera House. The fifteen-minute walk was brisk, and he used the time to review in his mind all that Ty Malcomb had told him the night before. Maddeningly the Halsford case kept intruding, so his thoughts were a jumble as he walked up the shallow steps to the huge gray building. He passed through the outer lobby and handed the pass from Malcomb to the fussy old man who stood at the one open door.

"Is Maestro Malcomb expecting you?" the old man demanded as he held the pass up to scrutinize it.

"He is. You'll see on the back that he's put the date and the time. Here's my card. Take it to him if you're not satisfied." Ty had warned him about the old man, whom he had called a dragon.

"Ogilvie, Tallant, and Moon," the ticket taker read from the card. "Attorneys-at-law. Offices Seven-ten Clay at Bush." The man looked up at Charlie. "And you are?"

"As it says on my card, I'm Charles S. Moon."

The old man sniffed skeptically but stood aside. "Maestro Malcomb is in his box. It's on the far left." He was interrupted by a muffled wave of applause from behind the closed doors that led into the theater. The old man's face was sour in irritation.

"If you hate opera so much," Charlie asked pleasantly, "why do you work here?"

"I don't hate it, I adore it," the old man snapped, his pointed ferret's face set uncompromisingly. "I abhor the loss of dignity. Listen to that!" He gestured disdainfully toward the closed doors. "There's no restraint any more."

"It sounds like they're having fun," Charlie said.

Behind the doors, the applause was dying, and a gentle orchestral murmur penetrated the barrier, washing across the marble-and-gold lobby like a soft spring tide.

The old ticket taker sniffed once more, then indicated that Charlie should follow him.

Inside the opera house, the music was much louder, and Charlie tried to glance around the heads of the standees who pressed close to the rails at the back of the orchestra seats. Seeing this, the old ticket taker plucked impatiently at Charlie's sleeve, drawing him away from the attraction of the loud, brilliant spectacle on the cavernous stage.

"Okay," Charlie whispered, and fell in behind his difficult guide. They mounted the luxuriously carpeted stairs that led to the box entrances and followed along to the farthest curtain-covered door. The ticket taker signaled Charlie to wait and then hurried through the red velvet that separated them from the boxes.

Another blast of slightly dissonant, opulently decadent music penetrated the curtains, then grew suddenly loud as the ticket taker emerged and held the curtain aside for Charlie. His manner had changed dramatically. His smile was wonderfully servile, and he very nearly bowed as Charlie slipped by him.

Ty Malcomb did not turn his head, but he said very softly, "I'm glad to see you, Charlie. Sit down. This act'll be through in about ten minutes."

Charlie took the indicated seat and tried to look interested. On the little bit of stage that he could see, a young woman in white and rose was being sung to by another young woman in silver men's clothes of the eighteenth century. They were singing in German, and after a moment, Charlie gathered there was some kind of presentation going on. He knew enough about music to realize that the composition was fairly modern, and he leaned toward Ty and asked, "What are they doing?"

"Strauss. *Rosenkavalier.* This is the last performance. It's been very popular." Ty sounded mildly distracted, as if he was studying much more than the stage, which, in fact, he was.

"It's very pretty," Charlie said, somewhat uncertainly. "That's a lavish set."

Ty kept his voice low, but he smiled at that. "You like all those curlicues and tendrils and scrolls? They're done with those pastry things that bakers use to decorate cakes. You make this puttylike substance and squeeze away. When it's dry, paint it or gild it, and there you are. It's surprisingly cheap, and the effect is great." He had leaned forward, and it was obvious that his whole attention was directed at the stage.

Charlie tried to feel Ty's fascination, but, as usual, the whole thing seemed somewhat absurd to him. The high, mincing sound of the violins irritated him almost as much as the overrich swell of music. Activity on the stage increased, and then, almost abruptly, the act came to an end and the huge gold curtain fell and enthusiastic applause erupted in the house. Charlie leaned back in his chair and looked inquiringly at Ty.

"Wait until the curtain calls are over, and then I'll take you backstage. Then we'll go to my office, and I'll do what I can to answer any questions you may have." He had begun to clap almost automatically as the curtain billowed and the principal singers walked out onto the apron.

"Lani is having trouble with Octavian today. She never sings well in the afternoon—strictly a night person." There was no condemnation in this evaluation. "We sang together in London about eight years ago. She was just getting started, and she wasn't up to Adalgisa yet. But she's a formidable technician. I've seen her wear herself to a frazzle and come through on nerve and technique alone." He applauded as the woman in men's clothes returned to the stage. "She's thirty-four, just hitting her stride. You'd like her."

Charlie stared down at the young woman in silver. "She's my age," he said, as much to himself as to Ty.

"Yeah, that's what I thought," Ty agreed as he rose. He checked the audience, watching the movement as some of the people in the house stopped clapping for the artists on the stage and began to make their way to the various exits for the intermission. "The bar'll be busy," he remarked to the air, then turned to Charlie. "Come on, I'll take you backstage." He was through the red velvet curtain and into the gorgeous little hall almost as quickly as he had spoken. To his right was a fairly inconspicuous door, and it was this door that Ty opened with a key which he carried on a separate ring. The hallway beyond the door provided a dramatic contrast, as if the world had been suddenly transformed, like a fairy-tale princess seen in the cold light of dawn with none of her finery. Instead of cream-and-gilt walls and red velvet curtains, this narrow hallway was sternly functional, uncompromisingly lit by wire-caged bulbs. There was a black-painted staircase, and at the moment, three women in frilly eighteenth-century servants' dresses were climbing it, one of them saying to the two others, "God, Maestro Eisenbach is a clod. Did you hear the way he screwed up that last ritard?"

"Hello, Maggie," Ty said rather sardonically.

"Hello, Mr. Malcomb," she said, without a trace of embarrassment. "How's it going out front?"

"Quite well. They like it. They even like Maestro Eisenbach." Ty stood aside to let the women pass, and said, when they were gone into a dressing room farther down the hall, "Don't mind Maggie. I doubt if she's approved of a single conductor here since 1947. But she's one of our best *comprimari* . . ."

"Your what?" Charlie asked.

"Supporting singers, utility singers. They do the minor roles, and most of them have several dozen they sing. Maggie has something over a hundred roles in her personal repertoire. We'd be lost without her and singers like her." He had started down the stairs as he spoke. "We're going backstage. I'll see if we can make a quick circuit of the plant, but try not to get in the way. There's a pretty extensive scene change going on."

This proved to be a mild version of the truth. As they went through the heavy, counterweighted door that led to the backstage proper, singers and stagehands hurried around them, a few exchanging terse greetings with Ty Malcomb. At a table not far from the stage manager, one of the prop men was checking the sheet for the next act with the same desperation that a Swiss banker would have used on an unbalanced account.

"Stand back," Ty ordered, putting his arm out to hold Charlie back. Two stagehands pushed past, shoving part of a staircase ahead of them.

"Efficient, are they?" Charlie asked.

His sarcasm was lost on Ty. "That they are."

"Was it like this when Feuier died?"

"Pretty much. There was a scene change going on, the male chorus was backstage, and then went onstage, and they were changing costumes backstage because there was very little time between the Venetian act and the epilogue."

"Venetian act?" Charlie repeated. "Hold it. I did some checking this morning at the library. The Venetian act is the second act."

"No." Ty stepped back against the concrete wall. "It's the third. At least, Offenbach wrote it as the third. He died before it premiered, and somehow the two acts got changed around. Offenbach's order makes better musical and psychologi—look out!" He shoved Charlie to the side as a section of balcony came barreling through, pushed by three stagehands.

Charlie had dropped to his knees, and as he rose, he dusted off his slacks. "Like Friday night on the Bay Bridge," he said to Ty.

Ty paid no attention. He grabbed Charlie by the elbow and pulled him away from the stage area toward the door on the far side of the stage. "We'd better get out of here."

There was a gentle whoosh behind them as part of the set dropped from the fly gallery and was steadied in place as it touched the floor. One of the stagehands was about to make an insulting comment to the strangers backstage when he recognized Ty Malcomb and his ire turned to a sheepish wave.

A few yards farther on, Ty pulled Charlie into another hall, the twin of the one on the other side of the stage. The noise here was less, but there were more singers, and the level of excitement was higher. "As I told you last night," Ty said, almost shouting to make himself heard, "it was almost like this when Feuier died. Not so hectic backstage, but not very calm, either."

"Is there anyone who keeps track of this?" Charlie asked, and had to repeat the question over the din.

"There's the stage manager. There's the conductor. That's about it. The rest is left up to the crews and the performers. We have a P.A. system to the various dressing rooms and crews, and there are three pages if they're needed. Other than that, everyone knows where they're supposed to be, and we take reasonable precautions to be sure they're there. But we don't ride herd on them, if that's what you mean. There's too damn many people and too much going on for that." Ty glanced at his watch. "Better make it fast, Charlie. I have to be getting back to my box. Intermission will be over in about five minutes."

Charlie glanced down the hall. "Do you mind if I prowl around back here? Is it permitted?"

Before Ty answered, he thought seriously. "If that's what you want. I'll get you a friendly native guide. Will one of the makeup women do?"

The P.A. system drowned out Charlie's answer. "Onstage, please, act three. Octavian, Baron Ochs, servants. Octavian, Baron Ochs, servants. Places, please."

Now the movement seemed to change tempo. There were other people rushing backstage, and there was a hush. A tall man in elaborately awful clothes and a hugely padded paunch came down the stairs from the dressing rooms above. He nodded to Ty and flourished a lace handkerchief before slipping backstage.

"Baron Ochs," Ty explained. "He's Helmut Sternhaus. He's superb, but he's getting near the end of his career. He's announced that he's retiring at the end of the seventy-eight season. Too bad. But he'll be sixty-one then. That's longer than most of us get." There was a wistful quality in his last words, and he quickly set the thought aside. "I'm heading back. But I want Nicole Johnson to take you around. Stay here." He touched Charlie's shoulder as if arranging him, then ducked into one of the dressing rooms in the hall. A few moments later, he came out again with a young woman behind him. "This is Nicole Johnson, Charlie. Nicole, this is Charles Moon. He's helping out with the Feuier business. I want you to take him around so he can get a look at the place. When the performance is over, please bring him to my office. Thanks." He was obviously hurried and made no excuses as he rushed away from them.

Nicole Johnson regarded Charlie levelly. "What do you want to see?" Her voice was low and pleasant, and the chaos around her did not affect her at all.

"Everything. But I want to know what happened backstage when Feuier died." Charlie was disappointed by her reaction; she clicked her tongue and nodded exasperatedly.

"It was a madhouse. At first, no one believed it, and then everyone was either trying to get backstage to get a look at Feuier or they were trying to get away from backstage because they'd seen him. The doctor who looked at him was very disappointing. He only determined that Feuier was dead and refused to move the body or to carry on in the appropriate manner." She studied Charlie critically. "You didn't know Feuier, did you?"

"No." Charlie wondered why she asked.

"That's part of it. Feuier was a rat, and most everyone wanted him dead, but they had to be horrified by his death. It's very complicated." She folded her arms. "Where do you want to start?"

"I don't know," Charlie admitted, and was startled by a muffled blast of music.

"Act three," Nicole Johnson explained. "Come this way," she said as she pointed down the hall. "Ask me anything you wish."

Charlie fell into step slightly behind her and tried to shut the music out of his mind.

Ty Malcomb's office was on the second floor of the Opera House, on the south side. It was an elegant room, thickly and conservatively carpeted and hung with bottle-green sculptured velvet draperies. At the moment, they were open, and the wan afternoon sun shone in on the gorgeous mahogany desk that dominated the room. Ty sat behind it folding one of the discarded paper programs into an airplane.

"It's worse than a rabbit warren" was Charlie's first remark as he was ushered into the office.

"Um-hum," Ty agreed as he finished his airplane and sailed it toward the window. It did well, banking only once, and then its paper nose hit the window, and it fluttered to the carpet. "Nicole show you everything you wanted to see?"

"For the moment. I'll let you know if I need to look around again." He studied Ty, concerned; Malcomb was being pressured, and it showed. "How did it go this afternoon?"

"They loved it," Ty said darkly. "Of course, no one dropped dead, so they can't dine out on the performance. But Sternhaus did upset one of the little tables accidentally, so the afternoon wasn't a total loss." He gestured to one of the Louis XV chairs across from him. "Sit down. Don't wait on ceremony, please. I've had so much courtesy today that I'm ready to slug the next unctuous bastard who smiles at me." All at once, he turned, facing Charlie squarely. "I shouldn't take this out on you. I'm sorry."

"It's understandable," Charlie allowed as he sat. "Did you manage to get the information I asked for?"

Ty nodded. "I got it." He reached into the center drawer of his desk and named off the files as he handed them to Charlie. "Gui-Adam Feuier, Cort Nørrehavn, Jocelynne Hendricks, Richard Tey, Peter Hamilton, Theresa Santos, Elise Baumtretter, Everard Lakey, Yvette Restigne, Domenico Solechiaro, Anastasia Tievieff. And Tory Ian Malcomb."

"Where did you get these?" Charlie said as he glanced through the files.

"In our records. We try to keep up to date on everyone who works here. Part of publicity." He appeared to lose interest in the files.

"And this is everyone you can think of who might be pleased by Feuier's death or might in some way profit from it?" Privately Charlie was worried to discover that the dead man was so heartily disliked.

"No," Ty said slowly, "that's everyone who's in town just now who had reason to dislike Feuier. Look. Feuier had an affair with Nørrehavn's wife; Hendricks was 'rumored to be involved with' him about three years ago; Richard Tey hates . . . hated his guts; Peter Hamilton had a big fight with him in London last spring during a production of *Werther;* Theresa Santos was another one of his women; Baumtretter hasn't been getting along with him, and I don't know why; Lakey has vowed never to direct a production with Feuier again; Restigne claims that he deliberately made her sound bad in two different operas in two different countries because she refused to sleep with him; Solechiaro was his biggest young rival; Tievieff has refused to work with him recently. And you know my reasons for disliking him."

"Some of this could be exaggerated," Charlie ventured, knowing how damaging a difficult reputation could be. "It might be a case of needing someone to point to and choosing Feuier."

Ty looked at the files and then at Charlie. "Maybe. But you didn't know him."

Charlie had to accept that. "Okay. I'll want to see every person whose file you've given me. Instruct them that if the police ask to see them, they shouldn't agree to talk until they've spoken to me. Set up appointments with my receptionist. Her name is Lydia Wong. I want to start seeing these people on Monday, after twelve-thirty. I'll be in court until eleven or so; that'll give me time to grab a bite of lunch and then get back to the office."

"Who did you want to see first? I'll try to set it up for you." Ty put his hands flat on the desk top and stared down at his spread fingers. "If it's urgent, I'll do my best to get the singer to you. We're dark on Mondays, so it won't conflict with anyone's performance."

"Well, what about the people who were in the building when Feuier died? That's Hendricks, Nørrehavn, Baumtretter, and Tey, I think," Charlie said, looking at the files.

"Let's see. Nørrehavn should be available. Baumtretter

is doing a concert at Flint Center, so she won't be. Hendricks is clear. Tey's in New York and won't be back until Tuesday noon." He thought for a moment. "And Solechiaro?"

"He wasn't around, was he? He's not in *Hoffmann.*"

"No, he's not in *Hoffmann,* but he was here. He came in for a costume fitting,and I guess he stuck around to watch. Singers do that occasionally. And I know Nico is doing a new *Hoffmann* in Munich next spring." Apparently Ty felt he had to supply Solechiaro with a reason to be backstage, because he added, "He likes to watch operas as well as to sing them. He's around for a lot of the productions when he's in town."

Charlie tapped the file, his flinty eyes intent as he calculated. "Okay," he said. "If you can arrange it this way: I'll want to see Solechiaro, Nørrehavn, and Hendricks on Monday. I've got to appear in Martinez on Tuesday, so I won't be able to see anyone else until Wednesday. By then, we should have a better idea of what happened to Feuier. I'll call you Wednesday morning, say around ten-thirty, and you can tell me who I have to see that afternoon. Does that sound okay to you?"

"Sure," Ty shrugged miserably.

There was obviously something more on his mind, and Charlie prompted him kindly. "Why don't you say it now and get it out of the way?"

There was the slightest hesitation before Ty answered. "I wasn't entirely candid with you on Friday."

"Yes," Charlie said, accepting this.

"When I lost my voice . . . it was very rough for a while. I mean rough. Depression. A suicide attempt . . ."

"Real or botched?" Charlie asked, knowing that Ty's answer would be very important.

"Oh, real enough. I had every intention of dying. I was staying with friends in Barcelona. I took a handful of sleeping pills and then went for a long swim in the Mediterranean. The people I was with knew something was wrong, and . . . my host . . ."—apparently he had decided not to involve the other person by name—"came after me. He's a singer. A good one. He's big and one of the strongest sons of a bitch I know. He pulled me back, kept me awake. And he made sure one of his three kids was with me every minute for the next four days." He looked down at his big hands. "Word spreads very fast in the opera world, and things that aren't supposed to get out do get out. Feuier was singing in Paris, and he made a few remarks in public, and the press picked it up. The next time I saw him, which was about a month later, I said some things that were . . ."

With cold certainty, Charlie added, "You said the things in public and the press picked that up, too."

"Yes."

"What did you say?"

This time Ty's hesitation was particularly noticeable. "I said it would be a service to music if he died. I . . . I kind of volunteered to help him along. When I became General Manager here—and my friend in Barcelona did a lot to make sure I got this job—Feuier made other disparaging comments. I didn't rise to the bait that time, but it dredged up what I'd said before. Then, to have him die here!" He started to get up, then sank back in his chair again. "God, I wish this had never happened. As much as I loathed Feuier, I wish he hadn't died. Not here. Not now."

Reaching into his pocket, Charlie pulled out a tightly folded zippered plastic case. He paused as he opened it, saying, "I do understand why. And I won't pretend that circumstances aren't very awkward, even if Feuier's death should turn out to be misadventure. But be careful what you say now and to whom."

"Why? The damage is already done." There was the beginning of anger in Ty's question, and he waited, challenging Charlie to answer.

"There's no need to make it worse. You say that the damage has been done. That's probably true," Charlie conceded, "but don't bring it up unless you have to."

"Okay." Ty nodded. "But the cops know about it. I had a call from an Owen McAllister. He knew all about Feuier."

"All?" Charlie asked, politely incredulous.

"Not all. But everything public. He hinted that it might be difficult around here if it turned out that Feuier didn't die of natural causes."

"And what was your response?" Charlie had never met Owen McAllister, but he knew his reputation for intelligence and tenacity.

"I said that he knew what kind of man Feuier was, and . . . I'm afraid that was stupid of me." This ended with an unhappy smile.

"It was stupid. You've made yourself a target. Look, Ty, you don't have to be personal. Tell the world that Feuier's death means a great loss to the opera world. It's true, isn't it?"

Ty gestured awkwardly. "I suppose so. Tenors are always in short supply."

"Good. Just keep your own feelings out of it. If you admit that you disliked Feuier, then you become a villain, and if you say how sad you are he's dead, you'll be labeled a hypocrite. You don't need that kind of hassle. You've got to be politic." Charlie had put the files into the case now, and he looked at Ty in sympathy. "You aren't the kind of man who takes to politics, but you're in a political job. For what it's worth, I don't like politics, either, but I have learned they can be useful. My senior partner, Willis Ogilvie, absolutely thrives on politics, the more Byzantine the better, and it's the process he loves." He looked steadily at Ty. "You love this company, don't you?"

"Yes."

"Then do the politic thing. If you don't, there's no one else who can." Charlie held out his hand. "Thank you for these." He patted the files, secure now in the plastic case. "I'll talk to you later, Ty. But if you have any questions in the meantime, or if there are any new developments, call me."

"As you wish," Ty said as their hands clasped.

Charlie, who in general was reserved with other people, startled himself as he added, "Have courage, my friend."

Eureka information took a fair amount of time coming up with the number for Gerard Gustavsen, but at last, Charlie scribbled the number on the memo pad at his elbow. Then he stared out the window for several minutes, his mind blank. The sun was gone now, and there was a touch of fog like a film over the sky. The sounds of traffic were faint, and the crowd that had filled much of Golden Gate Park was gone. Charlie drummed his fingers on the top of his cluttered desk.

Finally he sighed and began to dial. The phone was answered on the eleventh ring, and the voice was deep and stern. "Hello?"

"Mr. Gerard Gustavsen?" Charlie said, infusing his tone with purpose.

"Yes. Who is this?"

"This is Charles Moon of Ogilvie, Tallant, and Moon, attorneys, in San Francisco." He could feel the suspicion and resentment in the silence from the other end of the phone. "I'm representing a relative of yours, Sandy Halsford."

"Is Sandy okay?" The question came fast, and Charlie was relieved to hear concern in Gustavsen's voice, not just condemnation.

"Sandy's as well as can be expected," Charlie said

deliberately. "But she's in serious trouble, Mr. Gustavsen. That's why I'm calling you."

"What's wrong?" Again the question was fast, and this time guarded. "What's happened?"

"Nothing yet," Charlie said, thinking as he stared at the wall of the bedroom that would be his study that unfinished, rough wood would be nicer on the walls than paneling. "Have you ever met Bret Halsford, Mr. Gustavsen?"

"That arrogant prick she married?" Gustavsen asked. "I met him once, and that was more than enough. I told her last year she ought to leave him. What's he done to her?"

"Sandy's taken your advice. I'm handling the divorce." It was strange, Charlie reflected. In California, the word "divorce" had been replaced in law with "dissolution," which Charlie rather cynically thought of as "disillusion." But people still said divorce. "Bret isn't very happy about it. He's threatened Sandy and the kids. And lately he's taken to threatening her boss."

"Bastard!" Gustavsen said, venom in the word.

"Which is why I'm calling you," Charlie said, taking advantage of Gustavsen's anger. "She needs help, Mr. Gustavsen. She isn't safe here. But if she could come to you . . ."

There was a pause on the other end of the line. "Come to me?" Gustavsen repeated.

"Yes. She needs protection. You said yourself that Bret Halsford's a bastard. You know that he's serious about his threats."

"Well, can't you get a court order?" Gustavsen asked, his voice rising in pitch and becoming quieter. "That's what the law's for, isn't it?"

"Of course," Charlie agreed, masking his concern for Sandy. "But even with a court order, she's still very vulnerable. There's no way she can have a cop around all the time. And there's always the question of the kids.

Bret's threatened to hurt them, too. And Sandy is very badly frightened."

Very slowly Gerard Gustavsen said, "Well, I can understand that. I warned her about Halsford. But she's got friends in the city, doesn't she? She can stay with them."

"She *had* friends, Mr. Gustavsen. Ever since Bret got out on bail, most of her friends have been afraid to associate with her. She's isolated, Mr. Gustavsen. And she's terrified." He wished that Gerard Gustavsen could see the apartment where Sandy lived, see the way she looked, watch the tremor in her hands, hear the fright in her voice, listen to the hateful words Bret spoke over the telephone.

"But Eureka's a long way, Mr. . . . Moon, did you say?"

"That's why it would be an excellent place for her. That's the reason I called you."

"I don't know . . ."

Charlie leaned across his desk, determination filling him. "Mr. Gustavsen, if you're afraid of what Bret Halsford might do to *you*, think of how Sandy feels. You'll be getting a letter from her and from me in the next week. In the meantime, think about it. Don't answer me right now. Just think about what it would be like, living here in a run-down apartment, in fear of losing your job because of threats to your employer. Think about it, Mr. Gustavsen." He was tempted to hang up then, but he waited to hear what Gerard Gustavsen would say.

"It's not that I'm afraid. My wife doesn't like Sandy very much. They wouldn't get along."

"And you think Bret Halsford is better for Sandy than your wife?" He had not intended to show so much contempt, but it was unavoidable, and he knew that he did not regret it.

"Of course not," Gustavsen argued, sounding suddenly petulant. "But I owe it to Violet to take care of her. She's a nervous woman, Mr. Moon, and something like this would upset her." He sounded relieved to have hit on this solution.

"A martyr to your wife's delicate sensibilities?" Charlie said sarcastically. "Then tell me, Mr. Gustavsen, how would you feel if your wife were being threatened and her family refused to help her? Especially considering how nervous she is." For once, there was silence from the other end of the line. "Think about it, Mr. Gustavsen. Good night." He hung up without waiting to hear what Gerard Gustavsen would say. Then he stared out the window again as his anger faded, to be replaced with worry.

The lamp on his desk had been set up haphazardly; the light it shed gave more glare than illumination. Charlie moved the shade and, after a little experimentation, was able to focus the brightness so that he could read easily. With a sigh, he opened the plastic zipper case that lay atop one of the two-drawer files beside the desk. He pulled out the manila folders and looked through the various biographies. The files were all photocopies; presumably the originals were still with Ty.

"Jocelynne Hendricks," read one of them. "Born Canton, Ohio, February 9, 1940. Graduated Juilliard, 1962." He thumbed through the various clippings and reviews about Jocelynne Hendricks, looked at her costume measurements—she was 5′ 9′, 192 pounds. The accompanying photo was quite handsome, showing a tall, big-bodied woman in a light-colored brocaded gown. The photo was dated two years before. Beyond that there were a number of letters, most of them from Hendricks or her business manager. The only thing that caught Charlie's eye was a review of a production of *Don Carlo* in The Hague. Hendricks had been playing Eboli, according to the review—and Charlie made a note to himself to find out who Eboli was—and Feuier had been Carlo. The reviewer had been harsh in his criticism of Feuier, and there was an obscure reference to an incident onstage involving

Hendricks. Charlie stared at the review, and after a while, made a few terse notes to himself. Frowning, he set the Hendricks file aside and started on the next one.

"(Ryder) Cort Nørrehavn: Born Aarhus, Denmark, August 28, 1928. BS: Stockholm, organic chemistry. MS: Edinburgh, biochemistry." Charlie raised his eyes, surprised. An opera singer who had begun life as a chemist. He read the biography with increased interest and discovered that Cort Nørrehavn was a kind of family maverick. Both his brothers were scientists, one an astronomer and the other a herpetologist. Cort's musical training had begun early in his life and was a slow-developing obsession. At the end of World War II, Cort Nørrehavn was a hero of the anti-Nazi underground and had already given three concerts of lieder. He had married late, to a young American pianist. The reviews were uniformly positive, ranging from mildly complimentary to outright raves. His letters were brisk, businesslike, except for one to Ty Malcomb which revealed a touching humanity. "Linnet is gone. I say that to myself every morning. But her photograph is on my desk, and I must stop myself from waiting for her call. I have tried to listen to her recordings, but the very sound of her playing makes fresh wounds in my soul. You are kind to write to me, T.I. Yet reading your affectionate, charitable words brings me new anguish. Please forgive me if I am short with you. I know that, through your loss, you will understand mine. Grief is not taken lightly."

Charlie skipped over the fitting sheet and picked up the photo. It was recent, less than six months old. The face just missed being handsome, though middle age had revealed a craggy strength that would have been absent in youth. It was an intelligent face. A private face.

Curiosity got the better of Charlie then, and he picked up the file for Gui-Adam Feuier. "Born July 17, 1937, in Sausset-les-Pins, France. First musical education in Mar-

seilles, paid for by contributions from members of the
church where he did his first singing." Charlie half smiled.
Small-town-boy-makes-good seemed to be the tone of
Feuier's first reviews, but that gave way to more individual
reactions. Feuier's rise had been comparatively fast, and
the reviews were full of words of guarded praise for the
beautiful young French tenor. But even early on, there
was a sporadic quality to his work, judging from the
varied reaction Feuier got. Some reviews were overflow-
ing with applause, but others were cautious, a few uncom-
plimentary. Charlie studied the picture, slightly more
than a year old. Feuier was absurdly good-looking. He was
tall, and, for a singer, quite slender. His dark eyes were
large and dreamy. The smile that curved his mouth did
not reach those eyes.

The letters included in the file were fascinating. Charlie
spent the next half hour reading outpourings of re-
crimination and statements of demands as well as a
number of carbons of letters from Ty and his predecessor
attempting, with varying degrees of patience, to coax
Feuier into cooperation with conductors, directors, other
singers, and, once, with a dancer.

When he was through with Feuier's file, Charlie read
straight through it again. Somewhere in all that tempera-
ment there was something more, something so dire that
Feuier had died for it. He put the file aside, apart from
the others. He would review it later.

Richard Tey, Charlie discovered, was forty-five, had
trained in Philadelphia at the Conservatory, lived in Mill
Valley, was married, and had three teenaged kids. His
letters were energetic, forceful, and infused with an
unexpected humor.

The sound of a siren cut through the night, and Charlie
looked up with a start. The room was cold, and the
windows in the houses across the street were almost all
dark. He glanced almost guiltily at his watch, not entirely

taken aback to read the time as one-forty-eight. As always, his glance lingered on the fine Loloma watchband that had cost him almost every cent of the first fees he had earned. Silver, turquoise, and cinnabar gleamed back at him.

He rose slowly, stretching with care as he moved away from his desk. He gave the open file on his desk one last perfunctory glance. "Domenico (Giovanni Benedetto) Solechiaro: Born December 10, 1940, Rimini, Italy." It was more than Charlie could face. He put the file on the unread stack, telling himself sternly that tomorrow, after he had brought Rufus home from the kennel, he would spend more time on the files. He yawned and turned toward the door, trying to remember whether or not he had put the night latches on the doors, and considered forgetting it. But then, accepting his duty to the house, he made the rounds of the doors, checked the windows, and at last fell into bed a little after two. He was afraid that his mind was too occupied to let him relax, but by the time he had read two pages of the espionage novel on his nightstand, he was asleep.

Sunday, October 31

The overcast morning sky was clearing to blue as Charlie swung off Highway 101 toward Greenbrae and Kentfield. He was glad to have this time to himself, and driving out to the kennel gave him the excuse he needed; he told himself that he wasn't loafing.

In San Anselmo, he swung off Sir Francis Drake Boulevard onto a narrow road that wound west into the hills. In the spring, it was intensely green under the trees, but now, in autumn, the scrub oaks were almost bare, and the occasional redwoods served only to punctuate the barrenness around him. Charlie drove carefully, for, although he was familiar with the road, it was quite narrow, and he didn't relish meeting another car unexpectedly. He wished it would rain and saw the bushes at the side of the road with their heavy load of red berries as an ominous sign. It meant they were in for a hard winter, but continued drought would be even worse. He laughed mirthlessly as he recalled the letter he had had from his grandfather just a week ago. On the Iron River Reservation, which was located toward the north end of the Alberta-Saskatchewan border, the snow had been falling early and with a persistence that threatened the tribe with unusually severe cold. At that moment, Charlie wished some of that Canadian snow would fall in California to succor the parched land.

He was so lost in thought that he almost missed the turn at the discreet sign on the high redwood fence. MONTOYA KENNELS, it said in simple brass letters. Charlie dragged on the wheel and made it through the gate with almost six inches to spare.

The Montoyas kept an attractive place, kennels and dog runs on the south side of the house, a small stable and a paddock on the east where Amelia Montoya trained her two saddlebreds for show. The house itself snuggled against the hillside, and Charlie, as always, admired it. It was close to the land, like an extension of the earth.

"Hey! Charlie!" Roldan Montoya waved as he came out of the house. "Good to see you."

Charlie was out of his car by the time the fifty-year-old Spaniard came up to him, the slender hand that never roughened with work extended toward his guest. "Come in. Have coffee with me."

"Good to see you, Roldan. How's Rufus?" Charlie fell into step beside Montoya as he started back toward the house.

"Rufus is pining, but he's well. He's a very intelligent dog. Your grandfather trained him well. He'll never attack needlessly or turn on you. But the new house will disturb him. You have done as I suggested, have you not?" He held open the front door and allowed Charlie to walk into the living room. "Sit down and tell me how you like your coffee."

"Cream, no sugar, if the coffee is strong. Otherwise, black." He sat in one of the beautiful leather chairs.

"Bueno. I will be back in a moment." He left the room but continued to speak from the kitchen. "Make sure that you give Rufus a place that's his own. Put down his blanket for him. Don't be too severe if he starts shedding or he needs to be let out to relieve himself more often. Moving is hard on dogs. If he starts vomiting or shitting in the house, let me know about it. That's more serious, and you don't want it to become a habit with him."

Charlie tried to imagine his well-mannered pet behaving the way Montoya described, and found it was impossible. Rufus had been a gift from his grandfather, the pick of the litter of his own seeing-eye dog. Rufus, with his mixed husky and Highland collie breeds, was steady-tempered and had been excellently raised. "I think he'll be okay when he gets used to it. But if I have any trouble, I'll call you."

There were some confusing sounds from the kitchen, but in a moment they stopped, and Roldan Montoya went on, "Amelia's over in Oakdale today. She's competing in a horse show, but I think the real reason she went is to see if she can buy one of those Andalusians from that man with the horse farm down near Riverside. He's bringing some stock up." He came back into the living room with a tray. "If you ever get tired of practicing law, Charlie, I'll take you on out here. Anything you want to do—train dogs, work horses, anything. You've got a feel for animals, and that's rare." He put the tray down and looked up quickly enough to see the uncomfortable expression at the back of Charlie's eyes. "What did I say?"

"Nothing." Charlie's shrug was uncomfortable. "I guess it's that old stereotype problem. Blacks have a natural sense of rhythm, and Indians are close to animals and nature. We're supposed to have some extra sense." He half smiled. "It *is* tempting, though."

"But don't you have such a sense, Charlie? Not Indians in general, you in particular." Roldan Montoya pulled up a chair and gave Charlie one of the large mugs on the tray and indicated the little sugar-covered cakes piled on an elaborately painted dish. "Amelia made them last night. Have some. And I hope the whipped cream doesn't ruin your coffee."

Experimentally Charlie sipped the bitter, strong coffee through the floating cream. "Very good."

"Gracias. But you still haven't answered my question." When Charlie didn't respond immediately, Montoya added, "I have seen you with animals, and you have a talent. Such ability is rare. When I was young, still living in Pamplona, there was a man who was better than anyone else in the district in taking care of animals. He was very well known, believe me. They all brought their horses and donkeys and goats and dogs to him, and he would cure them if there was the slightest possibility of saving the animal. Everyone said strange things about him, and a few accused him of witchcraft, for belief in witches is not dead in Spain. But I wasn't afraid of him, and sometimes he would let me work with him. I saw what he did, but I never learned to do it myself. I didn't see him once the Civil War was under way, and after that, of course, my brother brought us all to America. But I have never forgotten him, and I see something of him in you."

For one wild moment, Charlie wondered what Roldan would say if he told him the truth—that, aside from being an attorney, he was the medicine man of the Iron River Ojibwas. The impulse passed, and Charlie was able to say, "I like animals. That's probably the difference: liking them, respecting them."

Roldan Montoya took one of the sugared cakes and popped it into his mouth. When he was finished, he said, "Finish your coffee while I get Rufus."

Before he reached home once more, Charlie had seen several troupes of young goblins and witches, and, as always, Halloween made him feel uncomfortable. He disliked making light of the forces around him. He felt insulted that a ghost should be made an object of scorn by a child in an old sheet. When he was a child in Vallejo, before he and his father had returned to Canada, he had played trick or treat at Halloween, but even then it had made him uneasy. Later, as his grandfather began teaching him the ways of magic, Charlie had come to understand his dislike of the mocking ritual.

Rufus whined as he sat on the seat beside Charlie. This was not the way home, and it bothered him. He looked anxiously at Charlie and flattened his ears as he waved his tail tentatively, whimpering a little as Charlie patted his head. "It's okay, fella. You're going to like the new house. You're going to have a backyard all to yourself, and there's a sun porch upstairs where you can hide out until you get used to the place."

Rufus stared out the window with forlorn eyes and was still staring when Charlie pulled into the driveway. He got out long enough to open the garage door, then drove in and closed the door behind him. In the car, Rufus started to bark.

"Come on, fella, get out. We're home." Charlie reached back into the car and rubbed the dog's head. "Come on upstairs, and I'll get you some food." He didn't try to force the dog out of the car, waiting until Rufus emerged of his own volition. Rufus was still apprehensive, as the nervous way he carried his head revealed more than his curious sniffing.

While Rufus explored the main floor, Charlie went to the kitchen to set out food for the dog and to do something about supper for himself. It was slightly after five, and the dark was settling in fast.

He had just turned on the light when the phone rang. He looked at the pans on the stove and called Rufus to the kitchen before he reached for the phone. "Charles Moon speaking," he said as he clamped the receiver between his ear and his shoulder.

"This is Ty Malcomb," said the voice in his ear. "I've got to talk to you."

"Go on," Charlie invited as he stirred browning chicken livers with sour cream.

"I had a call this afternoon," Ty said with difficulty. "It was from the coroner's office. It was a Dr. Lee . . ."

"Nee," Charlie corrected. "What did he have to say?"

"They've done the autopsy on Feuier," Ty said, but there was none of the relief that Charlie had expected this news to bring.

"What happened?" As he asked that, he reached and turned down the fire under the chicken livers. Dinner would have to wait. "What did he die of?"

"Well, there was heroin in him . . ."

"Great," Charlie said caustically. "An OD. Wonderful."

"But that wasn't it, not according to Dr.—is it?—Nee. He said that there wasn't enough heroin and there were not enough indications to conclude that a drug overdose caused death. He said that Feuier had to have taken something else, something that reacted to the heroin, perhaps . . ." He stopped quite suddenly. "He might have been killed deliberately."

"Murdered," Charlie supplied, feeling very tired. He dragged a chair nearer the kitchen wall phone.

"God. Could it be? Really? I mean, we talked about the possibility, but I never really thought . . ." There was a sudden silence on the phone. "Someone actually *killed* Feuier."

More for Ty's benefit than his own, Charlie suggested, "He might have done it himself. He might have wanted to go out with a bang."

"But why? Why any of it?" Ty's voice had risen.

"I don't know." Charlie thought carefully about what to say next. "Tell me what Dr. Nee said, as precisely as you can. I'll check with the coroner's office before the meetings tomorrow, but give me anything you remember so that I'll have something to go on."

"All right." Ty made an effort to steady his voice. "Dr. Nee said that although there was heroin in the body, it was not in sufficient quantity to cause death, even given the nature of what Feuier was doing. He said that from the state of the internal organs it was difficult to tell how long Feuier had been on the drug, but he thought it could not be long . . ."

Charlie interrupted. "Wait. Did he say why he couldn't determine how long Feuier had been taking heroin? It usually leaves pretty definite signs."

"He didn't mention . . ."

"I'll find out tomorrow. Go on." He looked at the stove and sighed to himself as he watched the sour-cream sauce for the livers grow cold and lumpy.

"There were some indications of other drugs in the body, but nothing conclusive, he said. I had a call from the police and from one of the bigwigs on the Board of Directors of the Opera Company."

"Who was that?" Charlie asked idly, planning to call Elizabeth and ask her to deal with this person.

By Ty's answer drove that idea from his mind. "Rocco Lemmini," he said miserably.

Charlie cursed. Rocco Lemmini was the President of the Board of Supervisors and the wiliest old fox of a Florentine in San Francisco. His sons were hotel owners, jewelers, and, Charlie thought with a shudder, lawyers. "Shit," he said, not realizing he'd spoken aloud.

"He's going to make a statement to the press tomorrow afternoon," Ty added. "He could blow the whole thing wide open. There won't be any way to keep it private, if he does."

Inwardly, Charlie doubted that there was ever any chance to keep a case like this private, but certainly having the Lemminis taking a hand made it much more difficult. "I'll call the cops in the morning and find out what their opinion is. They might ask him to postpone his announcement for a bit."

"Would that make any difference?" Ty sounded hopeless now, and defeated.

"It might." That was all Charlie could say. He looked at the stove and the boxes in the kitchen still waiting to be unpacked. It would take him weeks to get this house organized. He said to Ty Malcomb, "Do any of the singers know yet? Are any of the people on your staff aware of what's happening?"

There was a pause. "I doubt it. I didn't hear until halfway through the performance this afternoon. Two matinees on the weekends is a hectic schedule. I doubt if anyone else heard what was said during the call."

"But someone told Rocco Lemmini." For a moment, Charlie debated phoning David Lemmini, Rocco's lawyer son, and asking him to speak with his father, but immediately thought better of it. The Lemmini clan did not tolerate interference from the outside. "Do you think you can find out who else knows about Feuier's death? If you call Dr. Nee, he should be willing to tell you. The report is a matter of public record, but it hasn't been officially released yet. You have good reason to want this information."

Ty responded doubtfully. "Do you think that's wise? I mean, if someone really did kill Feuier, wouldn't this give them a warning? The secret's out now. The . . . killer isn't safe any longer."

"Look, Ty, it's going to come out anyway. All you can do is cushion the blow. That's why you want to find out who knows about Feuier. Can you imagine what would happen if the *Chronicle* called up"—he picked a singer at random from the files he had read the night before— "Domenico Solechiaro and asked him to comment on the autopsy results? Or suppose they talked to Jocelynne Hendricks, who didn't like Feuier. The whole thing would blow like Vesuvius."

"I'll call Dr. Nee back," Ty said very calmly. "If you're going to be in later tonight, I'll call you again after I've talked to him." He added, "Do you think I should call the singers? The ones who are most likely to get asked about Feuier?"

Charlie considered this. "Okay, if you think it would help, do it. But remember that you'll start rumors moving when you do that. Tell your people whatever is wise. And tell them that if the cops start asking anything other than the most general questions that they should call me. General questions are okay, but anything specific is another matter. And for God's sake, tell them to err on the side of caution if they aren't sure what the difference is between general and specific questions." He stood up. "I'll let you get back to Dr. Nee. Call me when you've talked to him."

"I will." Some of Ty's confidence was coming back into his voice. "I hope I didn't interrupt anything. Thanks, Charlie."

"No," Charlie said as he heard Ty hang up. "You didn't interrupt anything." He gave his cooling dinner a thoughtful stare and turned his attention to salvaging as much of it as he could.

Monday, November 1

His morning court appearance went even more quickly than Charlie had thought it would, which was rare. It gave him an extra half hour, and he used that time to drop by the coroner's office.

"Howdy there, Charles," Pete Coners said with unaccustomed joviality. "You've been a real stranger around here."

"My clients haven't been killing each other of late," Charlie said dryly. He stood in the door and glanced around the neat windowless cubicle that was Pete Coners' office. "Mind if I come in?"

"Come ahead." Pete, who was a big, deceptively slovenly looking man with a lived-in face and rumpled clothes, shoved a stack of file folders to one side of his desk and offered Charlie a seat where they had been. "I've been after another chair for a couple of years. But who visits coroners? Particularly deputy coroners?" It was a rhetorical question.

"Pete," Charlie said seriously as he slung a leg over the end of the desk, "what can you tell me about this Feuier mess?"

"Why? What do you have to do with it?" There was the usual sharp attention at the back of Pete's lazy eyes. "Are you getting mixed up in it, or is this just academic curiosity?"

"I'm getting mixed up in it. Tell me what happened to Gui-Adam Feuier." He sat on the edge of the desk and looked down at Pete's unruly thatch of graying hair.

"Gui-Adam Feuier was playing at being a junkie, Charlie. He had a few tracks on his arms, but nothing on his legs yet, so he was still a beginner. Now, either he took something that didn't mix with heroin, he developed an allergy or other reaction to the stuff, or someone slipped him something extra."

"Deliberately?" Charlie asked quickly, studying the reaction that Pete was quick to disguise.

"Who knows? That's for the cops. I'd like to figure out what else was in him when he died. If we could figure that out, we'd be a long way to knowing why it was done, and who did it." He inspected the backs of his hands. "Lucile thinks it was one of the women. There was a thing on the news about all the women he was chasing. Lucile thinks that one of them got mad, heard about the dope, and decided to get even. She thinks it might have been Feuier's wife that did it."

"His wife?" Charlie asked, trying to remember any mention of a wife in the file he had read on Saturday night.

"Yeah, apparently he had a wife," Pete said with satisfaction. Learning about the sins of the world always pleased him. "There was a big interview with her in one of those Paris papers, and some of the locals are planning to pick up on it. It's all full of the martyred wife bit."

"Maybe she was, Pete," Charlie suggested with an edge to his voice.

"Maybe she was what? A martyred wife? Look, a man like that, big, handsome guy singing all over the world, everyone hot for him, what'd she expect? You take your applause where you can get it, Charlie." He chuckled. "He must have had some time. They showed pictures of some of the women. A lot of 'em weren't much to look at, but some of 'em . . ." He rolled his eyes lasciviously and leaned back in his chair. "I wouldn't object if they spread their legs for me, not at all."

Charlie frowned.

"And if Lucile gave me a bad time, well, shit, it'd be worth it." Pete's expression changed. "You know, ever since she quit her job in September, she's been a real bitch."

Although he knew this was not leading to anything he wanted to know, Charlie said, "Too bad. Why did she quit?"

Pete gestured in obscene exasperation. "It was so fuckin' *dumb!* She tried to get the manager at Rossiter's to give her a job as a buyer. Well, he said he couldn't. And then he promoted this new guy he hired over her. Well, okay, so she had the seniority, but the new guy has a wife and two kids to support, for Chri'sake. And all he did was ask Lucile to give him a hand a couple of times until he knew the ropes. To hear her, you'd think somebody shafted her. *Women!*"

Charlie's voice was very quiet. "She should have sued."

"Yeah, that's what she said until I talked some sense into her." Pete shook his head. "You lawyers, you slay me. Anything to get a fee." He grinned appreciatively.

Charlie hated to admit that there was any truth in Pete's accusation, but he hesitated before he said, "Even if you're right, Pete, it doesn't change the fact that the law was on Lucile's side. And as her husband, you ought to stand by her."

"Stand by her?" Pete gestured helplessly. "What for? So we can lose a lot of money and she can have a couple years of worry and trouble? Fine husband I'd be." He stared up at Charlie, and his sleepy, canny eyes narrowed. "So what else did you come here for?"

Charlie weighed his answer carefully. "Are you planning to pursue the Feuier investigation? Is there any reason to suppose that he was the victim of premeditated murder?"

Pete almost laughed, then realized that Charlie was serious. "We'll pursue it as much as we have to, unless the widow stops us."

"Does she have that power?" Charlie wondered aloud.

"The Mayor doesn't want a big scandal unless there's no avoiding it. And you know that Horatio Cronin won't start an investigation or prosecution in the full glare of the international press unless he's damn sure he's gonna come out of it shiny as healthy fur." He smiled at the image and turned an ingenuous glance on Charlie. "If you want my personal opinion, I'll give it to you."

"Okay," Charlie said, firmly conquering his reluctance, "what do you think happened?"

Pete leaned back again and laced his fingers behind his head. From his cynical smile, Charlie knew that Pete was enjoying himself. "I think that one of those jealous bastards he works with found out about the heroin and decided to play a little game on him. He probably got one of those drugs that you can buy over the counter and thought he could make Feuier real sick, right in front of God and everybody. But maybe Feuier was allergic to the drug or maybe the two drugs together were too much for him. And he dropped dead instead of barfing all over the stage."

"A practical joke gone wrong?" Charlie mused. "Why do you say that?"

"Well, look, if it were something like arsenic or one of the other standards, he'd be a garbage heap inside. We'd spot it. But there's nothing really wrong other than what the heroin did. So it figures that this was an amateur."

"Or a very clever professional," Charlie countered. He got off the desk. "That's it, Pete. I'll think about what you've said. And if you come up with anything, will you give me a call?"

Pete pretended to think about it. "I might. If you tell that receptionist of yours to be nice to me next time." He put his right hand to his chest, over his stomach.

Charlie paused in the door. "Did Lydia offend you? That's not like her." Too late he realized that Pete had set him up.

"Offend me? A classy Chinese chick like Lydia? I tell you, Charlie, I was gal*lant*." He chuckled again. "She told me to fuck off. Do you let your receptionist use language like that to a public servant like me?" He beamed at Charlie's discomfiture.

"Whatever you said to Lydia must have been very unpleasant for her," Charlie said levelly.

"You know, Charlie, the trouble with you is you want to lay that bitchy little ball-cutter Studevant, so you go around saying the same shit she gives out. She's probably a les anyway, and about as much good in bed as a board full of tacks." Pete saw that this had struck home and he laughed outright. "She's got a great bod, though."

Charlie forced himself not to be angry. "I think you spend too much time with corpses, Pete. You forget what it's like to be human." He didn't wait for a response; he knew that Pete was in a mood to trade insults all day. "Thanks for the info about Feuier. If you find out what else he took, let me know."

"Sure thing," Pete said with an easy wave.

Charlie had just come in from lunch when he saw his partner, Alex Tallant, coming down the hall, a wide, charming grin on his handsome face. "Charlie," he said at his expansive best.

"Hello, Alex. I thought you were going to be in court today."

"I am, I am. The voir dire is taking forever. The veniremen they've got!" He shook his head indulgently.

"What's the case?" Charlie asked as he glanced at his watch.

"Oh, you know the one. The mother's accused of child abuse. The ex-husband is trying to get custody of the kids. He claims that the upstairs neighbor has seen her beat the kids, and claims that she does some very kinky things to the kids as punishment."

"And does she?" Charlie asked in spite of himself.

"How do I know?" Alex favored him with an innocent smile. "My job is to see she keeps her kids. The father isn't any too savory, either. He's living with a woman with kids of her own, and he works as a janitor at Washington High. Not very promising material, really." He gave Charlie an arch look. "I hear through the grapevine that you're in on that Feuier thing. You're a very lucky Indian."

So that was it, Charlie thought. Alex was jealous. He waited for Alex's next words.

"Want to trade cases? You're the one who's always going on about human rights. My case is much more in your line. And let's be honest, Charlie. The kind of social affairs that go with opera singers, that's my home turf . . ."

At this point, Charlie interrupted him. "Jordan Alexander Tallant, if you make one move, any move at all, to interfere in this or any of my cases, I warn you right now I'll resign from the firm and take my clients with me."

He would have said more, but the door opened and the receptionist, Lydia Wong, came into the room. Both Charlie and Alex turned away, Alex's color slightly heightened.

Lydia looked at Charlie and said in her collected way, "You have an appointment in five minutes, Mr. Moon.

Mr. Tallant, there is a phone call for you, a Ms. Ellen Chambers."

Glad for this chance to break away, Alex became very businesslike. "Thank you, Lydia. I'll take the call in my office." He pushed past Charlie and left the room.

Lydia stared after Alex, and said at last in a soft voice, "I used to be in love with that creep. He's the most beautiful man I've ever seen, and that charm . . . But he's a creep." Even in anger, her elegant Chinese face was composed. She turned toward Charlie and almost smiled. "If you ever do break away from Willis and Alex, I'd love to go with you. You're the best attorney in this firm, and you deserve better."

Charlie was completely taken aback. He blinked at Lydia and found it difficult to speak. "You don't have to say that," he muttered, then, knowing how graceless that was, he added, "But Lydia, thank you very much."

"You're welcome," Lydia said, then looked down at the file she held in her hand. "Mr. Malcomb called this morning and made these appointments for the afternoon." She handed a photocopy to Charlie.

"What did we do before copying machines?" Charlie asked the air.

"We used lots and lots of carbon paper," Lydia said bitterly. "Will you take calls, or are these meetings closed?"

"If it's an emergency, put the call through. But otherwise, get me a name and number for callback." He nodded toward his office door. "Will you show them in when they get here?"

"If you like." Lydia started back toward her desk and then added, "Willis called an hour ago. He's going to be in Washington through Friday."

"He sounds pretty damn confident, then." Charlie wasn't really very interested in the presidential election. He had often castigated himself for his indifference toward politics, and excused himself on the basis that most of his interests were tied up in the politics of his own tribe, which was in Canada.

"If the Democrats win, he'll be impossible."

"He'll be impossible if they lose, too." He wanted to make up for his lack of enthusiasm, so he said, "If you aren't going to vote for Carter, promise me you'll never tell Willis."

Lydia laughed, and the sound was strangely enigmatic. "I'll remember that," she said.

Jocelynne Hendricks was wearing a tweed pantsuit and carrying a handbag the size of a briefcase. She looked once around Charlie's office, then came across the room. "You're Mr. Moon."

"And you're Jocelynne Hendricks," Charlie said as they shook hands. "I'm glad you have the time to speak to me. Please sit down."

She took the chair he indicated and looked at him. Her features were too strong to be pretty, and her candor reminded Charlie uncomfortably of Elizabeth. "Ty Malcomb said this had to do with Feuier's death. Is that right?"

"Yes," Charlie said, wondering where to start.

"Ty's afraid that there might be trouble, is that it? He doesn't want any of us to make it worse." There was an ironic edge to her lovely, low-pitched voice.

"That's part of it," Charlie agreed. "He also wants to be certain that you understand the law in this matter." She motioned him to continue. "There has been an autopsy, and certain . . . questions have resulted. You will probably be asked to tell what happened . . ."

"But I already told the cops that," Hendricks objected. "The night Feuier died, and then some questions on the phone yesterday."

Although he didn't change outwardly, Charlie was very

much on the alert. "What did they ask? And what did you say?"

"Oh, nothing very much. Where was Feuier when he died? What did he do? Did he say anything? Did I say anything? Did he appear ill or upset? That sort of question."

"What were your answers?" Charlie took out a pen and scribbled a few notes to himself.

"You know, what else was there to say? I told them that we were finishing *Hoffmann,* and Feuier was making a mess of it as usual. Tey cued me to take Hoffmann's responses, but I couldn't do the recitative for him, so I nudged him, and he fell over. He didn't say a damn thing, and I was too . . . shocked, I guess, to say anything. I told him that Feuier and I didn't see each other between acts, so I didn't know how he was feeling. He was singing really wretchedly."

"Did you say that?" Charlie asked. With his left hand, he began to tap restlessly on the desktop.

"Sure. Everyone in the damn Opera House knew it. All you had to do was listen. He was strained on top and muddy on the bottom, and his breath control was nonexistent." She looked at her hands. "Was it unwise of me to say that?"

Charlie sighed. "Probably not, if he was as bad as you say."

"He was. But . . ." She looked away toward the high windows, where bright, unseasonable sunshine made the room glow.

"But?" Charlie prompted her gently.

"I wasn't very kind. I hated Gui-Adam," she mused, unaware that she had called the dead tenor by his first name.

There wasn't an easy way to ask the next question. "But I understood you were . . . involved with Feuier once."

Jocelynne Hendricks flushed. "It was some time ago. I

learned better, Mr. Moon." Her eyes were brilliant with anger. "It was part of what made me hate him. That and the way he treated Linnet Nørrehavn."

"And what way was that, Ms. Hendricks?"

"Vilely," she said concisely. "He deserved to be flayed for it."

Charlie made certain mental allowances for Jocelynne Hendricks' theatricality as well as her own experiences with Feuier, but he was still worried about the hostility she revealed. "Why? What did he do?"

She swallowed with distaste and compassion. "He tried to make her be like him. And when he couldn't, he destroyed her."

"Isn't that too severe?" Charlie suggested mildly.

"No! Linnet was a beautiful woman, inside and out, and Gui-Adam ruined her. And," she added with sudden vehemence, "you've got no idea how much I wanted to tell the cops that. Gui-Adam Feuier deserved to die." She pushed up out of the chair and walked over to the window, standing with her back to Charlie.

"Ms. Hendricks?" Charlie said impatiently. Then he saw that her shoulders were trembling, and he relented. He went across the room and put gentle hands on her arms. "Don't be ashamed, Ms. Hendricks." He felt her stiffen under his fingers. "Let this out now, not where it might do harm."

But Jocelynne Hendricks was already wiping her face with a monogrammed handkerchief. "I'll be all right in a moment," she said, sternly controlling her voice. She folded the handkerchief and stuffed it into her pocket, and with a slight toss of her hair, she turned around, saying too brightly, "I don't usually act this way, Mr. Moon. But holding this all in the last few days, and with Enrique in Munich, I've been beside myself."

"Who's Enrique?" Charlie asked.

"My fiancé. He's a director and a designer. He's working on a new *Boccanegra.* I called him Thursday, but it's not the same thing." She said the last forlornly, and for an instant, Charlie understood that Jocelynne Hendricks was lonely. He stepped back and motioned to the chair again.

"Please, Ms. Hendricks. There are a few more things we have to discuss. I'll try to be brief." Charlie waited until Jocelynn Hendricks was seated once more, then he said, "This whole thing could blow up in our faces, you know." He kept his tone very even and pleasant. "There would be a lot of extremely nasty publicity. If possible, we want to avoid this."

"If possible?" she echoed him.

"We don't know yet how Feuier died. That's one of the reasons I'm talking to you now. If it turns out that this was merely a terrible accident, well and good. However, it might be something more."

This time Jocelynne Hendricks turned pale. "More? Do you mean suicide? Gui-Adam?"

"It's one possibility," Charlie said quickly. "If the police should talk to you again, please give them general answers. Keep personalities out of it if you can." He studied her face and decided she could take a little more. "Ms. Hendricks, an investigation of this sort is never pleasant. Everything you can do, within the limits of the law, to minimize the upheaval resulting from this . . . accident, the better for you and all the others. If, for example, there are questions about Mr. Nørrehavn's wife, it would be wiser to suggest that they talk to Mr. Nørrehavn. If they ask you if you knew about bad feelings between Nørrehavn and Feuier or any other singer, you can say that Feuier was generally unpopular, but please, please don't elaborate. And if, for some reason, the police insist that you answer questions, call me first. There are certain sorts of questions that you need not and should not answer." He handed her one of his personal cards. "That's my home address and phone number. If you have any questions, call me here or at home."

Jocelynne Hendricks took the card and stared at it rather blankly. Then she looked up. "It's real, isn't it, Mr. Moon?"

Charlie had heard enough dazed questions to understand. "Yes, Ms. Hendricks. It's real."

She looked at him. "But no matter what, Gui-Adam deserved it!"

"Under the law, Ms. Hendricks, no one deserves it. Look, unless your life is in immediate and certain danger, you have no right to kill another human being. Manslaughter and murder are crimes, and the law is not concerned about the personality or morals or peculiarities of the victim. It's the act that counts. And the person who does the killing is punishable under the law." He had spoken sternly, hoping that Jocelynne Hendricks would be persuaded to curb her tongue. He leaned forward and added, "No matter what Feuier did, the law says it doesn't justify killing him."

Somewhat numbly, Jocelynne Hendricks apologized. "But it doesn't seem right. And no matter what you say, there *are* people who ought to die. Think about Hitler. Or the terrorists who killed those Israeli schoolchildren." She put Charlie's card in her purse. "All right, Mr. Moon. I'll try to remember. But the cops will have to be painfully dumb not to figure out about Gui-Adam."

"That, Ms. Hendricks, is their problem. Keeping you out of trouble is mine."

Half an hour later, Charlie finished a second cup of coffee and looked at his notes on Jocelynn Hendricks. He thought he should keep an eye on her; her temper was under control, but there was an explosive rage in her that he could not afford to overlook. He knew he would have to talk this over with Ty Malcomb later in the evening.

His thoughts were interrupted by Lydia's voice on the

intercom. "Mr. Moon, there's a Mr. Solechiaro to see you."

In his mind, Charlie quickly reviewed the file on Solechiaro. When he was certain he'd sorted it out, he said to the intercom, "Very good, Ms. Wong. Please send him in."

A few moments later, there was a knock on the door. Charlie had risen to answer it when it was flung open and Domenico Solechiaro strode into the room. He was one of those men who seem much larger than they really are, which, in Solechiaro's case, was truly impressive. Standing just under six feet, Solechiaro had the massive good looks of a professional football player. His chest, Charlie knew from the singer's costume records, was fifty-four inches around, and, judging from the way he moved, very little of it was fat.

"You are Sr. Moon?" he demanded in accented but excellent English. He smiled as he took Charlie's hand. "I am very proud to have this honor of your acquaintance."

In his ten years of law practice, Charlie had never met anyone of such incandescent charm. It was an effort of will to be stern with the big Italian. "How do you do, Mr. Solechiaro. Please come in."

Domenico Solechiaro glanced around the room. "*È bella questa camera,*" he informed Charlie. He selected one of the three chairs, not the one opposite the desk, and sat down. "*Ebben,* you wanted to speak to me. *Ecco.* I am here."

Charlie resisted the urge to pull one of the casual chairs nearer. It would be so simple just to chat with Solechiaro. But he resisted the magnetism and walked back to his chair behind his desk. "Are you comfortable there, Mr. Solechiaro?"

"Of course," he answered with a wave of his hand. "This is a very nice chair." He beamed at Charlie.

Ordinarily Charlie would have been irritated. Now he

felt himself smile. "Thank you." In order to regain direction of the interview, he picked up his notepad and said, "I understand the police have asked you some questions about the death of Mr. Feuier."

"*Ah, si.* They have come to me. I have told them that it was true that Feuier and I were rivals. But I did not mind that. I'm a better singer." This last was a simple statement of fact, and Solechiaro accented it with a shrug. "What more could I say?"

Privately Charlie thought that was quite enough. "Did they ask you anything more?"

"They asked if I saw him die. As it happened, I did not."

"Why?" Charlie asked, more out of form than from any real desire for information. Since his own tour of the Opera House backstage, he realized that it would have been remarkable if Solechiaro had seen Feuier die.

"It is greatly sad, but I cannot tell you that." He folded his arms and smiled.

Immediately Charlie was curious. "Why not?"

"Others are involved." He stared at Charlie, then said with disarming frankness. "I have not seen someone like you before. You are not of the Orient, I think. Perhaps you are mixed?"

"I'm an Ojibwa," Charlie said shortly. He regarded Solechiaro evenly, secretly pleased that the tenor was confused.

"What is Ojibwa?" he demanded with the same eager curiosity that had marked his entrance into Charlie's office.

At that, Charlie relented. "An Indian tribe. In Canada."

"*Ah!*" Solechiaro sprang to his feet and crossed the room to lean on the desk, studying Charlie's face intently. "An Indian. It is a marvel. Your face is the color of ripe grain. How beautiful. You should be proud, Sr. Moon. Always I have wanted to meet an Indian."

Anger filled Charlie, and left him almost at once. There was no condescension in Solechiaro's expression, only an odd respect. He was about to rebuke the Italian gently when Solechiaro said, "You must not feel shamed, Sr. Moon. It is a most fortunate thing to be rare. I know. I am a tenor. And tenors are rarer even than Indians."

Charlie had heard similar remarks before, and they had always offended him deeply. He looked up at Solechiaro, his eyes keen. The smile that answered his glance was one of genuine delight, and to his surprise, Charlie found himself starting to laugh. With an effort, he controlled this, saying, "Mr. Solechiaro, please. Sit down again. There are a few things we ought to discuss about Mr. Feuier's unfortunate death."

"But it was not unfortunate," Solechiaro said as he returned to the chair. "Oh, *si*, it was most unlucky for the opera company, but men like Feuier, it is not a bad thing when they die."

"I hope," Charlie said, "that you haven't said so."

"No. No. But, of course, I have not denied that it pleases me greatly that he is dead." Solechiaro opened his hands innocently. "Why should I lie, Sr. Moon? All the world knows that he and I were not friends."

"Whom did you say this to?" Charlie had abandoned taking notes for the moment.

"I do not precisely remember. It was at dinner, yesterday evening. The food was excellent . . ."

Before Domenico Solechiaro could digress onto the subject of food, Charlie interrupted him. "Who was with you, Mr. Solechiaro?"

The Italian studied Charlie a moment. "You have a very good accent, Sr. Moon. You pronounce my name correctly. *Mille grazie.*"

"That's very kind of you," Charlie said, determined not to be sidetracked again. "But I wish you would tell me who else had dinner with you last night."

"We were at a restaurant on the other side of the Bay," Solechiaro said thoughtfully. "An excellent restaurant. Expensive, truly, but superb food. Americans," he added slowly, "do not in general understand food. They eat too quickly and fear to be fat. This restaurant is not for such. They served the food well. The wines were good."

Charlie wanted to interrupt but thought it would be better to let Solechiaro ramble a bit longer; it would be easier to find out whom he had dined with. "Where was this, again?"

"Near Berkeley," Solechiaro answered promptly. "A place named Narsai's, as I recall. A strange name, don't you agree?" He beamed at Charlie.

"And who was with you?" Charlie asked again, his patience beginning to wear thin.

"There was Agnes Sorrel. Do you know her?" He saw Charlie shake his head. "A superb pianist. I am a great admirer of hers. There was her husband, who is, I think, a teacher or professor of some sort. He is forever talking about 'mind-sets' and other absurdities. They had brought guests with them, of course, three others." He stopped long enough to think about these guests. "I found the woman most pleasant, even though she asked many foolish questions."

"Do you remember her name?"

Solechiaro's answer destroyed Charlie's dawning hope that perhaps the tenor's unfortunate remarks would be forgotten. "The inquisitive woman? Hers was a peculiar name. I will recall it . . ." He looked across the room, an expression of complete blankness on his face. "I think," he said cautiously, "that perhaps her name was Felicity. Felicity. A strange name. The last name, I am certain of."

"Yes?" Charlie said for form's sake, already picturing in his mind the assertive young newswoman working at KRON.

"Cooper. Yes. Felicity Cooper." Solechiaro considered

the matter a moment, then added, "She asked me a great
deal about Feuier. Foolish questions. It was annoying to
speak with her. She kept saying what a great man Feuier
was. She knows nothing about the voice, nothing about
the opera, nothing about the music."

Angrily Charlie agreed. It was an old reporter's trick,
asking simplistic, annoying questions and praising the
opposition to goad the subject into unguarded responses.
"Felicity Cooper," Charlie said aloud.

Apparently Solechiaro caught condemnation in
Charlie's inflection. "It was wrong to speak with her? But
why? I assure you I explained everything most thoroughly."

"You did?" Charlie sat back in his chair, wondering
what to do now. If Felicity Cooper knew about Solechiaro's feelings toward Feuier, the chance of avoiding
scandal was almost nonexistent. He realized he ought to
warn Ty Malcomb. He was about to ask Solechiaro how
much he had told Ms. Cooper when there was a knock at
the door. "Yes?" Charlie called out, hating to be interrupted at so crucial a moment.

"It's Morgan," said the person on the other side of the
door. "I'm sorry to interrupt. There's a paper here that
must be signed."

Charlie hesitated, then said, "Come in, Morgan." He
turned to Solechiaro to explain. "Ms. Studevant is my
associate, another attorney."

By then, Morgan had stepped into the room, a folder in
her hand, an apologetic expression in her eyes that
quickly faded as she recognized Charlie's companion.

Domenico Solechiaro had risen at her entrance and
now moved toward her. *"Bellissima!"* he exclaimed as he
took her hand and lifted it to his lips.

One time before, Charlie had seen Morgan in such a
situation. It was shortly after Morgan had won her first
case. Alex Tallant had stopped her in the outer office,

complimented her, and kissed her hand. Morgan had
been furious. So Charlie braced himself for a similar
explosion.

It never came. Morgan smiled awkwardly as she withdrew her hand. "Thank you," she said quietly.

"I am Domenico Solechiaro, kind lady. And you
are . . ."

"I know who you are," Morgan answered. "I've been an
admirer of yours for years. I have several of your
records." Her reserve lessened as he drew her toward one
of the chairs. "It's a pleasure to meet you."

"Ah, but this is not so. The pleasure must be mine. Is it
true, what Sr. Moon has told me? That you are *una
avvocata?*"

"I'm an attorney, if that's what you mean," she said, but
there was no rebuke in her tone. "I'm Morgan Studevant."

"Morgan? But this is a man's name, and, *cara,* you are
not a man." He had led her to a chair which he held for
her, waiting until she was seated before returning to the
chair he had occupied.

"It's sometimes a woman's name," Morgan explained
earnestly. "In the legends of King Arthur, there is a
woman who is a great enchantress, Morgan le Fay."

"Then you are well named, for you are enchanting."
Solechiaro leaned toward her, his whole attention on her.
"But why, when you are so lovely, do you practice the law,
which is surely for dull old men?"

At that, Charlie scowled, but Morgan answered, "Not
everyone in the law is dull, Mr. Solechiaro, and you may
think it foolish of me, but I believe in justice." Some of her
stiffness was back as she continued. "I must get Mr.
Moon's signature on this paper. Neither Mr. Ogilvie nor
Mr. Tallant is available, or I wouldn't have bothered you."

"And I would be desolated," Solechiaro said, rising as
she rose. "Do not leave, Miss Morgan Studevant."

Morgan stopped at the desk and looked back at the big

tenor. "I have two cases that need my attention. It's flattering of you to ask."

Solechiaro shook his head. "No, it is not your cases that take you away; you have permitted me to offend you. Truly, *cara,* I would rather perish than offend you."

Charlie finished reading the paper and reached for his pen to sign it, saying in an undervoice as he did, "I wish you would stay. I need help."

Morgan's eyes widened for an instant. "All right. What do you want me to do?"

"Get it through his thick Italian head," Charlie said with more resignation than anger, "that this is a serious matter and he could get into a great deal of trouble. He's already made a big mistake. He talked about Feuier at a dinner party last night. One of the party was Felicity Cooper."

"Grand." Morgan left the folder on the desk and turned back to Solechiaro. "Mr. Moon is being very kind. He's asked me to stay while he talks with you. If you don't mind, I'm going to make a few comments of my own."

"I could not mind," Solechiaro announced with a sweeping gesture of his hands developed more for the huge scale of an opera house stage than for the comparative intimacy of a law office. "It gives me the opportunity to see you more."

Morgan cast a quick glance back at Charlie, then walked over to where Solechiaro was sitting. "You must be very disturbed by Mr. Feuier's death," she said as she sank into the chair beside the tenor.

"Not too much," he said nonchalantly. "I attended the Requiem on Saturday, of course. It is a pity that there has been so much uproar on his account. But, *cara,* you must not concern yourself with Sr. Feuier."

Charlie watched as Morgan studied her fingers. He tried not to smile. She was succeeding where he had failed, and he could not keep from admiring her skill with the singer.

"You see, Mr. Solechiaro," she said shyly, "I am concerned for Feuier because his death could affect you."

"But why? How could it?"

This time Morgan's hesitation was longer, and Charlie
knew it was more genuine than the first. "Mr. Solechiaro,
you've admitted that you and Feuier were rivals. It's
common knowledge. Mr. Feuier died under peculiar
circumstances. Until the cause of his death is known, the
authorities will be forced to consider several unpleasant
possibilities. One of those possibilities is that you might
have . . . contributed to his death." As she finished the
words, Morgan looked squarely at Solechiaro.

"Impossibile! Non posso! Quest' è follia, la vergogna." He
stopped, confused. "I am sorry. *Mi dispiace* . . . It does not
please me to hear such things." His accent was much
stronger now, and it was an effort for him to continue
speaking in English. "I am unable to think that anyone
would imagine that I would do anything so despicable.
That I could want such a thing . . ." He broke off
suddenly and added in a quieter tone, "Of course, he was
a bad man and a worse singer. His fame was bad. He
behaved most deplorably. Certainly he upset me in the
past, with tricks of evil children, and for that and other
reasons, I was his enemy, and he was mine. It is well
known. But if you think that because of this, I would seek
his death in any way, you do me dishonor. I do not grieve
for him, but he did not die because of me. I swear this by
la Corona della Virgine. God sees it." His eyes flashed as
he glanced from Charlie to Morgan. "Sweet lady, you say
you have heard me sing. Could I make someone die and
sing so?"

Morgan said something incoherent, her confusion making her blush. Then she regained her composure and
said, "I don't doubt you, Mr. Solechiaro, but I don't think
you understand the problem. You see, under the law,
when there is an investigation, comments like yours

sometimes make for greater difficulty than is necessary. Difficulty for yourself as well as for others." She held his attention with her eyes. "You should not lie. But please don't say anything more than is necessary."

"That's a barn-door issue now," Charlie put in sardonically. "Felicity Cooper will make the most of what she heard."

Domenico Solechiaro got to his feet and paced across the room. He moved gracefully and quickly, and as Charlie watched him, he began to realize what the tenor must be like on stage. Suddenly Solechiaro stopped and said to Charlie, "How did Feuier die?"

"They don't know yet."

"When will they know?" He faced Charlie across the desk, his arms folded pugnaciously.

Charlie shrugged. "As soon as they run some more tests." He considered telling Solechiaro about the autopsy, then decided against it. "It isn't a simple matter."

"Why not?" Again the challenge was directed at Charlie, but this time Morgan answered.

"Singing is very strenuous, Mr. Solechiaro. It makes unusual demands on the body. It distorts test results." She was still in her chair looking very relaxed. "You should know that better than anyone."

He turned. "Ah, *sta ben'*. You are most right. The body, the heart, the lungs, how hard they must work when I sing. We must be strong." He clapped his hands to his chest. "In the opera, I sweat. I struggle like a slave."

Charlie could not help making the comment, "And then there's five minutes of curtain calls to soothe your nerves."

Solechiaro gave Charlie a pained look. "My friend, for every minute of glory in a curtain call, there are two years of study and three weeks of work. When I make a record, there is no curtain call, just the music and the work. If the music, the singing, was not enough by itself, the curtain calls could not make up for it." Then he smiled mischievously. "But I would not want to give them up. I love curtain calls." And he bowed slightly, as if waiting for applause.

Morgan actually chuckled. "You deserve them." She studied the tenor a moment. "You can understand why a death after singing might be out of the ordinary, then."

"But something is wrong." His half smile was canny as he looked from Morgan to Charlie. "If Feuier's heart had burst or if his lungs had failed, it would be a simple matter, would it not? But here the authorities are asking questions, and you are cautioning me about what I say. Feuier was disliked by many more than me. You will have to speak to a great number of people, I think, Sr. Moon. I pray you, do not dissemble with me."

"Okay," Charlie said. "There will be many questions about Feuier. I'm telling you now, don't answer them unless you check with me first. You can make the excuse that, being a foreigner, you don't understand the limits of the law or the nature of the questions being asked."

"Which is truly the case." Solechiaro smiled at Charlie.

"And in the meantime, if you get any more questions about Feuier at dinner or any other place, say that you're upset and very little more. I don't think it will help very much; there's trouble already from what you've said to Felicity Cooper. But if you can, head off the questions as long as possible."

Solechiaro shrugged. "Tomorrow I have a rehearsal, and on Wednesday, I sing. I will not be talking very much between now and then. I must save my voice, you know." He leaned back and grinned. "My wife objects, sometimes, for if I cannot talk to her, I often do other things. And we have five children already, with a sixth coming in February." Apparently it was an old joke with him; his laughter was warm and familiar.

"Then you'll refuse to talk?" Charlie hardly dared hope that Solechiaro would be so cooperative.

"Of course. I must. Otherwise my voice will be . . . cloudy, and that is very bad. My secretary will answer the phone. He will tell them I cannot speak, and it is not possible that he would give answers without my permission." Solechiaro glanced at his watch. "I am sorry, Sr. Moon, but I must leave."

"Why?" Charlie asked, suddenly afraid that all the talk had been for nothing.

"I must go to confession, and then I have an appointment with my accompanist. I'm doing a series of concerts later in November, and we have much to prepare." He went to the door and turned back to say, "Thank you so much, Sr. Moon," and then, to Morgan, *"Bellissima* Signorina Studevant, from the depth of my soul, I am grateful that you enjoy my singing. Tell me when you are coming to hear *Manon Lescaut,* and I will see that you are on my list to come backstage."

"My ticket is for Wednesday night," Morgan said diffidently.

"I will arrange for you to have two tickets, so that Sr. Moon may come, too." He looked back at Charlie one last time. "It is not so very painful, Sr. Moon, and Puccini is generally short. You won't have to endure too much." He bowed slightly and let himself out the door.

For a moment, Charlie and Morgan just sat, and then Charlie put one hand to his eyes. "I wonder if he's like that all the time?" he asked of the air.

"Probably," Morgan said and smiled slowly. *"Manon Lescaut* on Wednesday. And a chance to go backstage."

Charlie remembered the hectic tour of Saturday afternoon and suppressed an inward shudder. "What do you think?" He was about to clarify his question, but apparently Morgan understood it.

"He's not a man to cross, but I doubt he'd kill Feuier. Unless there was more and worse between them than we know. Solechiaro is a strong-willed man." She looked down at the folder in her hand. "I've got to give this to Annie."

"Morgan." The sound of his voice stopped her at the door. "If you have something bothering you, tell me. I'm at a loss with this . . . case."

"I don't know, Charlie, and that's the truth." She opened the door, but stood uncertainly there. "I've admired these people for so long, perhaps I don't see them clearly. I'll think about it and let you know." She didn't look at him as she left the room.

Charlie stared at the closed door. His thumbs were hooked together under his chin, and his fingers beat out an irregular rhythm on his cheekbones. He tried again to assess his impression of Solechiaro and found that he could not make up his mind. The large· Italian was too overwhelming for Charlie to judge him with any degree of understanding. At last, he abandoned his thoughts, lifted the receiver, and dialed for an outside line.

"Mr. Malcomb's office," said the cool voice. "This is Mrs. Seikert."

"This is Charles Moon of Ogilvie, Tallant, and Moon. I'd like to speak to Mr. Malcomb."

"Mr. Malcomb is in a meeting just now. Shall I have him return your call?"

The icy tone of Ty's secretary annoyed Charlie. "I think Mr. Malcomb wouldn't mind if you interrupted him. I'm afraid that I have some unpleasant news for him."

There was a slight pause, and then Mrs. Seikert said, "Mr. Malcomb said that he wasn't to be disturbed."

"Tell him that Charlie Moon wants to speak to him. About Gui-Adam Feuier. Please." There was a nasty edge to his voice, and his request seemed perilously near an order.

Mrs. Seikert clicked her tongue impatiently. "Very well. But Mr. Malcomb will not be pleased."

Charlie waited on hold for almost two minutes, and was

just about to hang up when Ty's voice came on the line. "Good afternoon, Charlie. It's good of you to call me. I understand you have some information for me." Under the heartiness, Charlie could hear a deep apprehension.

"Is there someone in the office with you?" Charlie asked.

"Of course there is. You're right to inquire. Why don't you outline the matter to me now, and we'll discuss it later, when I've had a chance to think it over." Ty hesitated, then plunged on, "If it's one of those things that can't wait, I'll do my best to finish up here early."

"Okay, Ty," Charlie said unhappily. "But get ready for something you won't like. If you don't want your visitor to know that this is important, make sure you think about this very carefully. Are you ready?"

"Go ahead." Ty's tone was almost bored, and Charlie was grateful that Malcomb was so willing to follow instructions.

"I've just talked to Solechiaro. He said he had dinner the other night with friends and their guests. Unfortunately he mentioned his feelings about Feuier."

"I doubt that's as serious as it might appear," Ty remarked.

"One of the other guests was Felicity Cooper."

There was silence on the other end, then Ty said, very softly, "Oh, Christ."

"I think you might try to talk to her, or call KRON and find out what, if anything, they're going to do with it. They might not want her remarks to be actionable. You can use that word if you like."

"Actionable?" Ty repeated uncertainly.

"It means you'll sue the hell out of her and the station if she goes beyond certain limits. They know what slander is, believe it. And they know that in cases of slander and libel the burden of proof is on the defendant. Even if she is telling the truth, if that truth is revealed with intent to damage, it's still actionable, and she and they are still liable for damages. Keep that in mind if you talk to the station."

"Will it be necessary?" From Ty's tone, it was obvious that he hoped it would not be.

"I don't know. I'll see what I can do. Just remember, they can get into a lot of trouble." Charlie was tapping his desk now, his thoughts moving quickly.

"Charlie, what if one of us is . . . blamed?"

"You mean arrested?"

"Yes, exactly."

"For what? They still aren't sure this is murder. And who? As you've pointed out, there are lots of people with pretty good motives for murder. The police would have to have evidence of murder and probable cause to arrest one particular person. They've got a pretty big number to choose from, don't you think?"

"Is it always this complicated?" Ty wondered.

"Not always."

For several seconds, the line was quiet. This time, Ty spoke gravely, and for the benefit of whoever was in his office. "Yes. I see. I certainly appreciate your call. It's good to be prepared for any eventuality, however unlikely. I'm confident that the situation can be corrected without misunderstanding."

Concerned, Charlie asked, "Ty, if you talk to KRON, will you give me a call first?"

"Quite likely."

"Look, Ty, it's election eve. Maybe they'll put the whole thing aside until after tomorrow, and by then, there should be more definite results from the coroner's office. We'll know where we stand." Desperately Charlie searched his mind, hoping to offer Ty some modicum of consolation. "Felicity Cooper is a scandalmonger. People are apt to discount a lot of what she says because of that."

"I doubt it."

Charlie had to admit that he agreed with Ty. "Well, I

wanted you to consider that. If there's anything I can do . . ." He left the matter open.

"Thanks," Ty cut him off. "I'll call you later." He hung up suddenly, and Charlie was left holding the receiver.

Charlie was on the phone half an hour later when Lydia buzzed his office once again. He glared at the intercom and interrupted his discourse on civil fraud. "What is it, Lydia?"

"Mr. Nørrehavn is here to see you. He's a few minutes early and says he doesn't mind waiting."

"Okay." Charlie flipped through his appointment book while the attorney on the other end of the line went on attempting to demonstrate why his client had not committed civil fraud. At last, Charlie closed his appointment book and said impatiently. "Brad, I've got a contract with Flowning's signature, and I've got a letter he wrote the day before to his uncle in Sacramento saying that he has to have certain releases from the uncle before he signs the contract. And I have the sworn statement of the uncle that at no time did he make the requested transfer, nor did he authorize Flowning to act in any way on his behalf in the matter. Flowning signed the contract knowing that. And that is civil fraud. Vallraughn is willing to settle out of court, and you know that the fifteen thousand is a reasonable figure. He's lost almost a year of work, legitimate work. Flowning's a crook, Brad. Admit it."

Bradley Howell sighed heavily. "I've got some time free next Tuesday, a week from tomorrow. Let's get together before lunch and go over it. If you've got what you say you've got . . ."

"I wouldn't say it if I didn't. Tuesday the ninth, say, eleven-thirty. We can have lunch afterward."

"Sounds good," Brad Howell assented. "See you then."

As soon as he had hung up, Charlie said to the intercom, "Okay, Lydia, send Mr. Nørrehavn in. And please apologize for this delay." He was about to click off but added, "Oh, Brad Howell is coming in at eleven-thirty on the ninth. Mark it down, please."

"Very good, Mr. Moon."

There was a short rap on the door, and Charlie crossed the room to open it. "Mr. Nørrehavn? I'm Charles Moon. Please come in." As he spoke, he took Nørrehavn's extended hand.

"Mr. Moon." Cort Nørrehavn's voice was low and musical. He wore an elegant, conservative dark suit with a silk shirt and tie. His serious gray eyes were reserved but not unfriendly as they met Charlie's.

"Please sit down," Charlie said, motioning to a chair as he pulled the door closed.

But Nørrehavn remained standing. He looked around the room which was now lit by a burnished sliver of afternoon sunlight. His gaze lingered on the bookcase that covered one wall. "So much to remember," he said.

From behind his desk, Charlie again motioned to the chairs. "I think you'll be more comfortable."

"Perhaps." Nørrehavn chose the nearest chair, a simple design of straight back and low arms. "Mr. Malcomb wanted us to talk."

"Yes." Charlie felt himself warming to Nørrehavn in a way that he had not responded to the others. He could sense the Dane's quiet, powerful discipline, and it touched a resonance in himself. Charlie admired privacy as much as he admired strength.

"I gather this is about Gui-Adam Feuier's death." Nørrehavn waited, and Charlie's nod confirmed it. "I see. I thought it likely."

"Ty Malcomb has asked me to talk with you about what your rights and obligations are under the laws of California. He's hoping to avoid as much scandal as possible." Though, Charlie reminded himself, it was not that he could keep the matter quiet. "It's probable that you'll be asked certain questions regarding Feuier's death. The final outcome of the autopsy isn't in yet, but there's reason to believe that Feuier's death was not entirely accidental."

Nørrehavn nodded. "You are saying that he might have been killed, either suicide or murder. Why do you think so?"

Charlie's answer was cautious. "The autopsy results so far have been inconclusive. Given Feuier's reputation . . ."

"He was foul!" Nørrehavn's outburst was all the more terrible for being quiet. He rose and moved across the room. "He was poisonous!"

Some of Nørrehavn's anguish touched Charlie, and he was silent while the Danish singer mastered himself. "Mr. Nørrehavn, for your own sake, don't say that outside of this office. You could put yourself in a very unpleasant position."

Slowly Nørrehavn came back to the chair. "I'm sorry. The last few days have been . . . difficult. And there are three more performances of *Hoffmann* to go."

"But not with Feuier," Charlie reminded him gently.

"No. Not with Feuier."

Again Charlie tried to explain the legal aspects of Feuier's death to Nørrehavn. "I don't want to distress you, Mr. Nørrehavn, but it is vitally important that you understand your position in this. You have certain obligations under the law, and certain rights. Mr. Malcomb is anxious to have you realize what these are. And, unfortunately, your situation is particularly difficult."

An expression of anger and pain crossed Nørrehavn's face so quickly that Charlie was not sure he saw it. "Mr. Feuier is a very unpleasant subject for me, Mr. Moon." He clenched his large square hands, then forced them to open.

"I've been told a little about your wife. I'm very sorry."

Nørrehavn said nothing. His eyes met Charlie's. "She died twenty-one months ago. It's as new to me still as the morning paper." There was a slight roughening of his English, an abruptness of pronunciation, and a lengthening of his *r*'s that reminded Charlie that Nørrehavn had taken a degree at Edinburgh.

"Do you hold Feuier responsible?" Charlie asked.

"Completely. He destroyed her." Nørrehavn said it calmly. "It's true, Mr. Moon. He used her, and when he was through, he destroyed her." There was a whitening now around his eyes and mouth. "I hoped, with Feuier dead, that it might soften her death, but it hasn't. I'm forty-eight years old, Mr. Moon. I've been a singer for twenty-seven of them. The only other thing that truly mattered to me was Linnet. Without her, even the music is not the same. Each morning, I wake up and tell myself that today it will be easier and I will forget. But it doesn't turn out so. In the night, I am still the same." He tried to smile but failed. "You are an excellent listener, Mr. Moon. In general, I don't say so much."

Charlie knew that this was the time to make the effort to get their interview back on the subject, but as he looked at Nørrehavn's dignified, ravaged face, he heard himself say, "Would you like to talk more about it?"

Nørrehavn shook his head. "I haven't been able to. It's too hurtful. You are kind to offer."

"I'm a stranger, Mr. Nørrehavn. I'm not part of your world and you're not part of mine. I'm not a fan of yours. To tell you the truth, I don't like opera. But you are very obviously in trouble. Don't you think it would be easier to face all the publicity and all the questions that are sure to come as soon as the newsmen"—he deliberately did not mention the police—"start getting details on your wife's involvement with Feuier? The strain is going to be very great. If you don't want to talk to me, talk to someone."

Cort Nørrehavn seemed to withdraw. "Perhaps you had better explain the legalities to me, Mr. Moon."

"If that's what you want." Charlie took a deep breath

and prepared to launch into what had become his standard explanation. "You will certainly be asked questions by the various officers who are investigating the case. Those questions which are general and which are designed to get factual information can and should be answered, as concisely as possible. Information about Feuier's state of mind might be requested. In that case, you'd be justified in saying that your relationship was such that you're not able to judge . . ."

"Dear God," Cort Nørrehavn interrupted. "But I know how Feuier thought. He was contemptuous of everyone." He looked at Charlie. "My wife committed suicide on February 27, in 1975. She killed herself because of what Feuier had done to her. And Feuier himself, in Paris last May, told me that Linnet had been a foolish woman to do so, and that . . ." He stopped suddenly. "I found her." He moved a little, his hands jerky and his voice tight. "The flat was cold. Milan is cold in February. She'd turned off the heat before . . . She was on the bed, lying very still. I knew when I saw her that she was dead, but it wasn't real. I saw the blood sticking to the blankets, but it didn't mean anything to me." Now that the words had started, they came more quickly. "I thought—it seems so foolish—that if I could get her attention, if I could assure her that I still loved her, if I could warm her, then she wouldn't be dead any longer and . . . she would still be with me. She'd left the window open and sleet had blown in, so the foot of the bed was soaked and icy. I bent over her, put my coat over her feet. And then I looked at her face. Her eyes were open. Open. Open and dusty." He choked on the last words and rose suddenly, turning away from Charlie. His shoulders quivered with silent weeping.

It was difficult for Charlie to watch Cort Nørrehavn stand alone in his suffering. Among his people, tears were rare and deeply respected. He realized that the Danish singer had the same attitude, and for that reason he waited without embarrassment until Nørrehavn spoke again.

"I'm sorry, Mr. Moon." He did not turn, but his voice was even. "I had no intention . . ."

Charlie interrupted him. "Grief is a sacred thing, Mr. Nørrehavn. It's wrong to deny it." He watched while Nørrehavn folded his handkerchief and returned it to his coat pocket. "If you want to say the rest, I'll listen." At Iron River, he would have done the same thing, reciting the mourning ritual and listening while his people spoke of the dead for the last time by name. Cort Nørrehavn had denied his hurt, and for that reason it was burning in him corrosively.

"There is little to tell." Nørrehavn went to the window and stood looking down at the traffic on Clay Street. "I was forty-one and Linnet twenty-four when we were married. I'd met her when I did a series of master classes at Juilliard. She was my accompanist. She was so quiet, so shy, that I paid no attention to her until she started to play. Then everything about her changed. She became bright and joyful and strong. What is it that cripples so many splendid women, Mr. Moon? Here was this radiant creature terrified of her own glory. She thought I was mocking her when I asked her to marry me. She refused me because she was afraid I only wanted to sleep with her. She even offered herself to me, in the hope that I would settle for that." He shook his head wistfully. "It was not the sort of offer I was used to turning down. Yet I did. And eight months later, she came to Denmark as my wife." He put up one hand to shield his eyes from the last glare of sunset. "I have never been happier. She delighted me in everything. In time, some of her fear faded, and she began to blossom. She traveled with me more often, enjoyed herself, and started doing a few concerts. You cannot imagine how splendid she was. Everything she did was lovely. Her music was as clear and perfect as jewels."

"You weren't jealous?" Charlie asked.

"Jealous? Jealous of Linnet?" Nørrehavn almost laughed at this absurdity. "Are you jealous when your best friend is praised? Are you jealous when the one you love best in the world achieves victory?" He put his hand down and turned away from the window. "I was never jealous. If you had known her, you wouldn't need to ask."

"Then how did Feuier get to her? If she was the sort of woman you describe . . ."

"Gui-Adam Feuier," Cort Nørrehavn said with loathing, "was quite capable of lying to get what he wanted. Linnet accompanied three of his concerts and piqued his interest when she refused his advances. It wasn't out of fear of me. She'd had two other lovers by then."

Charlie looked up, startled. "Two other lovers?"

"Mr. Moon," Cort Nørrehavn explained gently, "we were together perhaps eight months of the year. There were others she loved, not with the daily love we had, but it was love, all the same. I never asked her to deny herself loving. Why should I? She had been denied so much for so long it would have been cruel of me to insist that she force herself to refuse what she wanted. With Feuier, it was different." His gray eyes grew cold. "Feuier wooed her, flattered her, engaged her sympathy with false tales of his poverty-stricken childhood. Oh, he was not rich, but he was not the urchin he described. I was doing *Rigoletto* at the Met the first time they spent a weekend together. One of my colleagues heard about it and mentioned it to me."

"What did you do?" He was searching Nørrehavn's face for any sign of duplicity and found none.

"I called her that night and spoke with her. I asked her not to continue her affair with Feuier, and told her something about his reputation. I told her it would end badly if she continued to see him." Nørrehavn met Charlie's eyes. "Do you know what it is to see the person you love being drawn into peril?"

Charlie nodded slowly, eyes almost blank. He had indeed pictured how he would feel if the woman he loved best was in danger, and his shock had come in realizing that it was not his ex-wife, Lois, he feared for, but Morgan Studevant.

"I see you do know." Nørrehavn spoke more compassionately than before, as if he at last believed that Charlie did care about his grief. "Then you know how desperate I felt."

"Yes," Charlie said, more to himself than to Nørrehavn.

"When I got back to Denmark, I talked to Linnet at great length, but Feuier had anticipated what I would say, and I sounded petulant to Linnet. I asked her to come with me to London, where I was doing some recording, but she refused, and in the end, I had to leave without her . . . I hated doing that. I had reneged but once before on a contract, and that was for reasons of health. Yet I was tempted to then . . . If it hadn't been that I would have let down some of my closest friends, I think I would have invented a reason to stay in Denmark."

As he listened, Charlie continued to study Cort Nørrehavn's face, the way he moved, the tension in his body. "Was it that important, your work in London?"

"I thought so at the time," Nørrehavn said heavily. "As it happened, I saw Feuier there, and he made a point of telling me he was going to Rome, and I assumed that he had lost interest in Linnet and would not bother to tell her himself. He would much rather I hurt her, in case his interest should revive, or so I thought." He swallowed and let his gaze travel back toward the window. There was fog gathering over San Francisco, and what light there was filtered through shining mist. "I had next to go to Berlin, for a *Forza,* and Linnet had agreed to meet me there." It was a few moments before he could go on. "She never came. She had gone to Feuier in Rome."

Nørrehavn got up slowly and took a turn about the

room. At last, he stopped and looked down at Charlie. "I called her, but she wouldn't talk to me. I did the *Forza* that night, and took a plane to Rome at three in the morning. I stayed there four days, hoping to talk to her, to see her. But she refused, and Feuier offered to buy me a drink." He turned away on his heel, the rage still fresh in him.

"Finish it, Cort," Charlie urged him. Neither of them noticed that Charlie had used Nørrehavn's name.

"I went back to Berlin, for the rest of the *Forza* run there. I called Rome every day, but no luck. She wouldn't talk to me. And then they left, and I couldn't find them . . . I couldn't find her. I called everyone I knew, I pleaded with them to find her or Feuier. I think . . . I think that if I had located him then I would have killed him with my bare hands." He looked down at his large square hands and said distantly, "That's not an idle threat, my friend. When the Nazis were in Denmark, I did many things that would horrify me now. But I have not forgotten."

Very gently Charlie asked, "Then how did you find her?"

"I didn t. She called me. She was at our flat in Milan. Feuier had left her. Listening to her . . ." Some part of his mind was reliving that conversation as he spoke, and his features contorted as he remembered. "I thought my heart would burst, or that I would go mad. He had done such things to her, said such things . . . For the first time, I canceled a performance and took the first train I could catch to Milan. There was a storm or I would have taken a plane." His voice dropped. "You know what I found when I got there."

"Who else knows about this?" Charlie asked, some little time later. He had not spoken as Cort sank into a chair on the far side of the office. He was still struck by the rawness of Cort's pain, and he found it hard to concentrate.

"All of it? No one. Some of them may guess. There's

been a lot of gossip, but it has lessened in the last six, seven months."

"How much could the police reconstruct?"

Cort considered this. "Most of it, if they made a real effort. The other singers know some of it . . ."

Charlie remembered Jocelynne Hendricks saying earlier that she felt Feuier was at fault in Linnet Nørrehavn's death. "Have you said anything to the police about your wife that they might want to check out?"

"I don't actually remember." He gave Charlie a curious look. "I don't know why I·let you draw me out this way. I don't understand it."

"You had to tell someone." Charlie glanced over the few notes he had made at the beginning of the interview. "Exactly what have the police asked you?"

"Oh," Cort said in a different tone, relieved to put aside the memories of his wife's death. "They asked if I had noticed anything about Feuier. I said he was singing badly, but that was nothing new. He also mentioned that he would have guests in his dressing room during the opera. But that was before we began, and I don't know whether he did or not."

"You told the police this?" Charlie made a note to check with the investigative officers for verification.

"I believe so. I was startled at Feuier's death."

"Startled but not sorry," Charlie suggested.

Cort paused before he said, somewhat slowly, "I was sorry. I was sorry that he didn't suffer as Linnet had. I was sorry he died without being shamed. He should have had time to realize what he had done . . ." He broke off.

"I hope you didn't tell the cops that." Charlie almost held his breath as he waited for what Cort would say.

"No. I told them the truth. I was in my dressing room when he collapsed. I was changing from Dapertutto to Lindorf. The first time I realized anything was wrong was when they stopped the opera before the end." He looked at the law books on the shelves. "So many."

"The law is a complex field." Again Charlie considered the matter and said, "If it's pretty well known that Feuier had an affair with your wife, you shouldn't attempt to deny it. But you can say you would prefer not to discuss it. It's on uncertain ground, anyway. It's asking for specific information not directly bearing on the investigation. It's bound to come up. But you don't have to respond."

Cort shook his head. "You're wrong. I will have to answer questions, if not from the police, then from my colleagues. I'll have to say something or there will never be an end to suspicion, even if it is found that Feuier left a specific suicide note." Carefully he smoothed his fine coat and adjusted the dark tie. "I have been afraid that it would all come out. But perhaps it is just as well." It was obvious from his tone that he didn't believe it.

Was Cort thinking to make some sort of disastrous public statement? Charlie wondered. He resisted the urge to assume the worst, saying, "It would be wise to be circumspect while this investigation is going on. If it turns out that Feuier's death was accidental or suicide, you will have put yourself through a lot of difficulty for nothing. It's not just for yourself that you should consider what you say, it's for Ty Malcomb and the rest of the company as well as for the police. If you clutter up their inquiry with a lot of material that may have no bearing on the case, it will take longer and be harder on everyone." Charlie watched Cort closely as he added, "Unless, somehow, you killed Feuier."

"As you say, unless I killed him." There was a ghost of an ironic smile on Cort's firm mouth. He shifted position in the chair, his poised reserve returning. "Very well, Mr. Moon . . . or do I call you Charles?"

"Charlie."

"Charlie, then. I'll keep my answers within bounds, and if there is any difficulty, I will call you. Is that what you want?"

"Yes. And don't hesitate to ask any questions you may

have, at any time. It's important that the matter be cleared up as quickly and as cleanly as possible." The sudden ringing of the phone jarred Charlie, and he excused himself awkwardly to answer.

"This is Sandy Halsford, Charlie," said the voice on the phone. "I just had a call from Bret."

"What did he say?" Charlie motioned to Cort, indicating that he should stay a moment. Cort waited, one hand on the doorknob, while Charlie gave his attention to Sandy Halsford.

"He said that he was going to take the kids, that some of Daisy's friends would take them, and then we'd see about this divorce stuff." Her voice caught. "Charlie, what am I going to do?"

"First you call the cops. Tell them about the threat. Is there anyone else with you?" His expression darkened, and he made a quick note to himself.

"There's Suzanne. She's been keeping an eye on the kids. I took the day off because . . ." Here she faltered.

"Because your employer thinks it might be better that way?" Charlie suggested gently, keeping his disgust from his voice.

"Yes," she admitted miserably.

"Sandy, can you hang on just a minute? I've got someone in the office who's just leaving." Charlie put his hand over the mouthpiece and glanced at Cort. "This is important or I'd delay it. Where can I reach you?"

"I'll leave the number with your receptionist." Cort thought of something more. "Please don't call tomorrow. I don't talk on days when I sing. I'll call you after the performance, if that's satisfactory."

"Fine. Or call me tonight if you have any questions. Lydia will give you my card."

"Very good. Thank you, Charlie . . . I . . ." He opened the door and left the office before he said anything more.

Charlie turned his attention back to Sandy. "Did

Suzanne hear any of your talk with Bret? Could she tell
the police what was said?"

"No, but she knows what happened. She told me herself
that it would be fine if I wanted her to tell the police that
she *did* hear."

If Sandy had not sounded so frightened, Charlie would
have snapped at her for this obvious mistake. "Look,
Sandy, don't lie to the cops, okay? You can have Suzanne
say that she heard your end of the conversation, but don't
tell her to say she heard something she didn't hear. That'll
only get you into trouble." He thought a moment. "Did
you say Bret's name while you were talking to him?"

"I think so. Once or twice. I'm not sure. Why?" Sandy
was sounding more worried again. "Shouldn't I have?"

"No, no, that's fine, Sandy," Charlie said, hoping to
calm her down. "If Suzanne is asked who frightened you,
at least she can say she heard you say Bret, and that helps.
Now, when I hang up, call the cops. I'll give them a call in
about half an hour. I'm also going to call your employer
and find out what Bret's been up to there. Maybe we can
get him immobilized for a little while. Who's his attorney,
do you know?"

"I can't remember the name. It's Sig-something."

"Never mind. I've got it in my records somewhere. I'll
give him a call, too. If he's still in his office. It's four-forty
now." Charlie had not been surprised when Bret Halsford
had changed attorneys a few weeks before. David Man-
ichetti had been trying to get Bret to plead to a lesser
charge, but Bret had balked at bargaining. "What's your
boss's secretary's name?" Charlie asked, prepared to write
it down.

"Why?"

"Because I want to talk to your boss. If I know her
name, she won't be as likely to put me off." Somewhat
ruefully Charlie realized that two years ago he would have
scorned such methods, but he had learned, with time, and

he was less inclined to do things the hard way.

"Oh. Her name is Diane Foster. Miss Foster."

Charlie underlined the Miss on his pad. "Okay. Now call the cops, and I'll talk to you again in about half an hour."

"If you think . . ." There was defeat in her voice. "I hate talking to cops."

"There's a good guy who'll help you. Ask for Peter Alercon. Tell him that Charlie told you to call. He'll help you."

"Well, I'll try." She was sullen now that the worst of her fright was over. "I'll talk to you later." She put the phone down before Charlie could say more.

He was still flipping through his directory a few minutes later when the phone rang. "Charles Moon," he said brusquely.

"Charlie, Pete Coners here. Dr. Nee and a few of the rest of us finished the autopsy this afternoon. Thought you might like to know the results."

"Go on," Charlie said, suddenly quite still.

"Well, we haven't got a positive result on what was used, but your boy was poisoned. No doubt about it." Pete chuckled slowly and appreciatively. "Probably before he started singing. Maybe even after. As soon as we finish a few more comparisons, we'll know what did it. When will be a little hard to find out, what with the heroin and the kind of stress his body was under."

Charlie rubbed his eyes, knowing that, though he had suspected something of the sort, now that it was actual fact and not his own speculation the idea was much more distressing. "Go on," he said softly.

"Whoever did it made a couple of mistakes. Maybe he didn't know about the heroin." Pete drew out the next words appreciatively, "So-o-o-o, Charlie, you've got your hands full. I'll call you back when we get more on the poison."

Before Pete could hang up, Charlie said, "Do you have a guess as to what it might be?"

"Me?" Pete asked, startled. "Sure. I think it was aconite."

"Why?" Charlie asked, ready to write again.

"Because we can't find it. Aconite's like that. Feuier didn't die the way aconite usually kills you, but I don't know how aconite and heroin combine. You start mixing poisons, you get some very freaky results." Pete clicked his tongue and added slyly, "Good luck, counselor."

"Thanks," Charlie said dryly before he hung up. Then he sat staring into space, an expression of supreme blankness on his angular face. At last, he shook off the abstraction and found the number he wanted. J. V. Sigismondo. He muttered the number to himself as he dialed.

Sigismondo had not been in, and Charlie had left a message with the answering service, along with his home number. Sandy's boss had already left for the day. Charlie had one more call to make—this one to Ty Malcomb— when the phone rang and Lydia informed him that Rocco Lemmini was on the phone.

"Lemmini?" He wondered what the Board of Supervisors wanted of him, or, more particularly, what its President wanted. "Put him through, Lydia."

"Moon?" The voice was cracked with age but filled with energy. "Your name's been coming up a lot these days."

Charlie was unsure how to react, so he said, "I hope in good company."

"Famous company," Lemmini snapped. "I had a talk with Malcomb earlier today. And there are a few things we have to discuss."

So it was what Charlie feared. Rocco Lemmini had decided to get involved with the Feuier investigation.

"And what did you say to Ty? I assume you'll say some of the same things to me."

"I've also been talking with Dr. Nee," Lemmini went on ferociously. "And that conversation was not satisfactory."

"Go on," Charlie said, resigned now to bargaining with the old Florentine.

"There's still no certain sign that this is murder. Now, because of that and because we're proud of our opera company, I'm going to make a deal with you."

Charlie knew something of the nature of Rocco Lemmini's deals, and inwardly he cursed. "What's the deal, Mr. Lemmini?"

"You know that the Board of Supervisors has a certain say in that opera company. A lot of the people working at the opera house are employees of the city. That means we've got a degree of control as to what goes on there. I'm just reminding you of that because I want you to remember that I've got a lot of ways of accomplishing my ends."

"I believe you." Charlie pictured the old Florentine, seeing him in his mind crouched over the phone, his long hands gesturing and his bright old eyes gleaming.

"Okay, Moon, this is the deal; you can have a free hand as long as you cooperate with the investigation. I've got a press conference set up that would be hell on the Opera. I'd hate to go ahead with it, but I will if this isn't handled right. I'll tell the cops to stay off your back. And in return, Moon, you will reveal anything you learn about this terrible business to the cops. Very discreetly. You try grandstanding and I'll slap you down along with the Opera Company. I can do it, Moon. Your senior partner and I are very old friends. He's not about to back you if it means his political throat." Rocco Lemmini chuckled wryly. "You know Willis. You know who he'll side with if it comes to that."

"Yes, I know." Charlie forced himself to speak calmly.

"So I'll put off the cops and the press as long as I can if

you cooperate. If you don't, well, I'll have to open the whole thing up."

"Felicity Cooper may beat you to that," Charlie said sharply. He knew that this was probably a foolish move, but he was determined to meet Rocco Lemmini with spirit.

"Felicity Cooper is seeing my nephew. I think she'll listen to us. That's not official, because I don't want her yelling about the First Amendment."

"What about me?" Charlie wanted to know. "How do you know I won't go out and announce to the world what you're doing—leaning on the cops and pressuring me?"

"I know you won't because you're an honorable man, Moon. Oh, yes," Lemmini added quickly, not giving Charlie a chance to speak. "I know a lot about you, Moon. You may not believe it, but I respect you. If I didn't, I wouldn't be talking to you now."

"Thanks."

Rocco chose to ignore the sarcasm. "If you don't come through, then we'll assume it's murder and an official investigation will take place with all the publicity you might expect. That will be very bad for the opera company, but not as bad as leaving Feuier's death up in the air. You hold up your end of the deal, I promise I'll hold up mine."

Charlie hesitated, and in the silence, Rocco Lemmini added, "This is just between us, Moon. If you mention it to anyone at all, I'll say you made it up, and then no more deal. I don't want it bandied about that the Board of Supervisors leans on the cops. That's bad politics."

"Which is all you care about?" Charlie challenged him, very irritated.

"No, Moon, it isn't all I care about. I care about this city. And, believe it or not, I care about the Opera Company. I will not have this kind of mark against it. I want it free from any taint. If that means giving it a public acid bath, I

will. Frankly I'd rather use other means. I trust you to
find those means." Rocco's harsh voice softened, and,
somewhat unexpectedly, he said, "I know how much of a
joke it is about Italians and opera, but for me, it's true. I
love it, Mr. Moon. I've given money to the opera for the
last thirty years. I'd hate to see that scum Feuier destroy
the company."

"So you'll do it for him?" Charlie suggested.

"If that's what it takes," Rocco said, and the steel was
back in his voice. "I've already talked to Malcomb. He
knows about the press conference. I don't want him to
know about this. Is that plain, Moon?"

"It's plain," Charlie said as the pencil between his
fingers broke.

"Remember; you cooperate in the investigation, work
confidentially with the police, and I'll be sure it stays
private. Otherwise . . ."

Charlie imagined the fatalistic gesture Rocco Lemmini
was probably making. He looked at the broken pencil.
"Sure, Mr. Lemmini. I understand. Just clarify one thing
for me."

There was the ghost of a chuckle on the other end.
"You're a very intelligent man, Moon, but don't push your
luck. Treat me with honor, and I'll return the compli-
ment. But I tell you now I won't tolerate any hanky-
panky."

"I understand," Charlie repeated, glaring at the phone
as if it were Rocco Lemmini.

"Don't worry. I'll stay out of this as much as possible.
You'll only hear from me if it seems necessary. Do I have
your word that you'll cooperate?" Again there was a
respect in his tone, and Charlie was somewhat startled. He
considered what Rocco had said and admitted to himself
that he had hoped for just such an opportunity. He would
have chosen other terms and associates, but Rocco Lemmini was a formidable ally.

"Clarify one thing for me, Mr. Lemmini," Charlie said again.

"What?"

"How far does this cooperation extend? You know I will not break the law. I will not suppress or withhold evidence. I certainly wouldn't protect a confessed criminal beyond the limits of the law. But do you want my suspicions, too?"

Rocco Lemmini actually sounded relieved. "Hell, no. There're plenty of them already. To be candid with you, Moon, you know and I know that Feuier was a bastard just waiting for someone to off him. There's a certain chance that if this is murder the General Manager of the Opera Company did it. He certainly had the chance and enough of a motive to float a battleship. Keep your suspicions out of it. What I want is evidence, one way or the other, that we can take into court. Okay?"

Though Charlie wanted to sigh, he refused to give Lemmini that satisfaction. Very crisply he said, "Okay. But if you hold that press conference, I won't give an inch, and I'll reveal everything you've said to me. It might not topple you, but it would be damned embarrassing, wouldn't it?" He was not sure that he would indeed carry through with his threat, but he knew from watching Willis Ogilvie in action that he had to demand this for his own protection. He did not want him to leave himself open to Rocco Lemmini's manipulations.

"Well, if that's the way you see it . . ." This was part of the ritual. "I'll be watching you, Moon. And believe it or not, I wish you luck."

When he got through to Ty Malcomb's office, Charlie was told that the General Manager was busy taking notes at a rehearsal of the last production of the season, which would begin its run on Friday. Charlie wanted to tell Ty about his conversation with Rocco Lemmini, but he had given his word and would not. Nevertheless, he was curious to find out what, if anything, Rocco had said to Ty. So he identified himself to the young man on the phone and asked how soon it would be convenient for Malcomb to return his call.

The young man countered by telling Charlie enthusiastically that the rehearsal was apt to be a long one. He went on to explain that this was the first time that Domingo and von Stade had sung together in the Opera House and that *Mignon* would amaze everyone. When Charlie had the chance to interrupt this effervescent flow, he asked the young man to take a message to Mr. Malcomb.

"But I told you Mr. Malcomb has a very busy evening . . ." the young man said uncertainly.

At that, Charlie made up his mind. Rocco Lemmini had given him elbow room, and he was determined to use it. "Look. You're very deft at this, but it really isn't necessary. Tell Mr. Malcomb that Mr. Moon will be at the Opera House at . . ."—he consulted his watch and gauged the time to get there, given the traffic—"at five-forty. Where should I come to be let in?"

"I'm not sure . . ."

"If you think that Mr. Malcomb doesn't want to see me," Charlie said with exaggerated patience, "ask him. Or ask Mr. Solechiaro or Mr. Nørrehavn or Ms. Hendricks. Where do I come to get in?"

Relief was patent in the young man's voice. "Oh. You know them? We've had so much trouble with the press lately . . ."

"What door?" Charlie demanded.

"North stage door, sir. What is the name again? I'll give your name to the doorman."

"Moon," said Charlie tightly. "Charles S. Moon."

Sandy sounded satisfied to hear Charlie's voice. "I'm so

glad it's you. I was afraid it was Bret again. Every time the
phone rings, I jump."

"Did you talk to Alercon?" Charlie asked. "Will you
have someone there with you?"

"Suzanne has said she'll stay another hour, for free. But
she's got to go home after that. Alercon won't be here
until around seven. He said he wants to check the place
out and find out where Bret might get in."

Charlie nodded as he tapped his pencil on the desk.
"Good. I'll be by in about an hour. I have to see one other
client before I come by, but it won't take long," he said,
hoping it was so. "Don't let anyone in unless you know for
certain who it is. I'll ring twice, then pause and ring twice
again. Don't let me in unless I do that."

"Oh, Charlie, this isn't a spy movie. What's the point of
all this?" The weariness had crept back into her voice
again, and a kind of truculence.

"And if it were someone else ringing? What if it were
Bret? Or Daisy?" He paused to let her consider this. "This
is very serious, Sandy. You need protection. That's why
you called me. Remember?"

She sighed audibly. "I hear you, Charlie. God, I wish
this were over. I'm sick of living like a refugee or some
kind of fugitive."

"I know," Charlie said, feeling a strong compassion for
this unfortunate young woman. In his mind, he pictured
her sitting at the window, staring out at the street,
dreading to see who might be watching, but ready to
welcome her observer, as well, so that her ordeal would be
over. "Hang on, Sandy. We'll get you through all this
somehow. The law is on your side."

"Terrific," she said sarcastically. "Tell Bret that, will
you, Charlie? I'm sure he'd be impressed." Then she
stopped and said, quite flatly. "Two rings, pause, and two
rings. Have I got that right?"

"Yes." He found her inaccessibility frustrating and

worrisome. It might be dangerous later, since it might lead her to cut herself off even more, and in that way, leave herself open to the threats of her estranged husband. "I'll see you in about an hour, Sandy. You don't have much longer to wait. We'll make sure that you're adequately protected." He stopped the urge to wish her luck and heard her put her receiver down. The whole conversation left him feeling uneasy and dissatisfied.

The elderly Filipino doorman checked his list, then nodded diffidently as he opened the door to Charlie. "Yes, Mr. Moon, Mr. Malcomb is waiting for you."

"Where is he?" Charlie hoped that Ty had not gone into the labyrinth backstage.

"At the back of the house, sir. Orchestra section. He's watching the rehearsal."

"Thank you," Charlie said as he started down the hall toward the door that led to the front of the house. He had been shown the way on his tour on Saturday, but he still had to ask directions from a couple of chorus members in startlingly gaudy clothes. One of them pointed out the inconspicuous door and then walked on, remarking to the other that the pacing in the first act was off.

"It's the music; Thomas wrote it that way. We can't do anything," said the other with a disgusted wag of his head, and the two fell to arguing as Charlie went through the door.

His heels rang on the marble floor when he walked briskly down the long, wide side lobby. The opulence of the building, normally brightly lit, was oddly disturbing in the gathering darkness, and the muffled bursts of music from behind the curtained doors gave the place a haunted feeling. At last, Charlie reached the main lobby, went up a few red-carpeted stairs, and pulled open one of the heavily studded red doors. He recoiled at the sudden blast of intense sound that engulfed him like a genie uncorked from a bottle.

Off to one side, Ty Malcomb stood, a clipboard in his hand while he leaned on the high rail, taking notes. He shook his head once and muttered to himself.

There was a particularly chaotic moment on stage, and then the music straggled to a stop as an older woman in jeans and a fringed vest walked out on the stage and began to sort things out. Ty sighed and put his clipboard aside.

"Ty?" Charlie said in the darkness.

Ty turned. "Charlie. Dick said you were coming by. I didn't expect you so soon." He took Charlie's outstretched hand with a warm smile. "I understand you've been seeing more of my people today. How's it going?"

Charlie shrugged. "If you discount Solechiaro's slip the other evening when he bitched about Feuier to Felicity Cooper, things aren't too bad, not with that side of it."

"You mean the heroin, don't you?" Ty stared rather blindly toward the stage. "I didn't believe it when I heard it, and it still doesn't make sense. No singer does that, not if he wants to keep singing. It's crazy. It was bad enough that he abused his voice, but this . . ." He stopped. "Is there anything else, Charlie?"

"Yes." Charlie faced him reluctantly. "I had a call from the coroner's office, from one of the deputies there. It's not official yet because the results aren't final . . ."

"Oh, God, what is it?" Ty asked quickly, his face becoming drawn with increasing anxiety.

"It seems," Charlie said with difficulty, "that Feuier was poisoned."

"Poisoned?" Ty echoed, as if the word were foreign and quite incomprehensible. "You mean an OD? Too much heroin?"

"No, not an OD. There was another drug in his system. He might not have known about it," Charlie said, thinking that was as gentle a way as any to suggest that Gui-Adam Feuier might have been murdered.

"You mean he was trying for a greater high? What the

hell did he mix with heroin? He couldn't sing at all if he mixed much more with it." Ty's voice had risen, and he forced himself to speak quietly. "What was it?"

"They don't know. We should have final results tomorrow, or the next day at the latest." Charlie wondered for a moment if, indeed, Feuier had taken something to increase his high. Or possibly, he thought, somewhat startled, Feuier had tried to stop the effects of the heroin. He frowned intently. "Until the poison is identified, it'll be difficult to know more."

At last, Ty recognized the significance of what Charlie had told him. "It might mean, too, that someone killed him, isn't that right, Charlie? It could be that. And that's what you're trying to tell me. And we'll know tomorrow or the next day."

"Let's hope it's tomorrow," Charlie said grimly.

"Why?" Ty's eyes were hard, and the tone of his question was bitter. "So we can get this over with and have it out in the open?"

"No," Charlie snapped. "Because tomorrow is Election Day, and everything else will take a backseat to that, that's why. What will anyone care about a simple poisoning, even a glamorous one, while Ford and Carter slug it out at the polls?"

Onstage, the action was once again under way, and the noise of the orchestra irritated Charlie. "Can we go some place where it's quiet?"

Ty shook his head. "No. I've got to takes notes. We've had nothing but technical problems with this opera. The cast is great, the direction is fine, the orchestra is playing very well for an excellent conductor, but it's catastrophic technically. I don't know why." He glared at the stage, his mouth set in a sad line.

"Okay." Charlie accepted this reluctantly. "But listen to me, will you, Ty? You've got a volcano under you."

"I know," Ty said softly. "You think this is murder, don't you?"

"I doubt he poisoned himself. For whatever reason. If he wanted to kill himself, all he needed to do was fill himself up with heroin. Why would he do that at the end of an opera? If he was as vain as everyone seems to think he was, why would he die so disgracefully? If he was trying to stop the effects of heroin, why did he wait for a performance to do it?"

"Maybe the other drug worked slowly. Maybe he didn't know it would poison him," Ty said, his eyes on the stage. "It's tempting to think he was murdered, but how do you *know?*"

In spite of himself, Charlie smiled. "You might make a very good lawyer, Ty."

Ty shrugged.

"Just make sure you continue to think and talk like that. It's important that you handle the press that way. You can take a lot of the strain off the investigation if you keep asking questions like that—you'll put the burden of proof where it belongs, on the police." Charlie leaned back against the rail so that he faced away from the distraction on the stage. "If the investigation is as difficult as it could be, you'd better be prepared to have a lot more questions to ask. But don't make it a challenge, just keep it low-key and very reasonable. If you think you might get angry, keep quiet."

"If you think that's wise?" Ty murmured as he scribbled on the clipboard.

"You don't want to turn this into a shouting match, believe me. You're doing fine so far, but we're just getting started."

"Yeah," Ty said, preoccupied with what he watched onstage. Then his expression changed, and he faced Charlie, a bright intensity in his eyes. "What about the singers who have to leave?"

"Leave?" Charlie asked, puzzled.

"Sure. They don't sing just in this city, you know. As soon as *Manon Lescaut* is over, Nico is off for London.

When *Hoffmann* is done, Jocelynne goes to the Met, and Cort has engagements in Germany and London."

"When?" Charlie demanded. "Give me dates, will you?"

"I'll call you later this evening. I don't remember who goes when."

"Okay. And see if you can keep your singers and crews from too much public speculation. Particularly those who were actually in *Hoffmann* that night. It won't be possible to . . ." The music welled up and drowned his words. Charlie kept silent until the worst was over. ". . . to keep it all out of the papers, but you minimize the effect by discouraging careless speculation."

"Do you think that would make a difference?" Ty asked, disgusted.

Charlie recalled his conversation with Rocco Lemmini, and knew that the old Florentine would add pressure from his end if he thought it was necessary. He wished he could explain that to Ty, but it was not possible, so he said, "If you can persuade the public that there is a certain solidarity to the Opera Company, it might. You'll be in a much stronger position."

Ty gestured his resignation. "I'll do my best, Charlie. But I'm new at this job. There are a lot of old hands around here who are going to resent this. I don't blame them."

"Then convince them it's their idea," Charlie said, thinking of the many times Willis Ogilvie had told him the same thing. He had rejected the idea many times, but in the last few years had come to admit its value. "Call a meeting and ask for suggestions, and make sure this is the one they choose. You can do it, Ty."

"How?" Ty was suspicious. "It's distasteful to me."

Charlie gave him a rueful smile. "I know. But it works, and you don't have time enough to work out another way." He decided to press home on this. "If this becomes a wholesale murder investigation, it will happen very fast. You're going to have to be in a very strong position then."

Ty nodded. "I'll do what I can. But what about Felicity Cooper? Won't she blow the whole thing?"

Once more, Charlie recalled his bargain with Rocco Lemmini. "Don't borrow trouble. Between the election and the cops, she's going to have her mind on other things. You only have to worry about her if this drags on too long." What was too long? he asked himself. A week? Two? He had a sudden, wicked inspiration. "We could ask Elizabeth to have a talk with her."

"You sound like you're scared of Elizabeth," Ty said, allowing himself to smile slightly.

"Damn right." He saw the smile turn to laughter and went on, "I'm not afraid of Felicity Cooper, not yet, anyway. I'd rather she hadn't found out, but I'll do everything I can to make sure she doesn't give you any trouble." He thought of another thing, and with a quiet inner satisfaction, he suggested, "You might ask Rocco Lemmini to get the Board of Supervisors behind you. Old Rocco's always going on about culture in our city, and I understand he really does like opera."

"Yeah," Ty said with mock weariness. "That speech he gave at the concert in the park? 'As a child of Florence, how can I help but love opera, which also was born there, nearly four hundred years ago?' " he quoted, with a tolerably good imitation of Rocco's choppy, explosive speech.

"Sounds like you'll be able to handle him." Charlie smiled and moved away from the rail. "Okay. I'll check in with you later tonight, and I'll give you a call tomorrow after I get back from Martinez. Can I reach you here?"

"From six-thirty until eight-fifteen. After that, I'll be tied up with the performance."

"Fine. I'll reach you then." He gave Ty one last critical look. "You can't allow yourself to get taken over by this, Ty. You've got to stick to your job running the opera. If you let this Feuier business get ahead of you, you aren't going to be able to deal with anything else." He wondered

if it did any good to say this. In the dim light, he could not
see Ty's face, and the increasing volume of the music was
once again claiming full attention.

"I'll remember," Ty said absently as he made a motion
that might have been a wave. He was already engrossed in
the rehearsal again, a measuring, critical smile pulling at
his mouth.

The lobby had fallen into near darkness when Charlie
left the place, pursued by the extravagant music and his
own doubts.

The police had arrived at Sandy Halsford's about ten
minutes before Charlie did. There were two black-and-
whites in the street and another car that Charlie recognized as well. A few curious neighbors stood in the street,
apprehension making their voices hushed as they specu-
lated. In this part of the city, the presence of the police
meant trouble.

Charlie parked a block away and walked back along the
street. Night was taking possession of the city, and Charlie
could look toward the east as he walked, and saw the
white, bladed spire of the cathedral, which inevitably
reminded him of the agitator of a washing machine.
Beyond that hill, the slim snouts of skyscrapers and high-
rise hotels poked at the sky. Darkness rounded the steep
hills, and lights distorted the buildings, making them all
anonymous. Who was it? Charlie thought as he walked.
Was it Art Hoppe who had said that this city was actually a
peninsula surrounded on three sides by water and one
side by reality? He turned into the entrance of Sandy's
building and buzzed twice, waited, and buzzed twice
again.

Instead of the usual sound that meant the release of the
lock, a light went on over Charlie's head, a very new, very
bright light, and then a uniformed police officer stepped

out of the little entry hall. With the light in his eyes, Charlie could not see the cop well enough to recognize him, if, indeed, he knew him.

"You Moon?" the cop asked.

"Yes. Would you like some identification?" He did not reach into his jacket for his wallet, sensing that it might be a dangerous move. Instead he waited, standing quite still.

"What kind of ID are you carrying, Moon?" the cop asked.

"In my wallet, inner jacket pocket," Charlie responded. "Left side. It's oversized, English-made."

"Don't be clever, Moon."

Charlie was tempted to make a retort when he heard Sandy say from some invisible place on the stairs, "It's Charlie. He's okay. You don't have to treat him like some kind of criminal!" She had come up behind the cop, irritation making her move with jerky intensity.

The cop turned ponderously toward her. "Look, Mrs. Halsford, you're the one who asked for protection. That means I gotta check out everyone coming through this door. If it embarrasses you, that's . . ." He swallowed the word that came most readily to him.

"Lamentable," Charlie ended curtly. He turned his attention to Sandy. "Okay, I'm here. Let's go upstairs and see what's going on." He took her by the arm and walked quickly through the hall, a quick, fierce glance quelling the questions that Sandy was about to ask. As they mounted the stairs, he said, "Who else is here?"

"Two other officers, in the apartment. There's one out back, and they say that there are others in the buildings around us. They're determined to get Bret."

"Bret or Daisy." Charlie went up the last half flight to Sandy's door. "Don't antagonize the cops, Sandy. I know it's tempting but don't do it. Because if you need them, you're going to need them very much, and very quickly."

Sandy sighed in annoyance. "I know it, but damn it, I'm tired of it all." She reached automatically for her key and could not conceal a scowl as one of the uniformed officers opened the door for her.

"You're Moon?" The man by the old fireplace looked Charlie over from head to toe, once, very comprehensively. "I'm Lieutenant Jacobs." He did not offer his hand, nor did Charlie expect it.

"Good to meet you," Charlie responded without hearing the words. He decided that he would call Frank Shirer in homicide and ask him what he knew, if anything, about this Lieutenant Jacobs. "Has there been any more trouble?"

"No. No trouble. No phone calls." There was an unspoken hint that there had been no phone calls and that Sandy was merely being hysterical.

"Do you know where Bret Halsford is?" Charlie asked at his most conversational.

"We haven't located him yet. His lawyer said he was visiting his folks." Jacobs had straight dark hair and slate-colored eyes, and when he moved, it was with the same determination shown by a caged leopard.

Sandy's knuckles were white, but she forced her voice to be emotionless. "Bret's mother is in a rest home in Arizona. His father is dead. He has one sister living in Oregon."

There was new accusation in Jacobs' expression. "Why didn't you mention that?"

"You didn't tell me what Bret's lawyer said."

Before the hostility could erupt into argument, Charlie said, "Then you haven't found him, Lieutenant Jacobs?"

For a moment, Charlie thought Jacobs might hit him. The dark gray eyes raked over him in fury; then Jacobs set his teeth and answered with assumed civility. "Apparently not, Mr. Moon. I'll talk to his lawyer."

"Why not let me do that? I have a couple of other

questions I want to ask him." The last was not quite the truth, but it calmed Jacobs, who gave Charlie a terse nod. "Would you prefer I call now or after you tell me what precautions you're taking to protect Mrs. Halsford?"

Sandy had moved away from the men and was now standing in a shadowed angle of the main room, her hands clutching her elbows, her lower lip caught by her teeth. "Do you have to?" she asked silently, her voice reaching no farther than the drooping and yellowed spider plant hanging near her head.

"We've got four uniformed officers and three plainclothesmen around this building. If that Halsford ever decides to show up, we'll get him." He looked at Charlie again, as if discovering him for the first time. "You're the new guy with Willis Ogilvie, aren't you?"

Charlie, who had been with the firm for seven years, resented being called the "new guy," but he answered, "Yes, I'm one of the partners."

"Ogilvie's like a barracuda," Jacobs announced, and waited for Charlie's reaction.

"If you're on the wrong side, I suppose he is," Charlie said, at his most bland. "What about Halsford? Don't you think you're being just a little too visible if you want to catch him?"

"I thought this was to keep him away from his wife?" Jacobs made an ironic question of it. "She said she needed protection, and we're here. Aren't we?"

Charlie gave Jacobs a long, measuring look. Then he crossed the room to Sandy's telephone. "Do you mind if I make a call, Mrs. Halsford? It's local."

Sandy shrugged, but watched with curiosity as Charlie dialed.

The answering service for the office of J. V. Sigismondo reminded Charlie that Mr. Sigismondo was gone for the day and would be in his office in the morning.

"Do you know how to reach him now?" Charlie asked

the bored young man at the answering service.

"I . . . I'm not supposed . . ."

"Look, Mr. . . ."

"Parker," the operator supplied, beginning to sound flustered.

"Mr. Parker, one of Mr. Sigismondo's clients may be in a great deal of trouble. It's imperative that I reach him tonight. Now. If you know where Mr. Sigismondo is, call him and give him this number"—he read off Sandy's number from the dial—"and tell him it's about Bret Halsford."

"I'll do what I can, sir. Your name again?"

"Charles S. Moon of Ogilvie, Tallant, and Moon." That was as much for the benefit of Lieutenant Jacobs as for poor Mr. Parker on the other end of the line. "I'll be at this number for about half an hour, and then Mr. Sigismondo can reach me at my home number, which you already have."

Mr. Parker promised that he would do his best to find Mr. Sigismondo, and rang off with the beginning of an obscenity ringing along the wires.

"Very neat, Mr. Moon," Lieutenant Jacobs said sarcastically. "And now, let's get down to business." He pointed toward one of the rickety chairs. "If Halsford is really threatening his wife . . . his estranged wife, pardon me. If he is threatening her, as she insists he is, then we've got good reason to put him away until his trial. But if this is being cooked up, you're going to be in a lot of trouble, Moon. And you, too, Mrs. Halsford."

Sandy sighed hopelessly. "I've told you I'm not making it up. Why should I?"

"All kinds of reasons," Jacobs said, somewhat obscurely.

"Be specific, Lieutenant," Charlie said with asperity. "Your job is to protect Mrs. Halsford, not cross-examine her. There is a court order that prohibits Bret Halsford from having contact with his wife at any time, in any way. That includes threatening phone calls."

"Yeah, but how do we *know* . . ."

This time Charlie interrupted without any pretense at cordiality. "If Mrs. Halsford were a banker who had fired an employee for some minor offense, and that employee had threatened her, assuming she were male and not female, would you be willing to enforce a court order of this nature without playing twenty questions? Well?"

"It's not the same thing," Jacobs said, scowling at the other policemen in the small room.

"No, it's not. Instead of a banker and a disgruntled former employee, we have a woman about to lose her job and a husband who's accused of dope dealing and setting explosives in public buildings. Hardly comparable." Very deliberately Charlie walked over to Sandy and stood beside her, his eyes like hard black stones. "She has two children and no help with them. Mrs. Halsford is broke, and there isn't much chance she'll get more money for a while. The only thing on her side is the power of the court, which you are choosing to make impotent." He waited a moment, thinking that Willis would be proud of him. "Tell me who your superior is."

One of the other policemen was about to speak when Jacobs cut him off. "There's no need to do this. It's just that you know how it is, a woman calls up and says her husband is trying to hurt her, she's probably just mad that he made her give him some head . . ."

Again Charlie cut him off. "Are you telling me she isn't entitled to protection because she's female?"

It was a trap, and both Jacobs and Charlie knew it. Jacobs glared at Charlie. "No, you know I'm not saying that."

"Are you saying that her husband isn't a dangerous man, potentially?"

"No, I'm not, but . . ." Jacobs stopped and resumed in his best, most clipped manner, "we'll have to work out a schedule so that the place is covered all the time. Will that suit you, Mr. Moon?"

"You know your job," Charlie responded as non-chalantly as he could. He could feel Sandy's distrust and fear like a cold front. He did his best to ignore it as Lieutenant Jacobs began to outline the methods of protection he could provide.

By the time he got home, Charlie was exhausted. Rufus was waiting on the other side of the door, whining uneasily. He was unhappy in the new house, bewildered. Charlie knew that he ought to spend more time with his dog so that Rufus would accept the place as home, but it wasn't possible. As he had often done, he told himself that it wasn't fair to keep a large dog in the city. He also reminded himself that Rufus was one of the reasons he had bought this house, with its yard where the dog could run. Somehow his conscience refused to accept this offering, and Charlie felt guilty as he bent down to hug and tousle his pet.

"Want to go for a walk?" he asked as he rubbed his dog's neck. "Want to go for a walk, huh?" He pulled his hand away and found it covered with hair. Rufus had been shedding since the move.

Rufus gave a yelp and followed Charlie very closely through the house.

"Let me get some coffee into me, and then we'll have that walk," Charlie promised as he headed toward the kitchen.

The coffee was almost cool enough to drink when the phone rang.

Cursing, Charlie went down the hall to the phone by the stairs. "Charles Moon," he said as he picked it up.

"It's Ty, Charlie," was the quick response. "Did you catch Felicity Cooper tonight? I've been trying to get you since seven."

It was after ten now, and Charlie gritted his teeth. "Was it that bad?"

"Worse. She's been on the phone to Italy. She knows someone who knows someone who knows someone who says that Domenico Solechiaro's sister has been seeing Feuier." There was both desperation and misery in Ty's voice now.

"Is it true?" Charlie demanded, mentally condemning Solechiaro to five different hells if it were.

"I don't know. I can't reach Nico. But Charlie, what if it is?" There was something in the way Ty spoke that told Charlie that Ty was more certain of the facts than he pretended to be.

"Do you think it is, Ty?"

Apparently Ty heard the implacable note in the question, because he answered flatly, "I'm afraid it might be. Serephina was wild about Feuier two years ago. I don't think she's changed."

"And Felicity Cooper said this on the air?" She must be very sure of her facts, Charlie thought grimly, or she would not risk the unfavorable reaction that irresponsible reporting might bring her, to say nothing of the lawsuit that might result.

"Not directly. She credited it to a Roman newspaper, and was coy about the circumstances, but I think she was delighted to get a chance at this kind of story."

Charlie fixed his eyes on the front door and forced himself to speak calmly. He imagined what he would tell his grandfather about this case when he went to Canada at the end of the summer for the tribal council. He could see the wicked disbelief and enjoyment in the old man's sightless eyes. "It's unfortunate. It means a lot of publicity now, no matter what happens, but it can't be helped. The worst has been done. Better pray that the autopsy report is either very complicated or very, very simple and shows that Feuier messed up on drugs." He reached down and patted Rufus's head, trying to be reassuring in spite of the edge of dissatisfaction in his voice. "If I were you, Ty, I'd have a talk with Solechiaro first thing tomorrow. Wednesday morning, I promise you, they'll be howling for his blood."

"Wednesday morning they can howl in vain," Ty snapped.

"What do you mean?"

"I mean that Nico is singing Wednesday night, and he simply doesn't speak to anyone on the day he sings. Not to anyone."

Charlie felt his jaw begin to relax for the first time since he answered the phone. "Does he always do this?"

"As long as I've known him, and that's close to fourteen years." Ty hesitated and then went on painstakingly, "A lot of singers are like that. They want to save their voices for the opera, and if they're going to do that, they have to rest. Some of them are lucky and"—Charlie heard the pain in Ty's voice when he referred to singers as *them*—"well, they don't have to be so careful, but most of them, it's necessary that they be silent."

"Then," Charlie said, feeling a reluctant hope touch him, "it wouldn't be thought capricious, would it, if he refused to talk to anyone, including the press?"

"Not at all." Ty sounded mildly startled, as if anyone should know that singers might refuse to talk. "I used to keep silent for at least five hours. It made a difference in my stamina, and that's a large part of the battle." As if this recollection was embarrassing, he added, "There's a lot of variation, of course. Some singers can go on gabbling right up until curtain time. But they're in the minority."

"Okay," Charlie said as his thoughts came together. "Tell Solechiaro to keep his silence, and make sure this is explained so that the press and the public don't get the idea he's trying to avoid them. Then make sure he keeps to himself. I don't want him writing notes for reporters to find. Keep the other cast members silent the same way. Be very polite. And call someone in Italy whom you trust who can tell you the truth about this rumor. If Solechiaro's sister *was* tied up with Feuier, you know it means a lot of trouble."

"I'll call tomorrow morning. I know someone in Milan who'll give me a straight answer."

"Good." Charlie looked down at Rufus, who was moving impatiently in the hall. "I'll call you in the evening, as arranged. Let's hope that the autopsy findings are made public tomorrow. It'll make everything a lot easier for us." He was toying with the phone cord, a subtle disturbance making him feel restless.

Ty hesitated a moment, then said, "Elizabeth has invited Nico to stay with her for the rest of his time here. What do you think?"

The image of Elizabeth flashed into Charlie's mind, her stocky indomitability and her enormous prestige. "Wonderful. Get him over there as soon as possible. She'll fend off the press, and they won't dare hassle her. No one hassles Elizabeth. And tell Nico to do just what she tells him." He considered a moment and added wryly, "Not that he'll have any choice."

"He'll go over in the morning. I'll attend to it myself."

"Good." So far, Charlie thought, this was the one positive thing that had happened to Domenico Solechiaro.

Again Ty hesitated. "I think," he said with a great deal of difficulty, "I think that Feuier was killed. I think someone murdered him. I just hope to God that it wasn't Nico."

There was little that Charlie could say to this. He sensed the anguish that Ty felt and that he tried to keep out of his voice. He gave Rufus a pat, and the dog whimpered, moving closer to Charlie. "I'll talk to Elizabeth tomorrow when I get back from Martinez. We'll need to work out how best to handle inquiries after Wednesday."

"Thanks. I appreciate it . . . Hell, Charlie, I'm scared of this whole thing. Thanks for helping me. I don't know what else to say. Elizabeth said that you don't like being thanked, but I have to."

"Then thank me when this is over, Ty. You might not feel like thanking me then." Many other times cases had turned out this way for him, but he found himself hoping that this would not be such a case. He had discovered he liked Tory Ian Malcomb.

"Don't be foolish," Ty said testily. "I'll talk to you tomorrow, Charlie. It was good of you to listen. Even if there's nothing you can do, I feel better."

After he had heard Ty hang up, Charlie stared down the hall at his front door. So much would depend on what Ty learned from Milan the next day. It was crazy, he thought. A small town that spread all over the world, with as much gossip and as rigid a social structure. He forced this from his mind and went to get Rufus's leash. It would be good to get out of the house—dinner or no dinner. He wanted some time to himself, to think.

Tuesday, November 2

As he began the long drive back from Martinez, Charlie had a terrible headache. He sighed as the setting sun struck at his eyes through the windshield. The cutoff through the rolling, dry hills was still a fairly new route to him, and he concentrated on the road. At last, one turnoff indicated the freeway to Oakland, and another pointed toward Vallejo. For an instant, Charlie was tempted to drive to Vallejo, where he had been born almost thirty-five years before. He put the idea out of his mind and took the Oakland turning, heading into the unusually light traffic. As he drove past the new Hilltop shopping center, he considered stopping for an early supper but recalled the tasks he had not yet completed that day. He stayed on the freeway, heading for home.

He was almost to the bridge when he turned on the news, curious to hear if the Feuier autopsy had been made public. Most of the time was taken up with reviews of the various crucial political contests around the country and some last-minute comparisons of Ford and Carter. He was on the other side of Yerba Buena island when at last there was mention of Feuier.

"Gui-Adam Feuier, the world-renowned French tenor who died suddenly last Wednesday night during a performance of Offenbach's *Les Contes d'Hoffmann* at the Opera, was today pronounced the victim of poisoning. Coroner Nee declined to speculate further." There was a scratchy sound and then a few taped comments in Terrence Nee's clipped manner. "I can't say whether the man was murdered. I have no evidence one way or the other." "But certainly, Dr. Nee, this rules out suicide." "Not necessarily." "Then how do you account . . ." "Young man, it is not my job to account. For that you must speak to the police and the District Attorney's office." The reporter went on, "District Attorney Horatio Cronin said that he would have a statement on Feuier's death tomorrow, following a meeting with Coroner Nee and Police Chief Hardwick."

By the time he reached home, twenty minutes later, Charlie had heard five traffic reports, three tallies of voter turnouts, and nothing further on Feuier. As he pulled into his driveway, he thought it could be worse.

When he had gone over the mail—three bills, a free sample of hair conditioner, two advertising sheets from nearby stores, a catalogue for office supplies, and two letters, one from his anthropologist cousin, who was currently on the faculty at McGill—he checked his book and started making phone calls.

Elizabeth was third on the list, and she herself answered the phone instead of Henry. "This is the residence of Elizabeth Kendrie. May I ask who is calling?"

If Charlie had not known Elizabeth, he would have been thoroughly daunted by this beginning, but instead he chuckled and said, "It's Charlie, Elizabeth. Has it been a hard day?"

Elizabeth sighed. "I've been thinking most of today that I should have stayed out of this Feuier nonsense. I meant it for the best, and it is certainly unfortunate that it's turning out to be so ruddy complicated." She stopped and said in another voice, "It's been quite hellish, Charlie. I didn't expect that, but I suppose I should have."

"Well," Charlie said gently, "that's not your fault. How's Solechiaro?"

"Energetic," Elizabeth snapped. "I don't understand how his family can stand it."

"Considering the kind of energy *you* have, Elizabeth, your protests sound a little hollow." Charlie picked up his notepad and grabbed a pencil. "What's he had to say about Feuier's autopsy?"

"I had a call from Ty about that a little after one. Since then, Nico has told me the story of his life, with footnotes, his opinion of half the operatic conductors in the world, which sopranos he likes, and why, how he feels about the twenty-six roles he sings, how he feels about the thirty-three roles he'd *like* to sing, what audiences he likes *best*, what conductors he likes best, what sopranos he likes best—and that's quite a fascinating list—what operas are performed too much, what operas aren't performed enough and why he likes silent movies, but I haven't been able to get him to say anything about his sister and Feuier, because he says it would be unfair to her."

"Don't you find that endless effervescence a little fatiguing?" Charlie asked, but not critically.

Elizabeth laughed. "Don't kid yourself, Charlie. The bubbles in Domenico Solechiaro are made of steel."

"Sure," Charlie said in polite disbelief.

"They are. Consider what he does. He's in one of the most demanding, competitive businesses in the world. And he's on his way to the top. That's not an accident. He's gone against family tradition to be a singer, and that takes a lot of determination."

Charlie was just curious enough to ask, "Why was going against family tradition so difficult? What kind of family was it?"

This time Elizabeth's answer was cautious. "You know how Italians are about family, don't you? Then you'll know that defying the family can be very difficult. In Nico's case, it was particularly hard, because he was bucking a thousand-year tradition. He comes from a very important military family. Three of his brothers are in the armed forces. One's a police captain. Can you imagine what they thought when Nico announced he wanted to be a singer?"

Charlie's answer was dry. "I know a little something about family traditions. He was up against it." This new information was disquieting, and for a few moments, Charlie wondered what more he could ask Elizabeth before she realized he was fishing. "He doesn't seem like the military type."

"That's because you aren't looking at him clearly, Charlie. I wouldn't want to cross Nico."

"When you say that, Elizabeth, you fill me with foreboding."

She chuckled. "But you know, Charlie, I like him."

"It figures. You're two of a kind."

Sandy Halsford had had a frustrating day and took most of this out on Charlie. Her cousin had refused to let her come to Eureka, the cops had not been on time, and there had been twenty minutes in the afternoon when she had been totally unguarded, and when she had called Lieutenant Jacobs, his reaction had not been good. "He said it was all a waste of time," she stormed. "Bret could have broken in here at any time, and there wouldn't have been anyone but me to stop him. I can't get Suzanne to come back. She says she's afraid of what Bret will do to her, but do you think Jacobs cares about that? No way, Charlie."

"Have you actually heard from Bret?"

"Oh, yes. He called while the cops were gone and said that he was waiting to get me. At least he's dropped the revolutionary rhetoric and kept to simple threats. None of this for-the-downtrodden-masses shit. This time it was plain, direct language. He wants the kids, and he wants me to stop the divorce and go back with him or he'll kill me. What can you do about that, Charlie? You can't get the cops to help, the courts can't hear the case for six years, and I'm broke right now. So you tell me, Charlie. Why the hell do I fight it?" Her voice had risen to a shout.

"Sandy," Charlie said when he was sure the worst of her wrath had broken. "I know how you feel. I can't defend the courts or the police. But I can defend the law. You have excellent reason to be angry and to be frightened. And you are entitled to protection. I'll see that you get it."

She was not much mollified. "That's great. I tried to call you earlier, and your receptionist kept telling me you were out."

Charlie knew a pang of guilt, but he said, "Well, Sandy, you're not my only client. You knew I was going to Martinez today. Why didn't you talk to Ms. Studevant?"

"I didn't want to. What could she do?" Sandy's voice broke as she started to sob. "Help me, Charlie. You've got to help me."

It was all Charlie could do to refuse her, but his survival told him he had to. "Is there an officer with you now?" he asked, his tone level but concerned.

"Yes, yes, there's two of them. One in the other room and one downstairs. But I don't want the police here. My neighbors hate the cops. It's terrible. Can't you come, Charlie?"

Five, even three years ago, Charlie would have surrendered to that appeal, but in that time, he had learned a great deal, and one of the things he had learned was not to be pulled into his clients' personal whirlpools. Sandy was grabbing blindly for anything that might offer her stability, but she was like a drowning woman who could drag her would-be rescuer under with her. Choosing his words very carefully, he said, "Okay, Sandy, get hold of yourself. If you're in that much danger and you don't trust the police, call La Casa de las Madres. They'll take you in. And they're quite protected. Their address is private, and there's no way Bret can get it. If you think you need that kind of protection, go there. I can give you a referral number if you want it. But you can't keep on like this. Either you fight Bret this way or you go to ground. At the beginning of this, you said you wanted to fight. I warned you then what could happen, and you said you were willing to undergo the pressure for the chance to stop Bret. You wanted it out in the open. That's the way it's been. If you want to change your mind, fine. We'll make new arrangements. Either with La Casa de las Madres or with another one of your relatives. Take the night to think about it. Whatever you decide, we'll do it."

She had stopped crying, though her breathing was still shaky. "Does it have to be that way?"

"Yes," Charlie said without hesitation.

"I see. Fine. I'll think about it." Before he could say anything, she hung up.

He had just returned from his walk with Rufus; in fact, he had not yet hung up his coat when the phone rang. This would be the fourth call of the night, and Charlie was tempted to let his machine take it. But curiosity got the better of him and he picked up the receiver as he closed the coat-closet door. "Charles Moon," he said as he reached to turn on a light.

"Moon?" The voice was plainly disguised, gravelly from being forced too low. "Moon, you stop messing with Sandy Halsford. If you don't stop messing with her, that nice new house of yours is gonna get all tore up."

There was real menace in the voice, but Charlie was unimpressed. "Stop the cheap theatrics, Bret. You're in serious trouble now, and if you add this threat to the list, you'll make it worse. Keep away from Sandy and the kids and talk to your lawyer before you try any more silly stunts."

This isn't Bret . . ."

"Like hell it isn't," Charlie snapped. "Call your attorney immediately. And don't call me again." He slapped the receiver down. "Damn," he said to the wall, then turned on his heel. It was bad enough having to be harsh with Sandy, but if Bret were going to start threats, Charlie would have to be willing to be more visibly protective of her, which would be a very bad thing. He was three steps away from the phone when it rang again. Quickly he reached back, snatching it from its cradle. "I told you not to call again," he said with ominous calm.

There was a silence at the other end. Then, "Charlie?"

"Morgan?" Charlie stared at the phone in embarrassment.

"Are you okay?" The worry in her words was genuine, he realized, and for an instant, he wanted to thank her, or recite poetry to her, or chant one of the private, potent songs his grandfather had taught him. But that was folly. He forced himself to speak lightly. "I'm sorry, Morgan. I just had a call from Bret Halsford, and because I hung up on him, I thought he was calling back."

"Threats?"

"Of course. What else? It'll be okay." He felt a tightness at the base of his throat, and he swallowed against it so that he could continue to speak.

"Are you sure you're all right?"

"I'm fine. It's been a long day." He still didn't know why she had called. "What's wrong, Morgan?"

"Oh, nothing. I was feeling down, and I needed someone to talk to." She was uncomfortable making that admission. He could tell from the slight halts between words and the softness of her tone.

"What happened?" It was his turn to show concern.

"Oh, nothing. The judgment went against the Millers today, and, oh, I don't know."

"But you thought it would." He knew that she felt the loss keenly, even though it was anticipated. "I'm sorry it turned out that way. It was important to you, wasn't it?"

"Yes." She was silent, and Charlie did not speak. "You *do* understand, don't you, Charlie?"

It would have been easy for him to say yes and leave it at that, but it would not be enough for Morgan. "I think I do. I know how I felt the first time I lost a case that I felt very strongly about. The trouble was, I knew it was a slim chance. And I lost. I thought at the time it was inexperience, but I think now that no one could have made a difference. There was an ambiguity in the law, and they found against us." He wished for a moment that he had not had that terrible insight yesterday; it was difficult to talk with Morgan. "Would you like to come over and watch election returns with me?" he heard himself ask.

"God, Charlie, I don't know . . ."

"A cup of tea or a glass of wine. The place is still a mess, but I've got the boxes in different piles." He was amazed at himself and felt genuinely bewildered by his own ease and confidence. "You don't have to if you don't want to, but it might keep you from brooding about the case. You've got other clients who are counting on you. You can't let this throw you. It may be the first time you've lost, but you can bet it isn't the last."

"You're right," she sighed. "Maybe I will come over, for an hour or so. Yeah. Thanks, Charlie."

It was nearly midnight, and the newscasters were all beginning to look haggard. Morgan leaned back against the sofa, not really watching the small screen, her eyes softly drowsy. A cold cup of tea sat on the packing box beside her. Charlie glanced up from the letter he was writing to watch her, chiding himself for his own blindness.

"Who're you writing to?" she asked, making an effort not to fall asleep.

"My cousin. James Raven Feathers. He's a professor of anthropology in Canada."

"That's pretty impressive," she said, reaching for the tea.

"Want me to warm that up for you?"

"No. It's okay." She sipped at it to prove it was fine, then put the cup down. "Did you grow up with him?"

Charlie stopped writing. "Well, I was born here, you know. I didn't go back to the tribe until I was six. After my mother died." He wished he knew more about her, not about the kind of lawyer she was, but what she had done as a child, what she had thought about in the morning before she got up, how she had felt about trees and sunsets.

"Was it very hard?"

"At first," he admitted, remembering his wretched loneliness, being the odd one, the California child in the wilds of Saskatchewan. He had never realized how out of place he could be with his own people. "James took pity on me, after a while."

"Is that what changed it?" Morgan was sitting forward now, elbows on her knees, her loose sweater sleeves pushed up her arms. With her hair slightly mussed and her face peacefully tired, she seemed strangely vulnerable.

"No, it wasn't that." He wondered if he dared to tell her. He feared her laughter more than he had feared anything in his life.

"Well?" She had picked up the tea again and was watching him, as if she had seen some of his fright.

"My grandfather . . . my grandfather is the medicine man. He found out I had magic. So he began to teach me." He was very still, and his eyes didn't leave her face.

"To teach you what?" She knew the answer, but had to hear it from him.

"Magic." The word hung between them. "It should have been James. He wanted it so badly—he still does, that's why he's a professor. He's a fine professor, but it isn't what he really wants."

"You're a medicine man?"

He nodded, waiting.

"Is that why you always go to those tribal councils?" He could see her fitting things into place in her mind, things he had said or done in the past, things she had not understood at the time.

"Yes."

"Is that why you're so good with animals, too?"

"One of the reasons." She had not asked him if he really believed it, and she had not yet laughed.

There was a defensive light in her eyes, and she moved on the sofa as if seeking shelter. "And do you do that with people?"

"Very rarely," he answered truthfully. "It's not easy, Morgan. It has to be important to use magic." He put his letter aside. On the screen, two local candidates were being asked what they thought about the election so far. The one who was trailing in vote count said it was too soon to tell.

"Not even on important cases?" Her face was intent, almost challenging.

"Twice. Only twice in ten years. You saw me after one of them. I had a bloody nose and was about to faint." He studied her again as she finished the last of her cold, unpalatable tea.

"Does it do that to you?"

"Sometimes. It depends."

She thought about what he said. Then she got up and poured herself another cup of tea from the pot on the dining room table. "I guess Carter's won," she said.

Wednesday, November 3

"I can't stay very long," Charlie explained to Ty as he entered his office. "I've got appointments at nine and at ten-thirty. What did you hear from Milan?"

Ty had dark smudges under his eyes, and he looked out into the last of the morning rush traffic without seeing it. "Carlo says that Feuier definitely made a play for Serephina. What a shitty way to say it!" Ty turned to Charlie. "What Carlo really said was that Feuier tried to seduce her." He nodded toward the folded paper on his desk. "Have you seen the *Chron* this morning? There's a big spread on Feuier on page six. A recap of his death and a lot about his career and a cleaned-up version of his Don Juan reputation." Ty was disgusted now, and he pushed away from his desk. "You're coming to the performance tonight, aren't you?"

Charlie had picked up the paper and was now glancing through the Feuier article. "They spelled your name wrong," he remarked.

Ty shrugged philosophically. "It happens all the time. My grandfather was barely literate, and that's the way he spelled it when he got his first papers. And that's the way I spell it." He paced the length of the office. "What do you think?"

"About your information? How reliable is this Carlo?" Charlie had hoped for a bit more of a diversion, but he accepted Ty's determination.

"Very reliable. I don't want to tell you too much, but he *is* honest, and he knows all the parties very well. And has known them for several years. He's never steered me wrong before."

Mentally Charlie decided that Carlo was a colleague, someone who knew Ty as well as Feuier and Solechiaro. A manager? A conductor? A director? Another singer? He put the question aside. "Did Carlo say anything about Solechiaro?"

"Just that he had had a talk with Feuier. I don't think they fought, because Nico could take Feuier apart. And apparently Nico insisted on Feuier's silence about the whole thing. Didn't want Serephina exposed to publicity. Or himself, for that matter."

Charlie dropped the paper on the desk. "I'll talk to Solechiaro tomorrow. He should have told me about this earlier. Whom else should I interview? You said that the conductor was back? Can I see him tomorrow or Friday?"

Ty consulted his large leatherbound appointment calendar. "He's busy those days. How's Monday? I think he's free around two."

"If that's the soonest . . ." Charlie glanced at his watch, fingered the silver, turquoise, and cinnabar of his Loloma watchband. "But earlier if you can manage it. The DA's office should be making an announcement about their investigation sometime this morning. Let me know what they tell you." He pulled his zipper case from under his arm and opened it, drawing out the file folders he had been given earlier. "I thought you'd want these back. I've made some notes, but no copies. Thanks for letting me read them."

"You're welcome," Ty said automatically. In spite of his height, today he seemed shrunken. "I've got a couple other things for you: a note that was found in the tenor's dressing room and a piece of paper with a phone number that Feuier had put into the pocket of his *Hoffmann* costume."

"No," Charlie said quickly.

"No?" Ty was puzzled. "But they might be important."

"Yes. And they might be evidence. I'm an officer of the court, and I have to surrender anything that's germane to this case. I'll take it, but only if you understand that."

Ty looked at the two bits of paper he held. "But surely between attorney and client . . ."

"Yes," Charlie agreed. He could feel Ty's distress acutely. "And *Elizabeth* is my client. I'm extending my services to you and the company on her instruction. In the eyes of the court, our relationship is tenuous, at best." His gaze lingered on the bits of paper. "Do you know, for sure, who wrote those notes?"

Ty bristled. "Of course."

"No," Charlie corrected him gently. "I mean *for sure.* Do you recognize the handwriting? Did you see the notes written?"

"Well, the phone number was found in Feuier's costume . . ." Ty began indignantly, and once again Charlie interrupted him. "What does that prove? Is it Feuier's handwriting?"

"Christ, I don't know. It's a phone number. A local prefix." Ty had slumped into his chair, his face set.

"How much of your company lives and works in the city?"

With a helpless wave of his hands, Ty gave it up. "They all work here. About forty percent of them live here. I get your point."

"And what about the note?" Charlie prodded.

"It's in Jocelynne Hendricks' hand. I've seen it before. We sang together a lot, my last season." He smoothed the note on the desk and stared down at it. "I don't know, Charlie. It doesn't sound very much like her."

"Why?" Charlie was beginning to hope that neither find would make that much difference to Ty and his singers.

"I think she was writing to Feuier. She mentions Enrique, that's her . . ."

"Fiancé," Charlie finished. "He's in Munich, isn't he?"

Ty nodded. "Yes. She told you about him?"

"Just enough to know that there is a fiancé named Enrique who is, I think, a director? The note was about Enrique?"

"Yes." Ty read the note carefully, although he must have memorized it by now. "If I turned this over to the cops, would it matter if I read it to you?"

"I guess not. What does it say?" Privately, Charlie was glad that Ty was willing to give such material to the DA. It would give Ty the advantage of cooperation as well as reduce the length of time the investigation took.

"It says, 'Forget it, Gui. Tell Enrique anything you want. He'll know who's lying. Next time you make a rotten proposition like that, pick on someone like yourself. J. H.' "

Charlie considered it. It was unpleasant in its inference, but it might be helpful. "The DA will want to see it. And the phone number." He considered a moment longer. "Be sure that you tell the DA's staff that you read the note to me. Say you weren't certain what to do with it, which is no more than the truth, and that I advised you to give it to them."

"Whatever you say," Ty agreed uneasily. "Today?"

"This morning. Now." Charlie paused again. "I've got to run. But I'd like to hear from you later today, after you talk to the DA's staff. I don't know what I can do, but there must be something." He went to the door, then said to Ty, "There isn't time for subtlety and subterfuge. Not with the kind of schedules those singers live. It's in your best interests to clear the whole thing up as quickly as possible."

"Sure," said Ty as he studied the two slips of paper in his hand. "Sure."

"There are four calls for you," Lydia said as she handed Charlie the memos. "Standridge wants to know about the limited partnership, that's not terribly urgent; Branneston wants a few minutes of your time on that wrongful death matter; a Mrs. Valdez wants someone to get her kid back from Reverend Moon . . ."

"Why on earth did she ask me?" Charlie asked the air.

"Who knows? Maybe because of your name. And this one, I don't know how to pronounce it, Nureh-something. He said he'd appreciate a call. Not urgent."

"Nørrehavn?" Charlie ventured.

"That's it. He called about twenty minutes ago. I told Branneston that you'd call him as soon as you got in." There was more than just a hint in her expression that Charlie should, indeed, call Mr. Branneston first.

Charlie took the slips from Lydia. "Like the elections?" he asked.

Her lovely, classic Chinese features changed into a wry, knowing smile. "Some. And some of it was awful."

Charlie nodded neutrally and was about to go down the hall to his office when the door opened and Alex Tallant, late as usual, breezed in. "Morning, Charlie, Lydia. Willis must be dancing a jig around the Washington Monument." He took his mail from Lydia, shuffled through it, frowning once, and started toward his office, then turned back to Charlie as if he had just remembered something. "Say, Charlie, about next Saturday . . ."

Immediately Charlie was on the alert. "What about next Saturday?"

"I'm having a little cocktail party. Didn't you get my invitation?" Alex flashed Charlie a wide, handsome smile as he adjusted his wide, bronze silk tie and smoothed his wide lapel. "You should have got it yesterday."

"I should have?" Alex had never invited Charlie to any of his exclusive little gatherings, and Charlie was instantly suspicious. "What's the occasion?"

"Oh, no occasion. Just a few of us getting together for drinks before going to the opera."

So that was it. Charlie's face set into hard planes. "I see."

"You can bring a guest, of course, or a couple of them. Since we're going to the opera, maybe you'd like to bring a couple of the singers so that they can meet their fans."

"How generous," Charlie marveled. "You're actually willing to let me bring along a couple of opera singers to your exclusive party. I'm amazed."

The smile had frozen on Alex's mouth. "Now, Charlie . . ."

"No, Alex, no 'now Charlie.' And if you've promised your friends that they would be able to meet Solechiaro or Hendricks or Nørrehavn, forget it."

Judging from the suddenly pathetic sag of his face, that was just what Alex had promised them. "But I'm your partner, Charlie. And it's not as if my friends were just anybody. I mean, these people really value singers. They support the opera."

"And they want to be able to boast to their friends what Domenico Solechiaro said to them over old-fashioneds at this terribly intimate little party." Charlie's grin was wolfish, and he shook his head. "No way, Alex."

"But what will I tell Margo?"

"Anything you like." It wasn't much of a game any more, this fighting with Alex. Three years ago, Charlie had promised himself that he would leave the Ogilvie, Tallant & Moon partnership after ten years, and he still had over two to go. It was moments like this that made him question the wisdom of waiting so long. He turned back to Lydia Wong. "Is Ms. Studevant in?"

"In and out again. She's gone over to Mrs. Halsford's."

Charlie felt a surge of alarm. "Mrs. Halsford's? Why?"

"Mrs. Halsford called a little before nine and said that the police protection hadn't arrived for the morning shift yet and she was alone for a little while. Ms. Studevant took the call and offered to go stay with Mrs. Halsford until the cops arrived. She said she'd be gone about an hour. She isn't busy until eleven, so she decided to save you the trouble."

The worry that had wakened in his mind refused to be quieted. He told himself that it was silly as he said to Lydia, "Look, Lydia, I want you to call a Lieutenant Jacobs. You can probably reach him through the Divisadero station. Find out why there aren't any officers at Sandy Halsford's place. I'll be in my office. And I may need Mr. Carpenter this morning."

"Okay," Lydia nodded. Mr. Carpenter was an invaluable asset to Ogilvie, Tallant & Moon; whenever an interruption was needed, or a pressing engagement took one of the attorneys away from a difficult client, it was at the insistence of Mr. Carpenter. The fictitious Mr. Carpenter had been with the firm for as long as Charlie had, and no one would have given him up willingly.

Alex had not quite finished with Charlie yet. "Charlie, I want you to think it over, about Saturday. You ought to know some of these people. They can help you, Charlie. And the singers won't mind . . ."

At that, Charlie turned on him, taking out some of his apprehension for Morgan on Alex. "Look, Alex, the whole Feuier matter could very easily turn into a murder investigation. I won't let these singers get paraded for your friends to gossip about. I'm trying to help them *avoid* scandal, not contribute to it." He knew that Alex was angry, but it was senseless to draw back now. "I won't do it. And if that makes me a social boor, so be it."

He had not been settled in his chair for more than a minute when the intercom buzzed. "Yes, Lydia?"

"Miss Wulffraat is here to see you. And I have Lieutenant Jacobs on the line."

"Thanks. Send Miss Wulffraat in in five minutes. I'll talk to Lieutenant Jacobs now." He pushed the lighted button and picked up the phone. "Lieutenant Jacobs, this is Charles Moon. We met at Mrs. Halsford's apartment."

"I remember you," Jacobs said with ill-concealed hostility.

"I realize you have a lot to contend with, Lieutenant, but perhaps you can tell me why there was no police protection around Mrs. Halsford this morning?" As he waited for an answer, his fingers drummed impatiently on his desk.

"There was a holdup attempt near Turk and Laguna. We had our hands full, Mr. Moon. I couldn't spare the men. And by the time it was cleared up, Mrs. Halsford called and said it wouldn't be necessary. Say, Moon," he went on in a different tone of voice, "I don't want to tell you your business, but I think this whole Halsford thing is exaggerated. Halsford's got one hell of a charge hanging over him already. He isn't going . . ."

"When did Mrs. Halsford call you?" Charlie cut in, his hands feeling cold as the first real dread hit him.

"What? About ten minutes ago. She said everything was okay. She'd expect the noon shift, but she had to stop by her office to get her paycheck and do some shopping."

Charlie rose slowly. "Sandy Halsford got her paycheck in the mail on Monday, and Suzanne, her friend, has done the shopping for her since this thing with Bret began."

For a moment, Lieutenant Jacobs was quiet. "Shit. Oh, *shit!* I'll get some black-and-whites over there . . ."

"No!" Charlie's fright made his voice harsh. "No, if Bret's there, no visible cops. Not yet." There was a voice in his head saying, *Morgan's there, Morgan's there, Morgan's there,* with his pulse. "I think one of my associates is there already. Let me make a call and find out. Stay on the line. It won't take long to find out." Without waiting for a response, he put Lieutenant Jacobs on hold and pushed the button for an outside line. He noted that his hands were steady as he dialed Sandy Halsford's number and waited while the phone rang once, twice, three times, four, five . . .

"Hello?" Sandy said, a tremor in her voice.

"Sandy?" Charlie said, hoping he sounded casual, normal. "Is Ms. Studevant there?" He didn't dare talk too long to Sandy, who was on the ragged edge of control.

"Yeah. She's here. I'll . . . get her for you." The phone clattered as she put it down, and there were a few muffled words, then the sound of footsteps and the receiver was picked up. "Hello, Mr. Moon? This is Ms. Studevant. Is it important?"

Through his worry, Charlie felt a touch of pride. Morgan was doing beautifully. "Yes it is." He was reasonably sure that Bret was listening, so he said, "You forgot you have an appointment with Mr. Carpenter in twenty minutes. He just called the office."

"Oh, yes. Mr. Carpenter. I did forget. He's so difficult, too. Will you tell him that I'll be delayed a bit? Sandy's not feeling well." Some of her cool assurance seemed forced now, but she added, "That medicine of yours you told me about?"

"Yes?" Charlie heard the desperation in her words. "I don't use it very often, you know. Some people get strange reactions to it."

"You warned me about that. But Sandy could probably use some right now."

Charlie thought he heard a sudden hiss of words, and there was a muffled sound of footsteps and something breaking. "Morgan?" Charlie said quickly as he heard her gasp.

"I'm sorry, Charlie. One of the kids needs my help. I'll talk to you later." She hung up quickly, but Charlie heard her say "Don't . . ." before the dial tone sounded.

As he held the phone in his hand, Charlie forced

himself to blot out the images his worry brought to his mind. Morgan shot. Morgan dead from knife wounds. Morgan dying slowly, horribly, alone. Morgan like Linnet Nørrehavn, with dust on her eyes. He punched the hold button. "Jacobs? This is Moon again. Halsford's there. He's got Sandy and the kids and my . . . associate."

"What's his name? Can he help us?" Jacobs asked quickly.

"He's a her. Her name is Morgan Studevant. Unless something happens to her, she'll help us." There was a brief, terrible constriction in his chest as he said that, but it passed quickly, and he forced himself to be calm and think clearly. "You'd better call the hostage-bargaining team downtown. You're going to need them."

Jacobs hesitated. "Is that really necessary?"

"Look, Jacobs, Bret Halsford is out on bail pending trial on a major narcotics charge. He's threatened his wife and his children on several occasions, despite a court order prohibiting him from any contact with them whatsoever. That means he's got to be fucking desperate. He's got two women and two children with him. Call the hostage-bargaining team. If you don't, I will." Then as an afterthought, "Bret's lawyer is this guy Sigismondo. Offices on McAllister. He's Spanish."

"Right. I'll call him. What are you going to do?"

"I'm going over to Sandy Halsford's."

There was wrath in the lieutenant's voice. "Now, wait a minute . . ."

"You may need me. I'll meet you there. Don't worry. I'm not going to do anything foolish." He was about to hang up, but said, "All that matters is getting them out alive, in one piece. Nothing else is that important. Nothing."

He parked two blocks away from Sandy's, on a cross street, on the off chance that Sandy or Morgan might recognize his Volvo and somehow alert Bret Halsford. He locked the car, knowing the crime record of that particular neighborhood, then went around to the trunk. It was a clear, chilly day, a golden autumn day of polished sky and brisk breezes. Charlie loved the autumn, its color, its light, its smell. Now he noticed none of it as he pulled off his jacket, his tie, and his shirt and flung them into the trunk. There was a small leather carry-on bag in the trunk, and he pulled this to him, opening it roughly. Ever since he had had to change a flat tire in the pouring rain, Charlie had carried a change of clothes in his car. From the carry-on bag, he took a dark blue turtleneck sweater, which he tugged on over his head. He was satisfied that it fit well enough and did not look too out of place with his gray slacks. He put the carry-on case back in the trunk. There was one last thing he wanted, and this was in a soft leather bag tucked into the trunk lining. There were special signs painted on the bag and certain dried herbs attached to the leather thong that closed it.

Carefully, respectfully, Charlie opened the little bag and drew out the thing it contained. It was a flattish wooden oval that snuggled neatly in the palm of his hand. A leather braid went through a hole at one end so that the wood might be worn around the neck. On the wood were the carefully carved and painted symbols of his name, Spotted Moon. He held the wood in his hands for a moment, warming it, then slipped the leather braid over his head and tucked the wood into the rolled collar of his sweater, so that it could lie against his chest. Although Lieutenant Jacobs or Lydia Wong would find the wood a curiosity, Charlie's anthropologist cousin or his grandfather or any member of the Iron River tribe of Ojibwa would instantly have recognized the wood for what it was—a medicine finger.

Charlie stood for a moment, his eyes on the middle distance as the finger began to work on him. He felt his sensitivity increase as his senses became keener. Now he felt both more calm and more alert. This honing of his perception intensified his focus, and he aimed his mind, his soul, to the thing he had to do.

When he was ready, Charlie slammed the trunk closed and began to walk back toward Sandy's. With his wheat-colored skin and dark hair, he was less conspicuous than Alex would have been on this street. The sweater he wore over his slacks seemed quite ordinary here, as a jacket, shirt, and tie would not. He changed his normally brisk walk to a saunter as he started down the street.

He went past Sandy's building and paused at the next corner to glance both ways, as if waiting for someone. Then he stepped back to lean against the bruised stucco of the ancient apartment house on the corner.

Ten minutes later, he saw two police cars go by on the street below, and then another two, less than five minutes later. At last, a somewhat battered Dodge Dart pulled around the corner and Lieutenant Jacobs, in faded Levi's and an embroidered denim shirt, got out of the car. He looked Charlie over once. "Not too bad," he admitted.

"I'm not a fool, Lieutenant."

"No, you're not." Jacobs looked away up the street. "Any activity?"

"None. No one at the windows. No one in or out of the building. I didn't try to go in," he added to forestall Jacobs' objections.

"What about the others?"

"One sign of Daisy, but I haven't met any of the other members of Bret's group. What do revolutionaries look like, Lieutenant? And how do we know they didn't come with Bret, plant a bomb, and leave?" He forced himself to be calm, to let the finger do its work.

"Daisy? Are you sure?"

"Well, I saw an albino black man go by on the street, dressed in white denim and a ruffled polka-dotted shirt. I didn't get close to him, but there can't be too many men like that in this city."

This time, Jacobs' nod was emphatic. "Daisy!"

"It certainly looked like him," Charlie allowed. "He went on down the street after he looked up at the Halsford windows for some time. There was a light on in the kids' bedroom. After Daisy went down the street, the light went out." Charlie touched his pocket, as if searching for his wallet, then shook his head.

Jacobs watched him with the dawning of respect. "You're doing very well, Moon."

Charlie's eyes went flinty. "My client, her children, and my associate are up there. I owe them a good job."

The answer that Jacobs made to this was an uncomfortable sound. "I've got cars on every block around here, but none on the street. There're plainclothesmen in two delivery vans that are like others that work in the neighborhood. One is a pizza delivery truck and one is a Methodist Visiting Nurse van."

"Very clever," Charlie said, realizing he had seen both the vans and had paid no attention to them.

"Standard. Officer Thacher of the hostage-bargaining team will be here in a little while. In the meantime . . ." He pointed the way around the corner, out of sight of the Victorian ruin where Sandy Halsford had her apartment.

Charlie hung back. "Are you sure it's safe? Not being able to see?"

Jacobs pointed. "The Visiting Nurse van is across the street. They're being watched. Don't worry."

With a nod, Charlie went around the corner, saying somewhat ruefully, "I've canceled my whole day's appointments. A couple of my clients are seriously displeased, they tell me." He gave Jacobs a steady look. "But it doesn't matter."

Jacobs nodded. "I hear you." He paused as he leaned against a telephone pole. "I had a talk with Frank Shirer over in homicide. He says you're okay—a civil-rights-happy lawyer but okay. He says you talk straight and you've got guts."

Charlie, for once, could think of nothing to say.

Officer Thacher rode up on an old BMW R40 that needed a tune-up. He got off the motorcycle and used a formidable chain to secure it to a telephone pole. He was a young man who looked younger, no more than twenty-five, and he was dressed in denim and fringed leather. He nodded to Lieutenant Jacobs. "Hi. What's happening?"

"Not very much, so far," Jacobs said.

Thacher busied himself pulling off serviceable leather gloves and stuffing them into his bright orange helmet. "Does Halsford know we're here yet?"

Charlie was surprised that Thacher knew Halsford's name, and said so.

The young officer from the hostage-bargaining squad smiled crookedly. "Bret Halsford is currently out on bail pending trial in a terrorist-type bombing. He's also known to be dealing in drugs. He's intelligent and has a psychological profile like the Grand Tetons. Currently he's second in command of a self-proclaimed revolutionary group that occasionally calls itself the Anarchist Freedom Front. He's a real crusader, that one. He's going to be very tricky to handle."

Charlie felt himself go cold. "How do you mean?"

Thacher squinted up at the building. "Well, if he's determined to be a martyr, we probably don't have much of a chance of getting those hostages out. Considering his previous record, he might just blow the lot of them to pieces. But if he's ego-tripping, then we've got a chance. Not much of one, but a chance." He looked at Charlie. "They tell me he's got his wife and kids and another woman up there."

"My associate," Charlie said, his throat tight.

Some of his feeling must have communicated to Thacher, because he gave Charlie a quick, intent look. "Are you willing to take a chance for your associate?"

"Any chance I have to."

Jacobs was about to object when Thacher silenced him. "Mr. Bretton James Halsford is a real sweetheart. He might get a kick out of killing you. He might decide to trade up. Would you be willing to make yourself a hostage?"

"Yes."

Thacher nodded. "Right. Then we better let him know we're here."

In the end, it was decided that Charlie should make the call to Sandy's apartment. There would be less suspicion if he phoned, because he knew both women, and they would not be alarmed by him.

Charlie chose a phone booth over a block away, at an incongruously new Texaco station. He dialed carefully and waited more than seven rings before he heard Sandy's voice on the line.

"Please, whoever you are . . ."

"Sandy, it's Charlie." He waited a moment for her to recognize him. "If you're not calm enough to talk to me, then let me talk to Morgan."

"I don't know . . . Charlie . . ."

"Wait!" Charlie ordered her. "I know what's happened. I know that Bret's there."

As Charlie said that, Sandy burst into tears and let the phone drop. He was ready to shout with frustration, but he waited until someone else picked up the phone.

"Who is this?" Bret demanded.

"This is Charlie Moon, Bret. I have a message for you." He was amazed to find himself calm now that he had Bret on the phone. He wasn't quite sure how to go on, so he tried the most direct approach. "Bret, you're in serious trouble. The only thing that's stopping the cops from blasting that apartment right now is your hostages. For that reason, they want to talk to you."

"*Fuck off, Moon!*" Bret screamed into the phone.

"Bret!" Charlie knew he must not let him hang up. "You can't do this. Wait! Wait, Bret!" The receiver was not slammed into the cradle, so Charlie ventured to go on.

"You hold all the aces, Bret. All the cops want to do is talk. That's all."

"Talk? Cops don't talk." Now his voice thickened with hatred. "I got what I need up here. I got two women. There's food. The kids are too scared to give me a hard time. What have the cops got to talk about that I need to hear?"

"That's fine for today, Bret, but what about tomorrow? What about when you run out of food?"

"They'll have to bring me some more." Bret was beginning to enjoy himself, and he spoke to Charlie with undisguised contempt.

"I don't know if they will," Charlie said, letting doubt color his words.

"They better. They don't, and Sandy and that lawyer bitch will come out in pieces."

Charlie shut his eyes and forced his anger to cool. He realized this would make him seem even weaker in Bret Halsford's eyes, but that apparently was what Halsford wanted. "Look, Bret, all we want are those hostages out alive. The cops will make arrangements with you so we can get them out, if you're willing to talk to them. Otherwise, it's a standoff."

"With newsmen and cameras?" Bret asked eagerly, taking delight in the chance to be so much the center of attention.

"Yes," Charlie said wearily. "Newsmen and cameras. Is that what you want?"

This time Bret's answer was prompt. "Yeah. I want that. I want everybody to see the cops eat shit." His chuckle was high and not quite controlled.

"I'll see what they say," Charlie said, hating Halsford.

"Yeah, yeah. I'd like to be on one of those KGO talk shows. Do you think they'd let me?" He chuckled again. "Who-o-o-e-e-e! What a beautiful trip! Okay, Moon, I'll talk to the cops."

Charlie choked down wrath and managed to say in a

quiet, civil voice, "There's an officer named Thacher, Jim Thacher. He's not in uniform. He'll come up if you'll let him."

"So long as it's just him and no one else." The threat was back in Bret's tone. "Remember, if you try anything, Sandy and the lawyer and the kids are dead."

Although he knew it wasn't wise, Charlie snapped, "If they're dead, you are, too."

By the time Jim Thacher came down from Sandy's apartment, a considerable crowd had gathered. Lieutenant Jacobs had set up an operations base at the corner, there were police up and down the block, and traffic was being diverted for two blocks on all sides. It was a little after eleven.

"Well?" Jacobs demanded as Thacher joined him at the squad car.

Thacher sighed. "It's gonna take time. He's in the fantasy stage right now; he wants the Mayor to give him a million dollars and a plane to get to Mexico, and he wants to take the kids with him. And he wants a presidential pardon, just, to use his words, 'like that bastard Nixon.'" He looked hard at Jacobs. "We've got to wind this up before tomorrow morning, though."

"Why?" It was Charlie who asked this question.

"Because of the hostages," Thacher said shortly. "Particularly his wife." He did not let Charlie object. "It happens a lot, this hostage syndrome. I've seen it before. You leave that woman with Halsford for more than twenty-four hours and she'll be helping him."

Charlie cut into this. "Come on, Thacher. She's been getting shit from him for months. She hates him. She's terrified of him, and the last . . ."

"That's the trouble, she's terrified." Jim Thacher's intense eyes met Charlie's. "She's already frightened. She's been fighting it for a long time, right?" He acknowledged Charlie's nod. "Then she's already softened up.

Either she has to accept her terror, which could mean some kind of psychological collapse, or she can get rid of the fear, get rid of it completely, by identifying with Bret. In her case, she's got a lot of reasons to choose the latter course. She's been his wife, he's the father of their children, she's familiar with him. All the bad things, yes. But if she identifies with him, they aren't bad any more."

Jacobs spoke first. "How long have we got?"

Thacher shifted his weight from one leg to the other. "At a guess, six hours. Any extension beyond that will have to come from what's-her-name."

"Morgan," Charlie said quietly. "Her name is Morgan Studevant."

"Yeah," Thacher nodded. "She's a very tough lady."

More quickly than he had intended, Charlie asked, "Is she all right?"

"She's scared, but it hasn't got to her yet. If it were just her, I'd say we had till this time tomorrow. I hope she can keep that tongue of hers under control. Halsford can't take much needling."

Involuntarily Charlie looked up toward the windows of Sandy's apartment, and for one swift moment there was a kind of anguish on his face. "Oh, God," he said softly.

But Jim Thacher was still talking. "I'm going to give Halsford about half an hour. He wants to talk to the Mayor, and I've told him we'll try. Don't connect him until I've had a second go at him."

"When will that be?" Jacobs was already becoming irritated.

"Forty, forty-five minutes. Time enough for a sandwich."

When Jim Thacher had gone up to Sandy's apartment a second time, there were newsmen in the street but no cameras. The police had asked for a four-hour news blackout, with the promise that at the end of that time, if the siege was still going on, they could bring in their vans and their cameras. One of the newsmen had just driven up in a silver Mercedes and took leisurely stock of the situation before getting out of the elegant car. He was dressed more for safari than a news beat, in a bush jacket and heavy jeans. He waved rather negligently to Lieutenant Jacobs.

Jacobs returned the wave and said under his breath to Charlie, "Bob Aragon. He's very sharp."

Aragon ambled across the street and stepped up to Jacobs. "I hear there's trouble," he said with a smile.

"Yes," Jacobs snapped.

"You gonna tell me about it, Jake?" The pushy question didn't seem pushy. "A wife and two kids, isn't it?"

"And Moon's associate," Jacobs admitted, nodding toward Charlie.

"Moon?" Aragon held out his hand. "Bob Aragon. How do you figure in this?"

Charlie looked at Lieutenant Jacobs questioningly.

"Sure, go ahead. If Bob uses this one second before we say he can, he knows he'll never get any early information again." Jacobs got into the squad car and began checking with the other squad cars stationed around the neighborhood.

"Tell me about your associate. Associate what?"

"I'm an attorney," Charlie said to Aragon.

"Moon. Moon. As in Ogilvie, Tallant and?"

"Yes."

"Hotshot firm. Who's this associate?"

"Morgan Studevant."

"What's he doing here?" Aragon wasn't taking notes, so Charlie assumed that somewhere in the loose bush jacket the reporter carried a tape recorder.

"She. She'd come to see Mrs. Halsford. Mrs. Halsford is a client of mine."

"What's your associate doing here if Mrs. Halsford is *your* client?"

Charlie knew the question was coming, but he still

disliked it. "She was doing me a favor," he said, blaming himself for the ordeal that Morgan was going through.

There was a flurry of motion in the Halsford apartment, then a scuffle, followed by the sound of two shots.

Everyone on the street looked up, and the police started forward, guns drawn.

"No!" Jim Thacher appeared in one of the windows. "No! Stay back."

Charlie had taken two steps toward the apartment building, but, unlike the others, he did not fall back as he heard Thacher's shout from the window.

From the apartment, there were cries and angry, indistinguishable words. The street was hushed, so the third shot seemed much louder than the other two.

"Morgan," Charlie said, starting toward the door.

There was a hand on his arm. Charlie turned and for the first time realized that Bob Aragon's rather hard greenish eyes were belied by a mobile, expressive mouth. "You can't help her that way," he said, much more kindly than Charlie anticipated.

It was more than three minutes before Jim Thacher came to the window again. "It's okay!" he called down. "Everything's okay. No one's hurt."

Lieutenant Jacobs took the bullhorn. "Are you coming down?"

"Yes," Thacher called back. "But tell everyone to stay where they are. The next shot won't be for show."

Jacobs muttered something under his breath, but he took the bullhorn and announced, "Everyone, stay where you are. This is imperative. Do not, I repeat, do not, change positions or attempt in any way to move nearer to the target building. Stay where you are. Stay where you are. Thacher is coming out."

"He's got two knives and an el cheapo Saturday-night special"—his tone was icily sarcastic—"just a little Smith and Wesson thirty-eight, nothing fancy. But it doesn't

mean he can't kill people," Thacher was saying a few
minutes later as he stood beside Lieutenant Jacobs' squad
car. "His wife is coming apart faster than I thought she
would. She's already saying that no one's on his side and
that we aren't giving him a chance. And she's mad at the
lawyer." He rubbed his face as if trying to wipe away the
strain.

Jacobs glared at him. "Now what?"

It was very difficult for Thacher to say the next, and he
began hesitantly. "I don't think I can get Halsford to talk
to me again, not for a while. That last time was very close."
He looked at the tense faces around him. "I think he
might talk to Moon here, if we handle it just right."

Charlie was startled but strangely relieved. He might
have a chance to do something at last. "Why do you say
that?" he asked evenly, anticipating Lieutenant Jacobs'
challenge.

"Well," Thacher looked him full in the face, "for one
thing, he doesn't like you. For another, he's a bigot about
Indians. And he thinks you're weak. For those reasons,
you might be able to get somewhere with him if you're
very, very careful."

Thacher's reasons made Charlie wince inwardly, but he
accepted them. "Okay. I'm weak and barely civilized and
maybe a cad. How does that help us?"

Thacher regarded Charlie with respect. "You'll do," he
said. "Halsford apparently wants you to tell his wife that
it's okay if she goes back with him, and he wants to make
sure that it's all legal so she can't get out of it again."

"But I can't do that . . ." Charlie began.

"The lady lawyer . . ."

"Morgan Studevant," Charlie corrected him with asperity.

"Yeah, Studevant. She's got him convinced that Mrs.
Halsford's hands are legally tied, and that until all kinds
of forms are taken care of, there's no way she can stop the
divorce, and that there's a certain kind of marriage

contract that would make it impossible for Mrs. Halsford
ever to leave him again." He stopped and gave the ruse a
brief consideration. "She's very clever, that girl. She keeps
Halsford off balance, like saying that even if the Mayor
wanted to give him the plane to escape in it would take a
vote of the Board of Supervisors and the FAA to allow it.
She takes risks, though. She might push him too hard."

The knot that had been in Charlie's chest since nine that
morning tightened again. "I'll try to warn her."

Thacher paused awkwardly. "There are a couple more
things. For one thing, Halsford wants to be interviewed.
By telephone, so there aren't too many people up there. I
was thinking, if we could get that interview . . ."

"You can," Bob Aragon said quietly. "I'll set it up."

"Good. If we can get the interview, there might be a way
to use it as a distraction to get the women and the kids out.
We've got Fire Department equipment at our disposal.
Maybe we could run one of those buckets up to the
window if Halsford could be kept out of the room."

Charlie knew what was being asked. "And then?"

"I don't know. It's a risk." He gave Charlie a significant
look. "He is armed and dangerous. If you don't want to
try it, that's up to you. I can't manage it. He's too
suspicious of me."

"But he isn't of me because I'm a dumb Indian?"
Charlie said without rancor. "I'll see what I can do. Maybe
when he has his interview, I can suggest he lock the
women in the bedroom with the kids. He might not go for
it."

"I'll make him go for it," Bob Aragon promised. "Just
make sure the kids are noisy when he starts to talk. I leave
the rest to you, once I get him convinced."

"Okay," Charlie agreed. He wanted to ask more about
Morgan, but the words would not come. At last, he looked
at Jacobs. "Look, I want you to call my office after I get in
there. If anything happens, tell them about it imme-

diately." He frowned impatiently. "Where's Halsford's lawyer? That's what I want to know."

"In court," Jacobs answered promptly. "In San Jose. He said he'd get here as quickly as possible once the session is over for the day, but even if court's already in recess, he's got at least an hour's drive up."

Charlie accepted this. "When do you want me to go in?"

"Whenever you're ready." Thacher added wryly. "But don't ask him to wait too long. He's touchy already."

Charlie actually smiled. "I won't." He looked over his shoulder at Bob Aragon. "Give me about ten minutes before you try to call him. If it isn't going to work, I should know by then."

Aragon nodded, then asked. "Is there a signal we can work out, some kind of password?"

"That's very risky," Thacher warned. "If he suspects anything, he could start shooting."

The image of Morgan killed filled his mind again, but Charlie blotted it out. "Look, Aragon, complain about the kids. If he goes for the bedroom plan, I'll be glad about it, maybe I'll say something about not being able to handle kids very well. If he's as bigoted as Thacher thinks, he might repeat that to you."

"I'll ask him what you said," Aragon said.

"Sure." Charlie looked at the three men. "Tell him I'm coming up, will you?" he asked Jacobs.

"I'll tell him."

As the bullhorn came to life again, Charlie walked up the street.

Bret Halsford himself opened the door. "Come in, Chief. We got to talk." He made certain that Charlie saw the gun in his hand, and for emphasis he used it to point out the daybed that Sandy used for a couch. "Join the fun."

The two Halsford children huddled together on the

daybed, Rats waving forlornly at Charlie. "Hello, Mr. Moon," he said, very near tears.

"Hello, Rats," Charlie said, hoping he'd be able to pull off awkwardness with these children. He looked around the room, at Sandy, who sat in the old wicker chair with her knees pulled up to her chest, at Morgan, who perched on the brick-and-board bookcase near the hall. The lapel of her coat was torn, and there were bruises on her cheek and forehead. For just an instant, their eyes touched like magnets, and Charlie had to suppress the urge to lunge at Bret Halsford and strangle the life out of him.

"I got some things I want to say to you, Moon," Halsford announced, straddling an old kitchen chair and holding the .38 negligently. "There's gonna be some changes around here, and I hear I need your help for that."

"Possibly," Charlie said, doing his best to stand awkwardly.

"That's what this smart-assed bitch's been telling me for the last hour." He examined his knuckles. "I made it clear how I felt. She's real tricky. Tried some of that fancy aikido stuff on me, but she forgot about the gun. Aikido's no good against a gun, is it, you ball-cutter?"

Although he could not keep his hands from clenching, Charlie did force himself to speak easily. "What do you want to talk about, Halsford? I can't give you my opinion until I know what's on your mind."

"*Lawyers!*" Halsford spat. "Can't you assholes ever say anything straight?" He shifted in the chair so that he could face Charlie squarely. "Y'see, Moon, my wife"—he emphasized the words harshly—"she's found out she made a mistake. She doesn't want a divorce. She wants to stay with me. Right, Sandy?"

Charlie had sometimes seen the expression in Sandy's eyes in the eyes of animals about to die. She pulled at a loose strand of hair. "That's right. He needs me on his side."

"That's horsesh . . ." Morgan started, ignoring the warning in Charlie's glance.

"That's what?" Bret Halsford asked, getting to his feet. "I'm running out of patience with you, you dyke."

Morgan looked at Halsford with withering scorn but was silent.

Slowly Bret sank back on the chair. He crossed his arms in unconscious imitation of James Bond and Dirty Harry posters, his .38 level with his head, aimed upward and outward.

"So Sandy wants to be your wife again?" Charlie asked in carefully neutral tones. "And you need me for filing the proper papers?" He came a little farther into the room, moving near the daybed where the children cowered.

"That's it. We want to be sure this kind of thing never happens again. Don't we, Sandy?"

"He needs me," Sandy said, barely audible.

Charlie looked at Sandy, and he felt her utter fatigue. Sandy was tired, tired of fighting, tired of decisions, tired of life. It was easy to give it up and be rid of all the things that had made her world unbearable for the last four months. She avoided Charlie's eyes and instead watched Bret with listless surrender. "I'm sorry, Sandy," Charlie said to her, but she refused to respond.

"The thing is, I want this taken care of now," Bret went on. "That ball-cutter tells me that it takes six weeks to clear everything up. I want it done now." He looked Charlie over as if to assure himself that Charlie could file forms. "I want it done today so that as soon as I get my money and the Mayor gets permission for that plane we can light out of here for Mexico without any of that border shit."

As Charlie watched Bret, he wondered whether Halsford might be on something. There was nothing in his record that showed addiction, but the records were ten weeks old, and Bret had been living differently. Unconsciously Charlie touched the wooden finger under his sweater, but learned little.

"I'll do what I can," Charlie said as if he had made up his mind. "If my client wants it that way, I'll do it."

"She wants it that way. Doesn't she?" Halsford favored Sandy with a malicious smile. "Doesn't she?"

Sandy drew her knees more closely under her chin. "Yes. She wants it that way."

Charlie had to strain to hear her, and using that as an excuse moved nearer the daybed. "You're speaking very softly . . ."

"She wants it that way," Bret said, as if explaining a simple task to an infuriating moron. "So you do it."

"Of course. But I must discuss the terms with you. You understand, Mr. Halsford, that I've got to know the terms of your agreement in detail."

"God, how can you lawyers stand all the crap? It'd drive me crazy." He motioned Charlie to sit down, and Charlie gratefully sank onto the daybed.

It was then that the phone rang.

"If that's the cops!" Bret lunged at the phone.

"No," Charlie said quickly. "It's not the police. It's Mr. Aragon. You said you wanted an interview, and he is very eager to talk to you."

Bret plucked the receiver out of the cradle. "If this is some kind of trick, I'll start shooting." He was about to go on in a similar vein but stopped. "How do I know you're Aragon?"

As Bret worked out a way to verify Bob's credentials, Charlie moved a little nearer the kids. "Hey, Rats, how're you doing?"

The boy looked up at him, puzzled.

"While your dad's on the phone, let's have a little fun. I want you two to tickle each other. You're ticklish, aren't you?" He reached out and raced his fingers along the boy's sides. Rats squirmed and shrieked. Heather, who had barely moved until now, tried to get away from her

thrashing brother and got her ankle kicked. Immediately
the boy and the girl fell to shouting and grabbing at each
other, partly from nervousness and partly to strike back at
something, anything, anyone, so that they would not feel
so helpless.

"Hey, you two! Stop the noise! I'm trying to talk!" Bret
took a hasty step forward while trying to hold onto the
gun and the phone at once.

Rats stopped almost at once, but Heather, who had
been so silent, now began a methodical screaming.

"Shut her up!" Bret waved the gun.

Sandy got out of the chair and gracelessly tried to hold
her children, but this seemed to reenforce their fear, and
even Rats whimpered.

It was at this point that Charlie said, quite diffidently,
"Is there another room where the kids could stay? And
perhaps the women? Sandy told me there was a lock on
the bedroom door. You could put them in there, then you
can conduct your interview and your discussion with me
in peace." He dared not meet Morgan's shocked eyes, for
fear her indignation would make him tell her what he was
doing.

The noise in the room was terribly loud, and instead of
growing softer, seemed only to be louder.

"That's the first sensible thing you've said since you
came in," Morgan snapped as she got off the bookcase
and came across the room, pulling Sandy to her feet.
"Come on, Sandy. We're going in the other room. Your
big, brave husband is going to lock us in." She turned a
scathing look on Bret. "We don't want to disturb your
interview."

Charlie added his own touch. "Would you like to put
me in with them?" He came nearer, so that he would be
heard over the phone, and made himself speak in a
strangely sycophantic manner. "I'm not very good with
kids, but I could try."

"Back off, Moon," Bret said, giving him a shove. "I want

you where I can see you. But the others, *shut up, you fuckers!*" He raised his hand as if to hit Sandy with the phone.

Morgan quickly pulled her out of the way and reached for the children, who were crying in earnest. "Come on. We're going into the bedroom." She pushed them ahead of her, into the hallway.

Bret was saying to Bob Aragon, "Will you wait a minute? There's something I got to do." He put the phone down and motioned to Charlie. "Come on. I'm not leaving you alone to talk to anyone. Come on!" He prodded Charlie between the shoulders. "I want you to lock the door," he said, and took the key from the inside of the bedroom door. "I want you to lock it right. 'Cause if I test it and it isn't locked right, I'm going to shoot your leg somewhere."

Charlie took the key and very deliberately turned it in the lock. He hoped that the Fire Department would have sense enough to raise their bucket to the window on the side of the building, rather than the one that fronted on the street. If they used the front window, there was little protection if Halsford should glance out at the street and see the truck. He handed the key to Halsford. "Try the lock. It's closed."

As they walked back into the living room, Bret shook his head in wonder. "I can't figure why you thought I'd fall for that. If I left you in that room, it would be real easy for you to signal the cops. They might get a sharpshooter up on one of the roofs around here, and then, blam! it's all over for me. I'm not dumb, Moon. I know what the cops are up to."

"Well, it was an idea," Charlie said, as if defeated.

Bret Halsford chuckled as he picked up the phone again.

To Charlie, sitting in the wicker chair and listening, the interview seemed interminable. Bob Aragon drew

Halsford out with a skill that Charlie respected profoundly. He thought that if Aragon had decided to be an attorney instead of a newscaster he would have been formidable at cross-examination. After the first five minutes, Charlie no longer listened to what Halsford was saying, or listened with divided attention. What interested him more were the sounds from the bedroom, which at first were the muffled sobs of Rats and Heather, and then a gradual calming. There were sounds from outside, too, and they were muted, but Charlie tried to pick out the sound of the Fire Department truck, hoping that it would arrive quickly and that it would be a swift task, for every minute it took to get Sandy, the children, and Morgan out of the house increased the risk of discovery.

Bret had been on the phone something more than half an hour when there was a shout from below. Bret interrupted a rambling discourse on why his two years of college had been a waste of time except for chemistry labs. He held the receiver to his chest and glared at Charlie. "What's going on?" he demanded.

"I don't know," Charlie admitted, although he feared a few of the men watching the siege had endangered it. "Maybe it's the cops again."

"Motherfuckers!" Bret yelled and slammed the phone down. "You!" he gestured at Charlie. "Up. Get up."

Charlie rose carefully to his feet. "What's the matter? If it was that sound, it might have been anything . . ."

"Sure. Anything." Bret's eyes were staring now, and there was a curiously set look to his face. He turned his head toward Charlie but did not see him. He had moved beyond reason now, and his exhilaration became maniacal. "Come on, Moon. We're gonna check on the ladies and the kiddies." His smile was devoid of humor. "Stay three steps ahead of me. I'll give you the key, and I want you to open the door to the bedroom. When it's open, you step inside first. I don't want no chairs bashing *my* skull. You hear me?"

"Yes," Charlie said flatly. He hoped fervently that when the door was open the room would be empty.

It was, almost. Morgan was at the window, just starting to climb into the white metal bucket that waited outside. As the door opened, she turned angry, despairing eyes toward it.

"Hold it!" Bret ordered, gesturing with the .38 for Morgan to step back into the room. "Move it!"

Slowly, deliberately, Morgan stepped off the sill, back onto the old, white-painted floor. She watched Bret Halsford, measuring the extent of his disorder by the way he moved, his terse speech, his expressionless face. Charlie saw this, and admired the way she concealed her rising fear.

"Hey!" Bret gave one explosive laugh. "You rotten little cunt!" He snapped his arm back into position to fire.

It was one of those moments when the world slowed down. Even as Charlie saw in his mind Morgan falling with blood spattering the walls and floor, he bent forward and kicked out with the full strength of the fury he had kept contained that day. His foot caught Bret Halsford on the hip and pushed him off balance just as he fired. Charlie saw him stagger, the gun falling from his hand, his arms flailing. It was only then that Charlie realized the heavy, sharply numbing blow he had felt on his shoulder was the bullet Bret had intended for Morgan, and that he was bleeding from a deep flesh wound.

Then pain sank vitriolic fangs into him, and he felt dizzy and wretchedly sick.

Bret turned on him, his hands bunched to strike, and the world came back to normal.

"Stop!" Morgan's voice was ragged and Charlie tried to turn to look at her, but the slight motion filled him with nausea.

Amazingly, Bret did stop. "Hey," he said uncertainly. "You don't want to play around with a thing like that . . ."

"Because the safety's off," Morgan said very coolly.

"And if I pull the trigger, you'll get a bullet in the stomach. Think about it."

Charlie had backed to a wall and leaned gratefully against it. His left sleeve and the side of his sweater were soaked in blood, and he could not yet bring himself to touch the wound. He tried to wiggle the fingers on his left hand, which added to the pain, but not in the grinding, sickening way that would mean shattered bone. "Morgan," he said softly, "the cops . . ."

"They're coming," she answered, and Charlie heard the beginning of a quaver in her voice.

"Hold on," he whispered. "It's almost over."

There were shouts and sirens in the street; the eruption of activity seemed a senseless distraction to Charlie, who still tried to keep his mind on Bret.

"Keep back!" Morgan said sharply.

Bret took another step nearer, some of his confidence returning. "You don't really think you can shoot me, do you, you foxy bitch? You like fighting."

"Come one step closer and you'll find out," she said very steadily.

A sound at the front door broke the spell, and it was what Bret had been waiting for. With a strangled shout he rushed Morgan.

Charlie lunged forward, reaching to grab Bret. As he stretched his good right arm, he was consumed with the thought, *If you harm her, if you harm her, I swear on the graves of my ancestors that I'll kill you if it takes the rest of my life to do it!* He shoved Bret, but it wasn't enough to break the force of his attack.

Morgan had fallen back, casting the gun aside, and then, in some way Charlie never quite understood, she turned away from Bret, seized one of his arms and tugged once.

Because the window was open there was no sound of breaking glass—only a short, unbelieving cry and then a metallic thud as Bret hit the Fire Department rescue equipment on his way down. The hectic sounds outside ceased.

But inside, the front door was being broken down.

Morgan stood up again slowly, her hands pressed to her face. "Charlie . . ." she said in a still tone. "Charlie, I . . ."

He had mastered the worst of the pain for the moment, though he knew he was shocky. He came up behind her, somewhat unsteadily, and with his unbloodied right arm pulled her close against him. His eyes were closed, his lips pressed to her shining hair. "You're alive," he murmured.

They were still standing that way when Lieutenant Jacobs rushed through the door. The gun lay on the floor where Morgan had dropped it, and around it were spatters of red.

"Moon! Oh, shit, your arm!" Jacobs blurted as he saw Charlie.

Both Charlie and Morgan turned at the sound, and for the first time she saw his shoulder, and the putty color his face had turned. Her eyes grew large and wet with tears; she tried to speak and found no words.

With his right hand, he touched her face, avoiding the darkening bruises. His fingers were gentle, lingering. "It doesn't matter, Morgan. It doesn't."

Then the room was filled with police and, shortly after them, ambulance attendants. Through the confusion, Jacobs gave orders to take Charlie to Mission Emergency Hospital.

When the stretcher was brought up, Charlie refused it. "I can walk," he said, and reached out for Morgan's hand. "Let's go, love."

"I'll want a full report from you later, Moon," Jacobs called after him.

"You'll get it," he answered, his voice showing his weakness. He gripped Morgan's hand tightly, and as they walked out of Sandy Halsford's apartment, he felt the wooden finger against his chest grow warm.

The doctors at Mission Emergency had wanted to keep him overnight for observation, but Charlie had refused. "I've got a very good physician of my own, and if there's anything wrong in the morning, I'll call him." He had balked at putting his bloodied sweater back on, and he had not had time to stop at his car to retrieve his shirt and jacket.

There was a familiar figure in the waiting room. "I'll let you have my bush jacket if you'll let me have an interview," Bob Aragon said with a slightly sardonic smile. "I'll even drive you home in my Mercedes."

Charlie attempted a shrug and gave up immediately. "Well, Morgan, do you mind?"

Morgan had been strangely silent through the whole patching-up procedure. She had consented to have her skull X-rayed, on the off chance that one of Bret's blows had done more than bruise her. Then she had stayed with Charlie, her mouth set in a tight line. Now she shook herself. "No. That's fine."

"I'll give you a lift too, Ms. Studevant. I'd love to know what went on in that apartment."

"I warn you," Charlie said as he signed a release absolving the hospital of any blame if his actions, which were contrary to medical advice, resulted in a worsening of his condition. "I probably won't make a lot of sense. My shoulder's full of something local, and they gave me some pills"—he touched his slacks pocket—"for pain. I don't know what they do for pain, but I tell you, they make me spacy." He studied the nurse a moment. "Is there anything else, or may I go?"

She pursed her mouth in a disapproving way. "You can go, sir. But you're a fool if you do."

"Thanks." Charlie touched Morgan's arm. "Ready?"

"Yes."

"Okay, Aragon. Give me your bush jacket." The drug and the aftereffects of shock had made him light-headed, almost giddy. He winced as he pulled the bush jacket around his bandaged shoulder; he found he could not fasten the buttons with his left arm strapped close to his body.

"I'll do it," Morgan said, and helped him button the jacket.

Bob Aragon shivered a little as he opened the door. The flowered shirt he'd worn under the bush jacket was not much protection against the sharp November wind, and now that the sun was almost down, it was getting cold fast.

"Thanks," Charlie said as he got into the luxurious back seat of the Mercedes. He made room for Morgan beside him, feeling strangeness around her now that the dreadful day was over.

"Out in the Avenues, isn't it? A couple blocks off Geary?" Bob asked as he swung the silver Mercedes into traffic.

"How did you know?"

"Ve haff our vayss," he said in a terrible parody of a German accent. "My way was calling your office and talking to your receptionist. A charming woman, your Lydia Wong."

Charlie looked bemused. "I wonder how you made her give out the information."

Bob Aragon smiled, "Well, I told her as much as I knew of what happened. And I told her your car was still somewhere near the Halsford place." He turned his attention to crossing Market Street. At five-thirty, it was rush-hour crowded, with buses, trolleys, and cars jockeying for advantage in the narrow lanes.

"God, I'm tired," Charlie said to the air. "You'd better

ask me your questions quickly, Bob. I think I'm about to fall asleep."

"Go ahead and sleep, I'll ask you questions when I get you home."

"Okay," Charlie said, and gratefully leaned his head back against the deeply padded upholstery.

Bob Aragon had asked his questions, Rufus had been fed, Charlie had tried to eat something and had settled for milk, hating himself for feeling weak and shaky.

"Maybe you should have stayed at the hospital," Morgan said as she made tea.

"No. I hate 'em. I don't have anything infectious. I can manage for myself."

"Can you?" she said, looking at him critically. "Then unbutton the jacket."

At that moment, Charlie wished that Bob Aragon had taken it when he left, rather than saying he'd drop by for it on the weekend. He fumbled with the buttons and at last managed to undo them, feeling smugly pleased with himself. "There. Unbuttoned." He dropped onto the only chair in the kitchen.

"Good," she said and turned to measure out the tea into the pot. The third spoonful tipped and dark, dry, tight-curled leaves littered the floor. Morgan bent forward, away from Charlie, and it took him a moment to realize that she was crying.

Charlie got to his feet. "Morgan . . . ?" he said uncertainly. He reached out to touch her, then dropped his hand. "What is it?"

"Nothing," she insisted, pulling away from him.

"No, it isn't," he said, suddenly very serious. The light-headed effect of the drug was beginning to wear off, and though it brought back a throb of pain, it brought back his senses as well. "You're crying, Morgan."

"So would you, after . . ." She stopped again and tried to control herself.

The kettle started to shriek as the water boiled. Charlie reached over and turned off the stove. He knew that she had been holding herself in check since that morning. "If you hurt, Morgan, let me help you. You can rest now."

"Why did you do it?" she asked as she mastered her emotions.

Charlie knew what she meant. "I couldn't leave you there alone, Morgan. I love you too much to do that." He'd said it. There was no mistaking him now. As he waited, he unconsciously pressed the little wooden finger on the braided thong around his neck.

"You don't have to say that." She refused to look at him. "Today was different. It doesn't . . . you don't have to say that."

"Morgan. Morgan, will you look at me?" He watched her indecision. At last, slowly, grudgingly, she turned, but her face was averted. "No, Morgan. Look at me." He made no move to touch her, to persuade her with anything other than his words.

"All right." There was a defiant angle to her chin as she met his eyes. "I tell you again, you don't have to say this." Her face was tired and blotchy from weeping, and the bruises were darkening. There was a place on her lip where she had bitten through the skin.

"You went to Sandy's as a favor to me, and now you're afraid that I have to say I love you as a kind of thank you, is that it?"

"I went there to prove something to Sandy, damn it. She said that women weren't any help in her situation. I wanted her to know differently." She started to cross her arms and compromised, grabbing her wrists in her hands.

"Okay, I had nothing to do with it, then." He was neither resentful nor vain.

She shook her head, but her eyes were wet again. "No."

"But you've been with me since we got out of Sandy's apartment," he reminded her, genuinely confused now.

"Well, Christ, you got shot trying to protect me!" She stammered a little on the word "shot" and her eyes flew from his face to the heavily packed bandage on his shoulder where the open bush jacket had slipped off.

He said nothing. He felt he had risked all that he had, and now the rest was up to her.

"You didn't have to, Charlie." She was trying to be reasonable, the same, competent, spiky Morgan she always was with him.

"Yes. I did."

She sighed, and there was a tremor in her breath. "You don't need to think that because you . . . protected me that . . . you have to love me."

"It's the other way around if you need protection." He reached awkwardly and turned the stove back on under the kettle. "Don't think about it, if you don't want to. We'll have some tea and you can do what you like." He had lost, he told himself. He'd tried, he'd done it wrong, and now he had lost, and the pain of it was deeper and worse than the wound under the bandage. He gathered his scattered thoughts together and added, "If there's a chance, you can let me know if you ever change your mind. But tell me if there's someone else, will you? And give me a little time to get used to it."

When she spoke, it was so softly that at first he wondered if he had heard her or only wished the words were said. "There's never been anyone else, Charlie."

He turned back to her quickly, so quickly that his head swam. He said the first thing that came into his mind. "You're not a twenty-seven-year-old virgin. It isn't fair to deny the love you've had before now. Love's too rare for that. Come on." He was shocked as he heard himself speak, fearing Morgan would think he had thrown her past into her face.

Luckily, with rare humor, Morgan laughed. "No. Of course I'm not. And I'm not forgetting anything or anyone. But what does it have to do with you?"

"Nothing," Charlie said, smiling at her.

"I wish I didn't keep falling asleep," Charlie complained when he had kissed her again. "This is too much like a dream if I keep falling asleep."

She pulled out of his circling arm and poured more tea. "Oh, thanks."

"Morgan." He waited until she looked at him. "Don't mock. For my sake, if not your own."

She nodded slowly and fixed her attention on the tea. "It's a habit I've got into. That's all." She took her cup in her hands and looked down into it. "How are you feeling? Really?"

"Why?" He knew there was more to her question than the words.

She continued to stare into the cup. "Shall I stay? Tonight?"

"If you want. There's a spare bed."

"That's not what I meant," she snapped, and put the cup down so sharply that it rattled in the saucer.

"I know." He touched her gently. "Morgan, I don't want to make love the first time while I'm exhausted, and you're exhausted, when I'm full of drugs and pain, and your hands are still shaking from what you've gone through. You're still seeing Bret Halsford falling out a window." He saw her flinch at the word. "Morgan?"

"I didn't think he'd fall. I thought he'd hit the floor. I didn't know I was so close." She put her hands over her eyes.

"Yes." He waited. "Don't you see, this is no way to begin? I don't want to hide in you, I want to discover you. And I don't want you to pity me for being hurt, I want you to welcome me." He stopped rather abruptly. "God, I wish I hadn't lost so much blood today."

She turned to him. "Charlie!"

"Well, I can't help it. I want to think clearly, I want to tell you things, and I can't keep two thoughts together for more than couple of minutes."

As she leaned back toward him, Morgan kissed him softly on the mouth. "You frighten me," she whispered.

"I do? Why?" He kissed her forehead, the line of her brow, the lids of her eyes.

"Because . . . you're so damn loving!" she said vehemently.

"Do you think you might get used to it in time?"

"*Used* to it?" She laughed, and her laughter was oddly strained. "I'm afraid I'll get *addicted* to it." This realization bothered her, and she drew away from him a little. "You don't have to take that too seriously. I'm not trying to get you to commit yourself to anything. I despise women who do that."

"Morgan, Morgan." He moved, and his shoulder hurt him. "You aren't trapping me." Awkwardly he took the braided thong from around his neck and held it out to her. "Here."

She took it from him, examining it carefully. "What is it?"

"It's magic. It's myself." Though he tried not to, he yawned. "When you are tired of me, or want to be free of me, take it off. But not until then. You have my word— and that wooden finger *is* my word—that I want to be with you as long as I am myself."

"Did Lois . . ." She bit back the words. "No, that's bitchy and spiteful. Forget I said it, Charlie."

The mention of Lois stung him with unpleasant memories. "No, Lois never wore it. She found such things . . . childish, I guess, is the best word for it."

"You mean it, don't you? That this is your self." The fear that had been in her eyes was replaced with awe.

"Yes. I don't know whether or not I can explain it to you, but I'll try, if you like."

"No. Maybe later. Do you put it on or do I?"

"You do. It's your choice." Charlie waited, his eyes never leaving Morgan's. Some of his dizziness had passed, but he still had to force himself to concentrate, and this was something he wanted very much to see, so that he could remember.

Carefully, slowly, Morgan brought the braided leather over her head so that the wooden finger lay on her shirt.

"Against the skin, Morgan." He nodded as she tucked the talisman inside her shirt. "Always wear it next to the skin."

"I will." She touched the piece of wood through her shirt. "Is there anything else I have to do?"

"Not now. In a week or two, perhaps." He wanted to tell her how much he hoped for, but he drew back, afraid to ask for too much from her.

Some of her apprehension had returned. "You mean after you've taken me to bed."

Charlie shook his head. "Please. No more mocking. There is a kind of ritual, very brief, that works best right after making love . . . Look, Morgan, when I'm inside you, I want to give you something more than my body; I want you to know how much I treasure you. That takes time."

"But Charlie," she said with difficulty, "what if it doesn't work out?"

"That's for later," he said drowsily. "I'm sorry, Morgan. I keep drifting off to sleep."

"Do you really want me so much?" she asked, frowning a little.

"Yep." He closed his eyes. "But only if you want me. So

think it over as long as you have to."

"What if my answer is no?"

"Well," he said, the words beginning to slur, "I wouldn't like it very much. But I don't want you to lie about it. Don't do anything against your will, Morgan. It's just that I want you so much. I hope it's yes . . ."

Her answer, if there was one, was lost to him—Charlie was asleep.

Thursday, November 4

Charlie had considered leaving the phone off the hook. He had had over ten calls since nine that morning; it was not yet noon, and the phone was ringing again. On the fifteenth ring, he gave up. "Charles Moon," he said, making no attempt to disguise his irritation.

"Charles, m'lad!" The hearty sound of Willis Ogilvie's oratorical tones boomed along the line.

"Hello, Willis," Charlie said, sighing. "When did you get back?"

"Last night, Charlie, about ten o'clock, and found the news full of you. An amazing story, Charlie. It's a pity Halsford was so badly hurt. He's not expected to live, they say; no more than a few hours. How are you? The eleven o'clock news said you'd been shot."

"It's superficial," Charlie said, doing his best to ignore the throbbing ache that was as wearing as a beating. "A flesh wound in the shoulder."

"It's truly incredible. Shannon said it will be the making

198

of you. You should have seen her in Washington, Charlie. They loved her, just loved her." With a fond chuckle he added, "The smartest thing I ever did was marry that woman."

Charlie pictured in his mind the petulant, attractive face of Shannon Ogilvie, who was Willis's third wife. There were close to thirty years between them, and Charlie had never made up his mind about Shannon; she was either very naïve or very cynical. "I'm glad it went so well for you."

"It was quite a time, Charlie. Too bad about the senatorial race, but maybe it won't matter that much." Again the appreciative chuckle. "You're moving in pretty glamorous circles yourself, so Alex tells me. Helping out the opera about that killing last week. Quite a plum for you."

Suddenly Charlie remembered that he had been expected to hear Solechiaro the night before. "Oh, Christ!" he said aloud.

"Are they being difficult?" Willis asked with ponderous humor.

"No, it's not that. I just remembered something. Willis, I have to make a call right now. I'll check in with you later this afternoon. After I've seen my doctor," he improvised.

"Oh. Of course. Yes. Of course. I should have realized. I'll talk to you later, Charles, m'lad. I just wanted you to know how proud I am of you."

Charlie knew that sulky tone and tried to lessen the offense to his senior partner. "I really appreciate that, Willis. It means a lot to me." How easily he said that, and how little truth there was in the words! His grandfather would be deeply concerned if he could hear Charlie speaking now.

"Thank you, Charlie. It's good to know that loyalty is still valuable." He cleared his throat. "I'll talk to you later, then. Be sure to take good care of yourself."

"I will do my best, Willis," Charlie said, wanting to hang up on him.

"I know you will. Remember to keep me posted on your progress. I admit it's hard for me to picture you and Morgan in a situation like that, but you both acquitted yourselves most creditably. Excellent work. Excellent work."

"Thanks, Willis."

"Well, I won't keep you any longer. Good to know you're all right. We'll have you over to dinner some time next week, and you can tell me all about it then."

"Fine," Charlie snapped.

"You're a hero, m'lad. I hope you get all your well-deserved praise."

"Morgan deserves praise, too, Willis. Why not give her a call and congratulate her, too?"

"I will. Later on. I've got to run now. I'll talk to you later." Very suddenly Willis Ogilvie cut the connection, and Charlie was at once pleased and furious.

When he had calmed down sufficiently, he called Elizabeth's house, and when Henry answered, he asked if he could speak to Mr. Solechiaro.

"Of course, Mr. Moon. I hope that your wound is not serious," he added.

Charlie cursed silently. Was everyone going to insist on talking about that? "Not particularly, Henry. Just inconvenient."

"Mrs. Kendrie will be pleased to hear it. If you'll hold the line a few moments, Mr. Solechiaro will be with you."

As Charlie waited, he thought over the previous night. He thought about Morgan, the nearness of her, the scent of her body, the coolness of her hands when she touched him.

He was shaken out of his reverie by Domenico Solechiaro's cheerful voice. "Ah, Sr. Moon. If you did not want to see the opera, you had only to tell me. You did not need to be shot."

Charlie almost choked on his laughter. "Mr. Solechiaro, I didn't do this to avoid your performance. I was, in fact, looking forward to it." Oddly he knew that was the truth. "But there is a matter I must discuss with you."

"But what? Not more of Feuier? What is there to say? He died, there are some unpleasant questions, and then it will be over, and the world will be a cleaner place."

"Mr. Solechiaro," Charlie said, determined not to get off the subject, "Gui-Adam Feuier was romantically involved with your sister. Why didn't you mention it?"

"No!" Solechiaro said emphatically. "No, never was it romantic. His interest in Serephina was wholly carnal. Had I thought it was a matter of love, I would have been sad, but I would not have objected. This was not love."

"Yes, Mr. Solechiaro, I understand that. But you should have mentioned it when we had our interview on Monday." Was it only three days ago? Charlie asked himself. It felt like weeks, a month.

"But it is over. It was already a thing of the past when we talked. It no longer mattered."

"It matters, Mr. Solechiaro, and it's not a thing of the past." Charlie wanted to rub his aching left arm, but the movement was difficult and painful. He put his mind on the conversation. "There's very good reason to believe that your sister's involvement with Feuier will make your position very difficult."

"But how?" the Italian protested. "I have said it is over, and for the honor of my family, I do not wish to discuss it."

"That's not your option if the police decide to talk about it with you. All I ask is that if you are questioned, will you please call me first, and say nothing until I arrive?"

"But you are much hurt," Solechiaro protested reasonably. "And you must rest assured that I will say nothing about my sister that would embarrass her."

"You can't do that, Mr. Solechiaro," Charlie began gently. "You will be asked about her . . ."

"Then," Solechiaro said with smug self-satisfaction, "I will lie."

Charlie mastered his temper and reminded himself that he was supposed to take it easy today. "No, Mr. Solechiaro, you must not do that. Lying will only make it more difficult, I promise you."

"But I will be gone shortly," he said, still blithely—it was apparent that he had worked it out to his own satisfaction. "In a year, who will bother about Gui-Adam Feuier?"

"It doesn't work that way," Charlie insisted, moving to make himself slightly more comfortable. "Mr. Solechiaro, there is good reason to believe that Feuier was murdered. If that's the case, you could find yourself suspected of the crime because of your previous trouble with Feuier."

"But no one would think so," Solechiaro protested. "I am not a violent man, Sr. Moon. I dislike such things. Even in the opera, I smile when I die."

Charlie was at once annoyed and amused. He made another valiant attempt to keep on the subject. "Mr. Solechiaro, this was not a violent act. Even you would have been able to put poison in Mr. Feuier's . . ." In his what? Charlie asked himself. When did the poison go into his system? And how? Did he take it before he began the opera? During? When had Feuier last taken heroin, and had this other poison been in his body before that?

Solechiaro seemed to sense Charlie's uncertainty. "I did not arrive at the Opera House until after the performance began, Sr. Moon. I dined until a quarter until nine. With friends, Sr. Moon. You see, we have your *Perry Mason* show in Italia, and I have watched it. From dinner, I went to the Opera House, and the doorman admitted me. By nine, I was with the costume mistress for my last fitting. During that time, Feuier may have been in his dressing room or on stage. When the fitting was over, I went to watch the performance. And to speak to . . . a friend."

"Will that friend vouch for you, Mr. Solechiaro?" Charlie asked aloud, thinking still that he had to know when and how Feuier had taken both heroin and the stuff that killed him.

"Perhaps, but I shall not ask it." Charlie had learned to recognize that tone. Solechiaro had said all that he was going to, and there was no way to change his mind.

"I will tell you one thing, Sr. Moon. Had Feuier harmed my sister as he has harmed others, I would have killed him. As it happened, I did not." He was very serious now, and much of his overwhelming ebullience was missing. This was another facet of Domenico Solechiaro, the part of him that accepted the hours of study, discipline, and hard work without complaint. "If you care about another, you accept certain . . . obligations."

"Yes," Charlie said to himself.

"It is not in the law, Sr. Moon, but it is stronger than the law. Is it not?"

"Yes," Charlie said again, somewhat louder.

"Ah." Then the seriousness was gone and the enthusiasm returned. "I will not speak unless you tell me to. And Mr. Malcomb and I will see you have tickets to *Manon Lescaut* next week. But I pray you, Sr. Moon, do not this time be shot."

"I don't intend to be." Charlie almost chuckled, but the movement was too hurtful.

"It was a very brave thing you did, Sr. Moon. I doubt that I would have the courage."

"It wasn't a matter of courage," Charlie said. "But thank you."

"*È niente.* I am flattered that you think of me after such an experience." He laughed, quite surprisingly kindly, and hung up.

*   *   *

Shortly after three, Lieutenant Jacobs arrived to get a full report from Charlie.

"I'm sorry to push you, but we want to move fast on this one." He summed up Charlie's condition very quickly and said with some concern, "Don't you want to get something for pain?"

"I've got something," Charlie said testily, "but I don't want to take it unless I have to. Why the rush on this Halsford thing, anyway?"

Lieutenant Jacobs chose one of the straight-backed chairs and left the couch to Charlie. "We checked with the hospital a little while ago, and they say there's no chance now that Halsford will make it. He could last a day or two longer, maybe as much as a week, but . . ."

"You mean he's still *alive?*" Charlie demanded.

"Yes. But his neck's broken, and there's a lot of internal damage. It's just a question of what quits when." Jacobs pulled out a tape recorder. "Do you mind if I record this? You'll see a transcription of it, and you can make changes then, or comments. It'll go faster this way."

It wasn't usual, but Charlie didn't particularly care. "Okay. What do you want to know?"

Forty minutes later, Lieutenant Jacobs had his tape, and Charlie had a crashing headache to add to the discomfort of his aching body. He got to his feet to show Jacobs out and was almost too dizzy to stand.

"Let me help," Jacobs said, holding out a solicitous hand.

Charlie found it infuriating. "I'm okay," he insisted through clenched teeth.

Jacobs stood back. "No offense, Moon."

"None taken. I'm just . . . very tired." That was the least of it, but it was the most acceptable.

"I'm not surprised. Bob Aragon called earlier to tell me a little of what the doctor said. You better take care of yourself." Jacobs finished putting the recorder away in its case. "I'll call you tomorrow. This should be typed up by then."

"How's Sandy?" Charlie asked, anxious to turn the conversation away from himself.

"Sandy? Mrs. Halsford? She's not very well. We had a call from a cousin of hers up in Eureka. He said he had no idea that Sandy needed help so badly, and he was offering to take her in until she felt better. He'll take the kids, too. He said his wife loves kids. It ought to help some."

Charlie recalled the frustrating conversation he had had with Sandy's cousin in Eureka, and he could not help smiling bitterly. "Isn't that fortunate?"

"She saw Bret this afternoon," Jacobs added thoughtfully. "He didn't recognize her, but that's not unusual in cases like his. I think it upset her, though, seeing him like that after what he put her through."

"Your compassion is admirable," Charlie said dryly, "but just a little late. If you'd given her the protection she deserved in the first place, there wouldn't have been anything for her to go through."

"Yes . . ." Jacobs had the grace to be uneasy. "But you know how it is with ex-wives. They're always complaining about their husbands. If it isn't a question of back alimony or child support, then they say that their husbands are harassing them." He shook his head. "We don't have the manpower to take care of those complaints, and most of them blow over in a day or two anyway." With that, he bent down to pick up the recorder and a zippered case that Charlie guessed contained notes on other similar interviews. "We can't do it, Moon."

"Tell me," Charlie said conversationally, "if it had been, say, a neighbor of Sandy's who'd been threatening her, and who had been restrained by court order from having anything to do with her, what would you have done then?"

Jacobs gave Charlie a nasty look, as if deciding how much he would be willing to take from him. "That's different. Entirely."

"Why?" Charlie let the question die between them. "I'll tell you why. Because you can't get it through your thick skulls that wives have a right to be safe from their husbands, that's why. And more so for ex-wives. Halsford had to try to kill her before you believed that it was more than petty spite." Charlie felt his shoulder grow more deeply painful, and it goaded him. "Halsford was prepared to kill Sandy, their kids, Ms. Studevant, and me, and you would have sat by and let him." He stopped then and leaned back against the cushions. His face was slightly flushed, and a feverish shine lit his eyes.

"I know you're upset," Jacobs said heavily. "You've got good reason to be. But you don't understand the realities." He started toward the door. I'll let myself out. Thanks for the report."

"Jacobs," Charlie said sharply before the lieutenant had stepped outside. "How much did that fiasco yesterday cost the city?"

"I don't know. Why?"

"Compare it sometime to what it would have cost to give Mrs. Halsford the protection she asked for and was entitled to. And don't use the manpower argument with me again."

If Jacobs said anything more, Charlie was too tired to hear it. He leaned back on the couch and closed his eyes.

His last caller of the day was Ty Malcomb. Shortly after six, while Charlie struggled to fix a simple supper one-handed, there was a knock at the door.

Rufus barked out a challenge, but Charlie quickly told him to be silent, letting the dog out into the backyard before going to admit his guest.

"Hello, Charlie," Ty said. He held a Styrofoam picnic

cooler in his hands. "I brought you something to eat. I heard about your shoulder on the news last night. I would have called, but . . . I didn't think you were in the mood for conversation."

Charlie held the door open. "Come in. You're right."

Ty glanced around and stepped into the dining room. "There isn't a lot here. But it's good, and it's hot. David and I made it up for you." He opened the container. "We tried to think of things that would be good for you. This is cream of spinach soup, it's hot. Um . . . This is chicken Kiev. Elizabeth said you like chicken. And here's some avocado in honey and sherry dressing." He put the dishes out on the table as he spoke. "I don't mean to intrude, but I really wanted to do something. You don't mind, do you?"

Perhaps Charlie had resented the interruption, but Ty's honest concern dispelled his resentment. "I appreciate it. To tell you the truth, I was making a mess of things in the kitchen." He took a seat nearest the food and gestured toward it. "You don't mind if I . . .?"

"Go ahead," Ty said, grateful to Charlie for his acceptance. "You probably don't want to discuss the Feuier thing . . ."

"What's happened now?" Charlie asked as he picked up the handsome silverware Ty had provided.

"There's a time problem. I talked with a police officer today and an attorney on the District Attorney's staff. They're trying to establish when Feuier had his latest heroin and when he took the other poison. They're almost certain it was aconite."

Charlie recalled his discussion with Solechiaro earlier and realized, rather grimly, that the Italian tenor must undoubtedly have talked to the investigators, too. "What's the trouble?"

"They figure that Feuier must have taken the aconite after he took heroin—aconite has certain paralytic properties that would become apparent very quickly. The investigators have already talked to the property master, and Tim insists that either he or Paul was at the table at all times and that no one handled the props who wasn't supposed to. There was no move to interfere with the props. There were no attempts to touch any of Feuier's mugs and glasses, and no one got near his wine."

"Wine?" Charlie asked. "Did he really drink wine?"

"Sure. He claimed it cleared his throat. It's not that uncommon. In the tavern scenes at the beginning and the end of the opera, he didn't drink, in fact. There was only a glass of champagne in the first act and a glass of wine in the last. He supplied his own wines—very expensive champagne and a particular burgundy he was fond of. The burgundy was opened to breathe by Feuier, at the prop table. The champagne was kept on ice and opened by one of the supers on stage." Ty threw up his hands and sighed. "I don't know what to think, Charlie. Either he killed himself accidentally or he wanted to implicate someone, or someone actually poisoned him on stage with more than three thousand people watching."

"What about the glasses?" Charlie watched Ty's face closely.

"They were washed, of course. After the opera and again before the next performance. If there was anything in either glass, it's probably gone by now."

"And Feuier opened his own wine?"

Ty nodded. "At the prop table. He wouldn't let anyone else do it. He claimed that no one knew how to handle his wine properly, and he forbade any of the prop staff to touch the wine. All they could do was keep it at the table and see that the bottle was on the tray when the super came to take it on stage."

"Um-hum," Charlie nodded as he finished the soup and started on the chicken. "This is very good." He could not use a knife yet and tried to cut the chicken with a fork.

The results were not neat, but the chicken was very tender. "And Solechiaro? What about him?"

"Well, one of the supers did see him over at Feuier's dressing room, stage left. Not going in or coming out, just near it. Nico won't say what he was doing there, but he indicated"—Charlie had, by now, a pretty good idea of the difficulty Ty or the police had had in getting that or any other indication—"that he did not see Feuier, did not go into the dressing room, and there was, he insisted, proof of that, which, for reasons of honor, he would not discuss."

"I can hear him say it," Charlie said, an amused resignation creeping into his voice. "The prop men are willing to swear under oath that no one but Feuier touched the wine?"

"They got the rough side of Feuier's tongue about it once. They were very careful."

"What about the super?"

"The super is an English teacher from Marin County, and he was very careful as well. Feuier put the fear of God into him about the wine. Do you want a number for the super?"

"I may need it," Charlie said, and cut more chicken.

"Do you think it was the wine?" Ty asked, doing a very good job of holding his anxiety at bay.

"I don't know. But it would be easy to demolish the question on the stand. If it was the wine, nothing short of a confession will stick." Charlie put down the utensils and rubbed his neck.

"Are you . . ." Ty stopped.

"I get stiff. You don't know how much everything is connected until you hurt it."

"It was your shoulder, wasn't it?"

Charlie disliked talking about the wound, but he sighed and said, "I was leaning forward with my arms out. The bullet grazed the back of my shoulder and along the top of my arm. The damage was more here, on the deltoid, than anything else."

"God." Ty shook his head. "Well, you really amaze me. When I heard about you on the news, I thought you'd be flat on your back for a week." He glanced around the room. "It's a nice house. Elizabeth said you just moved in."

"Isn't that obvious? I keep intending to unpack, but so far it hasn't worked very well." Charlie went back to work on the chicken, and at last, Ty said what was really bothering him.

"Charlie, what if they never find out what really happened to Feuier? It's possible, isn't it?"

Charlie considered it and the strangeness of the law. "Yes, it's possible. Even if something is pretty certain, it must be proved beyond a reasonable doubt. If it can't pass that test, then you don't have a case. Why?"

"And suppose there is no way to prove it?"

Very carefully Charlie put down his fork. "Are you trying to tell me that you killed Feuier?"

Ty whitened. "No. No. I didn't mean that. No."

"But you don't buy suicide, do you?" Neither did Charlie, as he thought about it. Feuier might commit suicide, but not so publicly, not so humiliatingly. "What about misadventure? You said yourself that maybe what he took was to counteract the heroin, and it backfired."

As he rubbed his big hands together, Ty said nervously, "I hope it was that. It would make everything else bearable. But why aconite? Where would he get it? Why would he use it? What did he do—go out and pick some monkshood and whip it up in the blender as a frappé?"

"Well, you know about monkshood," Charlie pointed out reasonably.

"Sure. When I was a kid we were always being cautioned to stay away from it. There's a variety of it that grows in Montana."

Charlie had learned about the plant from his grand-father, and had a great deal of respect for it. Monkshood, wolfsbane, the closed eye, no matter what it was called it was an effective and very powerful herb. There were preparations with very small quantities of monkshood that Charlie knew how to prepare. These were effective against certain kinds of pain, particularly neuralgia and arthritis. Monkshood was also used in a very strong sedative solution that Charlie had been warned must be used only when no other method would succeed. There was death in the plant: Even its virtues derived from death. "Do you know if Feuier had other physical conditions, something he might have used an old remedy for?"

"What kind of condition?" Ty asked wearily. "He was very skittish about his health, but he didn't do a lot about it."

"*Skittish?*" Charlie said, incredulous. "And on *heroin?*"

"Sure," Ty insisted. "He felt his strength going, and he thought drugs would boost it. He really wasn't built for the job, you know. He was too slight."

Charlie nodded, remembering the feeling he experienced around opera singers, the same feeling that a mustang might get turned out in a field of Clydesdales. "Is that a problem?"

"Damn right. It takes real strength to sing. Feuier didn't have it, but he had a slickness, a kind of vocal glibness that made him popular. But the drugs, well, that was the kind of man he was. It was easier than working." He stopped and looked at Charlie. "You're not eating."

"I am. I have to go slowly." He picked up his fork again but did not use it. "You've got a hunch, haven't you?"

"Not a hunch, really. A fear. I'm afraid the cops will think of it."

"They'll think of a lot of things. But they have to have a probable cause to accuse one person more than another of a crime. That's hard to do in this case. There are a lot of good motives around." He shoved the last of the chicken with his fork. "It's not Solechiaro?"

"No."

The room was still as Charlie considered the matter. When he spoke again, he was very reluctant. "Nørrehavn?"

Ty nodded. "What about the cops?"

"They'll consider him. And Domenico. And you."

There was a calm in Ty's face. "I see."

"It would be a simple matter to show that Cort didn't do it. Oh, he had motive. Perhaps—and it's a very big perhaps—he might have had the method. But opportunity? He never went near the prop area. He avoided Feuier. His time is completely accounted for." Charlie found that his protestations were born of his liking for the Danish baritone.

"I know." Ty got up and moved restlessly around the room. "Cort has been my loyal friend for years. I respect him. I admire him. When I was just starting out, Cort made a point of introducing me to Cesare Siepe, who's always been my bass ideal. Cort's that kind of man. He cares about people. That sounds so trivial, but it's true. You didn't know him when he and Linnet were married. I've never been able to talk to him about her death. It affected him too much, and he still hurts." He stopped. "God, I wish I *had* done it, so there wouldn't be this question hanging over all of us. I don't want to think my friends, my associates, are capable of something like this. And when I think about Cort . . ."

Charlie recalled his anguished interview with Cort earlier this week and felt oddly guilty. He was not the one to share Cort's feelings—he hadn't earned the right. But Ty, who had known him for years and who loved him, he deserved to receive that confidence which Cort had shown to Charlie.

"What are you thinking?" Ty demanded. "Your face . . ."

"Nothing," Charlie said, schooling his features to the appearance of calm. "My shoulder's giving me a little trouble, that's all."

"Should I leave?" Ty came nearer and gave Charlie a concerned scrutiny. "I didn't mean to tire you. I guess I shouldn't have talked about Feuier."

"No," Charlie disclaimed quickly. "It's a good thing you did. The case won't go away just because I've been shot. I want to help clear up this matter. And I want something to do other than sit here and feel sorry for myself." He finished the chicken and took a little of the avocado. Food still didn't taste like anything, it all seemed to be made of cardboard and old library paste. But he appreciated the thought and knew he ought to eat. "I like avocado," he said truthfully as he began on the salad.

"I've set up an appointment for you and Richard Tey on Monday. Is that okay or do you want me to cancel it?" Ty was studying Charlie again, and Charlie recognized that under his slightly self-effacing veneer there was steely determination. The Feuier matter would be solved because Ty Malcomb insisted that there be no blot on his company, on his tenure, on his singers, on his friends. And if that meant forcing Charles Spotted Moon, attorney-at-law, to expend effort far beyond the usual requirements, then he would be sure that effort was made. Ty smiled engagingly. "I can reschedule it if you need the time."

Charlie could not help smiling. "No, that's okay. I'll be happy to see him Monday. Maybe we'll have some idea then of what happened, and we'll be in a good position to clear it up."

"Great." Ty seemed to realize that this might sound strange to Charlie, so he amended it. "You're feeling better, then. I was afraid that you might be really out for a while. It's good to know you're tough."

"Keep that in mind for later reference," Charlie said rather sardonically as he finished the last of the avocado.

"I will." Ty crossed the room and stared out the window toward the wall of the house next door. Night was moving in fast, and with it a thin fog that had the effect of making the dark world glow. "I hated Feuier. Part of me was pleased when he died, and I can't help it now, hoping that no one I care for will be touched by his death. But it isn't going to happen that way, is it?"

Charlie answered carefully. "They've already been touched. You can't protect them from that. And no matter what Feuier did, the person who killed him, under the law, is guilty."

"Under the law," Ty repeated. "But is that enough?"

For the first time in his career, Charlie answered, "I don't know."

Ty raised his brows but said nothing.

"Look, when I was a kid, on the reservation, I was very lucky. We had one hell of a teacher there, Etienne de Groote. He'd gotten out of Belgium when the war started, and he came to Canada. He was highly qualified, but not by Canadian standards of certification, and so, since he couldn't teach in regular schools, he taught on the Iron River Reservation. We learned English and French—I already knew English, having spent my first six years in California—and German and Italian as well. We read Goethe and Rimbaud and Racine. De Groote was a devoted supporter of the oppressed. He told us that the law was our only hope, which was very much what my grandfather always said. So when the time came to go further in studies, I came back to California, went to McGeorge, and after a while, I was a lawyer. And then I started to learn about the law." His voice had gone bitter and he looked past Ty into the night. As he spoke, his accent had taken on a Canadian twinge, slightly Australian with a faint overlay of Scots. "I learned that the law was a tool, and that in skillful hands it could be made to perform the most wonderful tricks. I've seen my own partners use the law for despicable ends. But I've always believed that justice was an achievable, laudable goal. Justice and the law. They're often strangers to each other." For a moment, he was silent, then his attention came back to the room. "I'm sorry, Ty. Sitting around the house doing nothing, I've been brooding."

From the sound of his voice, Charlie knew that Ty was genuinely moved. "Don't apologize. Never for that."

Charlie rose, smiling still, but gently now. "Very well, my friend. I won't."

Friday, November 5

He was feeling well enough to be restless. He snapped at Willis when he dropped by and came dangerously close to having sharp words with Bob Aragon when he called to say that Bret Halsford was dead.

"Charlie, it sounds to me like there's something wrong," Aragon said after he had declined to fight.

"I'm fucking bored!" Charlie burst out. "Everyone's treating me like a hothouse flower"—he knew this wasn't true but aggravation made it seem so—"or a blithering incompetent." He was breathing fast, but the pain in his shoulder was muted. "I can't even unpack my moving boxes."

"Want some help?" Aragon volunteered.

"No," Charlie admitted wryly. "Help would only make it worse. Then I'd have to compare myself to you. And I'm in a terrible temper right now."

"I noticed."

At that Charlie realized he was being unfair to Bob Aragon.

"Maybe after this weekend, if you still want to help. The doctor says he'll unstrap my arm by next Wednesday."

"Great." Aragon was about to hang up when something else occurred to him. "Have you talked to Inspector McAllister yet?"

"About what?"

"That number that Feuier had in his dressing room. Turns out that it's a phone booth. It's where Feuier made contact with the dealers in the area."

"How do *you* know that?" Charlie demanded, as always amazed at the various sources newsmen had.

"I can't reveal that," Aragon said with mock primness. "But McAllister is trying to track down the dealer to find out when Feuier wanted to make a buy and how much of a buy. He's got the word out, and he's guaranteeing to take calls anonymously if he can get the information."

"Is that generally known?" Charlie asked, glad to have his interest engaged again.

"We're sitting on it for three days. If there aren't any results in that time, then it's news, and we start to talk about it." Aragon was quiet for a moment. "Charlie," he said hesitantly, "do you think any of the other singers . . ."

"If you push your luck with them, I promise you as tough a hassle as I can give you right now. And I'm spoiling for a fight." This was said earnestly, but the warning was plain.

"I'll hold off, then. For a while. Talk to you later."

"Okay. Thanks for the call." Charlie hung up, then sat musing, his eyes far away. What if it could be proved that Feuier had taken heroin at a specific time or in a specific amount? What would that do then? He tried rubbing at his shoulder, but the wound was still tender. He had stopped taking pain pills almost fourteen hours before, and though he found that his shoulder was still sore, his thoughts were clearer now, and there was no longer the heaviness of spirit that had held him for the last day and a half. There were ways to deal with pain, methods learned from his grandfather, and now that the drugs were out of his system, he could put them to work.

When he had assembled the things he needed, he went to one of two little rooms in his basement, a room that looked out onto a green tangle of branches and a small segment of lawn. Because of the plants and the angle of the window, he could not see any buildings around him, and because the room was at the back of the house, he rarely heard traffic. He had put many strange things in the room—There were several shelves of jars holding various dried herbs and other substances, a number of small hide bags, a few boxes with special kinds of wood stacked in them. On the floor, he had put a number of deer and bobcat hides.

He entered the room carefully, saying a few words in an undertone. Carefully, ritualistically, he stripped, and when he was quite naked, he made a few selections from the jars on the shelves. He placed these a small brazier, then sat on the skins, and when the herbs had been lit, he closed his eyes and repeated to himself the words his grandfather had so painstakingly taught him many years before. He wished vaguely that his shoulder were not so securely bandaged, but he knew he would not be able to put the bandages back on himself, and so he left them in place. His mind recalled the incidents leading up to the shot and the rake of the bullet along his arm. He made sure he saw each clearly, understood it. He forced himself to remember how the room looked, how he had stood, how he had moved, the kick that had thrown Bret Halsford off balance, the impact that had seem harmless until the adrenalin had stopped pumping through his body. Each detail was remembered and identified. Every sound, sight, feel, taste, and smell acknowledged. Nothing was rejected. The violence, the blood, the hurt, the pressure of Morgan's body as he stood behind her—he accepted it all. And then he began his healing.

*   *   *

Inspector Owen McAllister seemed resigned to the call from Charlie. "I didn't think you'd call till next week, but I knew I'd hear from you. What do you want, Moon?"

"I want to know as much as you're able to tell me. As legal adviser to Mr. Malcomb and the members of the Opera Company who may be involved in this unfortunate experience"—which, Charlie thought, was a very neat description of a possible homicide—"I'd appreciate having all the information possible made available to me."

"Under the rights of discovery . . ."

"Since there has been no formal accusation made, discovery isn't really the proper designation. But I think that if we work together we can protect the rights of the various innocent people involved as well as making sure that if there has been homicide the party responsible will be brought to justice." He had learned that particular kind of talk from Willis Ogilvie, and though he found it personally distasteful, it worked. "If you want the cooperation of other Opera Company members, it might be better if you and I worked together."

McAllister sighed. "I guess you're right. We've got a very tight deadline on this. Most of those singers go out of town as soon as the various operas finish their runs. Many of them will be out of the country. It would be time-consuming and expensive to bring any one of them back to stand trial." He paused, very plainly thinking it over. "I tell you what, Moon; if you're in any kind of shape tomorrow—I know it's Saturday, but I'm going to be on this full time, every day, until we get some questions answered—come downtown and see me. I could use your help."

That was quite an admission from the inspector, and Charlie was somewhat startled. "My help? Why?"

"Because you know those people. Jacobs and Shirer say you're okay. Even Thacher speaks well of you. If we can clear this up, let's do it." He was being much more reasonable than Charlie had expected him to be, and in

the next moment, Charlie learned why. "I've had calls
from Rocco Lemmini yesterday and today. He's suggested
I talk to you. He doesn't want the honor of this city
smirched."

Charlie could hear the ferocious old Italian say it, too.
He said dryly to Inspector McAllister, "Gives you a hard
time, does he?"

"Ever since he became President of the Board of
Supervisors, he's been impossible. He even sent *David*
down to talk to us." David was Rocco's attorney son; there
was another son who owned two hotels. Rocco made no
secret of the fact that he was grooming David for an
eventual senatorial seat.

"And what did David have to say?"

"Essentially the same thing. He doesn't like to see so fine
a cultural institution as the Opera Company embarrassed
in this way. He feels that it would be better if there were a
very discreet investigation so that any unpleasantness
could be avoided. If we make any accusations without a
shitload of evidence, you know we're going to be in
trouble." McAllister stopped suddenly, as if recalling that
he was talking to the opposing attorney.

Charlie was ready to take up the slack. "Is there any
chance, do you think, that it was misadventure? It's been
suggested that the other drug in the system was taken to
mask or lessen the effect of the heroin. Perhaps Feuier
didn't know what he was dealing with." He thought to
himself that this was exceedingly unlikely, but it was still a
possibility.

"We've thought about that. It's tempting, but I don't
know if it's viable." McAllister sighed again. "We've had
Feuier's current wife here for a week now, in tears,
demanding that we bring his murderer in and hang him.
And yesterday, his first wife showed up and insisted that
since her divorce was highly irregular she is still the wife
of Gui-Adam Feuier, and she wants to be the one to
arrange for the burial and honors for him."

"They're at each other's throats?" Charlie asked, picturing what McAllister might be enduring.

"Two o'clock yesterday, right here in my office. God, I don't know how he stood either of them."

"By his reputation, he didn't have to." Charlie changed his tone and went on briskly. "If these women are in town, I should contact Mr. Malcomb. It might be easier if you'll prepare some kind of brief for me—you know, something of the progress of your investigation so we'll have something to go on. I'll plan to come in sometime in the afternoon, if that's okay with you."

"Make it about three-thirty, then. I'm going to be interviewing some of the backstage personnel tomorrow." He shuffled some paper on the desk. "I understand that if I'm planning to talk to any of the singers you ought to be notified."

"That's right," Charlie said smoothly. "There's the problem of their rights. Most of them are foreign and don't know what is answerable and what's not. It might also be easier to get worthwhile information if I'm there. I've already had experience with them, Inspector, and you don't know what you're getting into."

McAllister was uncertain how to react to that, and so he chose the formal mode. "I'd appreciate it. Anything to speed the investigation."

"And to make sure you don't get thrown out of court on a technicality?" Charlie suggested pleasantly. "I'll see you about three-thirty tomorrow. I'll have to take a cab in, so I might not be right on time."

"I'll wait," McAllister said, then laughed. "I'll bet you want to be free of this damn mess as much as I do." There was a kind of humorous frustration in his voice.

"Possibly. But not at the cost of justice." As Charlie said it, he knew it was the truth. There was justice to be served. "Let me know what you find out about that dealer. If we can figure out what the state of Feuier's habit was, it might be easier to find out when and how and maybe even why he took, or was given, the second drug. By the way, how certain are they that it *was* aconite?"

If McAllister was surprised that Charlie knew about the aconite, there was no reflection of it in his voice. "We're pretty sure. We need to run a couple more tests. Aconite, you know, is damned hard to find, and the heroin indications mask what little there is quite well. But they're doing some work on the spleen and the kidneys. They might find it yet." Again he paused. "Tomorrow, then. I don't want this hanging over me much longer."

"I'll do my best," Charlie promised him. "Thanks for calling me. It's unusual to work this way, but in this case, I think it may be justified."

"Yeah," McAllister said neutrally. "Well, goodbye."

"Goodbye." Charlie hung up automatically, then went to the back door and called Rufus in from the yard, noting that the dog was still shedding too much. "I know how you feel," he said as he patted the dog awkwardly. "I'm not used to being here, either."

A little before six, Charlie turned the porch light on, more in hope than in certainty. He had talked to Morgan once, the day before, and at that time, she still had not made up her mind. Now he told himself not to be disappointed if she did not come, but he knew with deep certainty that her absence would hurt terribly. In the last year, he had had one or two short-lived, casual affairs that inevitably left him feeling empty and lonelier than before.

Morgan was different. Morgan roused him physically because she had the ability to reach him, to break through his reserve and privacy to his inmost self. If she came tonight, it would be to accept his love, and for no other reason. He considered that and had to admit that she might come to tell him she could not love him. Morgan was fair, and it was against her courageous honor for her to simply stay away or to call him.

At eight o'clock, he let Rufus out into the backyard

again and sat down to read. He pretended fascination with the book he had picked up a few days before at the supermarket. World War II, Nazis, spies, secret plans, hidden documents, hypocritical priests seethed on the pages before him, but though his eyes roved over the words, they saw little, and the hideous peril faced by a lone hero meant nothing to him. At last, he put the book down and went to the kitchen for a snack.

He was debating how best to cook the canned salmon he found in the cupboard when the doorbell rang. Charlie was so taken off guard that he almost dropped the tin. He gave the clock a swift glance—nine-forty. Too late for usual visitors. Nervously he wiped his hands on the canvas apron he had pulled on, then, as he started down the hall toward the front door, he tugged at the apron, trying to remove it. The task was difficult, and every time he tried to drag the neck strap over his head, his shoulder reminded him that it was far from healed.

He was still wrestling with the apron when he opened the door.

Morgan's eyes were a little too bright and her face slightly too set as she looked at Charlie. Then she saw his plight and a spurt of laughter softened her features.

"Oh, Charlie. You look terrible." She came through the door, and Charlie saw, with an absurd surge of hope, that she carried a small bag in addition to her purse.

"I didn't know when to expect you," he said lamely.

"That's obvious." She set the case down on the stairs and turned to help extricate him from the apron ties. "What did you do?"

"I don't know. When I heard the bell, I wanted to take it off." He wanted to shrug off his helplessness, but found that he could not. He stood still while she lifted the neck strap over his head.

"There. Just so long as you don't expect me to put it on."

Charlie had learned in the last year and a half that

Morgan had been with the firm that she was a fiercely competent attorney and a terrible cook. She had complained of being food-deaf once, but Charlie had corrected her. Food-deaf people, he explained, had no taste. Morgan had high standards in food, but no talent for cooking. For that reason he said, "Heaven forfend."

"Besides, I ate before I came over. There was some work I had to finish up before . . ." She broke off, making a complicated sound somewhere between a cough and a sigh.

"Before you came here," he said for her, very gently.

"Yes. Before I came here." She was facing away from him, and it was obviously an act of will for her to turn to him now. "I have to talk to you, Charlie."

The hope that had been born at the sight of the traveling bag was very nearly dashed at that. He met her eyes seriously, waiting. "I'm listening."

She went past him into the living room and stood looking into the empty maw of the fireplace. Her hands gripped her arms and under the fine woolen jacket, Charlie could see she was trembling. Her distress upset him, and it was all he could do not to cross the room and take her into his arms for comfort.

Finally she spoke, her tone very even and low. "I realize that on Wednesday you were . . . not quite yourself. And when you said . . . ah . . . how you felt, it didn't have to . . . mean that you really . . . feel that way. I know," she said a little louder to stop any objection he might have, "that you said you were certain. But you . . . you weren't feeling very well. So you might have said . . . things . . . you wish you hadn't."

"The only thing I wish I had said is how much I love you. I don't think there are words for it, though." He spoke very quietly.

"But . . ." She stopped. It was even more difficult for

her to go on, but in a moment she managed it. "It's been more than three years since I . . . had a . . . relationship with a man."

Charlie recognized her tension and knew that she had not said it all. "And with a woman?" There was no condemnation in the question, only a sadness that Morgan should fear him so.

Morgan nodded. "There was one woman. God, Charlie, don't hate me."

"Hate you? Why?" He was genuinely puzzled. He knew that many Caucasian men were fascinated and repelled by lesbian relationships, but he had always found that attitude foolish and oddly immature. "How do you know whom you want to love, and how, unless you try? That's why you're here now, isn't it? To try?"

She nodded, and her hair gleamed in the light from the dining room. Her answer was muffled.

He dared to move nearer to her. "Morgan, look at me." He stood silently until she turned swiftly to face him. There was a challenge in her eyes, but her mouth was sad. He touched her lips with his fingers. "Do you need more time to think?"

Morgan shook her head. "No. If I think much longer, I won't do it. And I think I want to."

"But you're not sure."

"No. I'm not sure."

"Are you wearing the token I gave you?" he asked.

She frowned; it was her turn to be puzzled. "Yes."

"Good." He wanted to explain why, but that would be for later. "What do you want now? Would you like to bathe? Or read? Watch TV for a while?"

She was exasperated now. "You act like this was any evening at home. We watched TV on Tuesday."

"But it is like other nights. Nothing's changed. There's an addition, but I still want to read with you, or watch TV, or scrub your back for you." He leaned forward and kissed her lightly. "You're part of my life, Morgan. Like breath is, like food and sunlight."

She moved away from him. "You still don't know . . ."

"If you're a good lay, is that it? I don't particularly care, one way or the other. If you are, great. And if not, it isn't that important."

Morgan rounded on him, her face flushed. "Will you stop being so damn *reasonable?*" At her sides her hands were clenched. "Take me to bed and get it over with, or read me poetry if you must, but, Charlie, you talk as if this were normal, and it isn't."

For a moment, he could not answer her. She wanted so much to provoke him, he knew. It was tempting to snap at her or to overpower her with argument and semantic tricks. But that way she would begrudge him one night and would—gratefully, perhaps—put him out of her life. At work, she would be professionally polite, so even their camaraderie would be lost. "Morgan," he said, letting some of his aggravation come into his voice. "I don't want to fight with you. If you want to leave, you don't need an excuse. Go. It won't change how I feel, but it will hurt. Don't you see that I'm not kidding? I want you so much that I'd rather not have you at all than have you resenting me. I want to touch you, to kiss you, to hold you, to move inside you, to lie beside you and feel the rhythm of your sleep. I want to be able to caress your hair while we're eating breakfast, or hold hands between the office and the parking lot. I want you in my life, Morgan."

"God, you scare me," Morgan whispered.

"Scare you? I don't want to."

"I know that," she said between tight teeth. "That's what's so scary." She shook her head. "Let's go to bed before I change my mind again."

"Just like that?"

"Yes, just like that." She glared at him.

"Okay. But I'm warning you," he said, smiling slightly, "if you have fantasies of being ravished by a noble savage, forget them. With my shoulder this way, you're going to have to help. A lot."

"Oh, shit. I forgot about your shoulder. Are you *sure* you want to do this?" She was sounding like herself again, and she moved closer to him. "It might hurt."

"Probably will," he agreed, very nearly grinning, "But it's a small price to pay. If all you ever cost me is a twinge in my deltoid, I'll be very lucky."

Morgan folded her arms, but there was the beginning of a smile in her eyes. "What would your doctor say?"

"He recommends exercise." Charlie's words were bland, but he felt lighthearted. It was wonderful to have Morgan herself again, and at last, he began to hope that she would stay.

"Well, what do we do then? Bathe? Read? Watch TV?"

In three steps, he was beside her, his arm around her. "Or go to bed?"

Her mouth was open when it touched his, and as his arm tightened around her, she pressed against him. Slowly, slowly, Charlie disengaged his arm and took her hand in his. "Come with me," he said, the tone of his voice low and clear.

She nodded, and though her hand tensed, she did not draw back.

As they got to the top of the stairs, Charlie let go of her hand and touched her face, tilting her chin up. He studied her, searching for anger or contempt, and found none. He read uncertainty and doubt, but no condemnation. With his one free hand, he touched her body lightly. "There are terrible green stripes in the bedroom. Do you think you can stand it?"

"I won't have to see them, will I?"

Charlie did not answer at once. "I'd like to leave a small light on. I want to see you. I want you to see me."

Morgan frowned. "But why?"

He took a chance and gave her the real answer. "For truth."

She pressed her head against his good shoulder. "Leave it on."

Morgan lay sleeping beside him, curved slightly against the line of his body. Only the ache in his shoulder kept Charlie awake, but it was welcome, for he wanted to remember everything that had passed between them in the last two hours.

The long, slow preparation had been necessary because of his shoulder, but he would not have wanted to give up one moment, one caress. When at last he had stretched out beneath her and waited while she had lowered herself onto his ready flesh, his whole body had felt ready to burst. She had moved freely on him, straddling his thighs, tuning her movements to the short thrusts of his hips.

Charlie had hoped for affection and pleasure, and had surprised himself and Morgan in finding much more than that. Lovingly, he reached toward her, running his hand along her arm and smiling as she moved in her sleep. It was good to be with her. He was curiously content, feeing an ease he had never thought possible. He reached for another pillow and braced his shoulder more.

Before he had slept, as she lay close against him, her legs still tangled with his, she had thanked him. Charlie had almost pulled the strapping off his chest in an effort to take her in both arms.

He reached across the nightstand to flip off the little light that was still burning, and thought to himself, somewhat smugly, that he had not noticed the horrid wallpaper until now.

Saturday, November 6

Morgan left for aikido shortly after breakfast, and Charlie had several hours before he had to see Inspector McAllister. He tried to occupy the time by emptying cartons, but he got as far as uncrating his stereo when he got too tired and sore to go on. His records were all packed away in another box; he thought it might be one of those stacked in the hall, but he wasn't up to finding out. For want of something else to do, he set up the stereo and dialed one of the music stations at random; quickly he grew bored.

At last, he turned it off and made a phone call. "Henry," he said to the cultured voice on the other end of the line, "is Mrs. Kendrie there? I'd like to talk to her. This is Charles Moon."

"I recognized your voice, Mr. Moon," Henry Tsukamoto assured him. "I hope you will not be offended if I tell you how much respect I have for your courageous act last Wednesday."

Feeling distinctly awkward, Charlie said, "Thank you, Henry, but it was much more desperate than heroic."

"If you insist, Mr. Moon. I'll fetch Mrs. Kendrie. She's playing cards with Mr. Solechiaro." It was obvious that Henry thought cards to be beneath Elizabeth Kendrie's dignity.

"Thank you. I'll be glad to hold." He waited until he heard the sound of a second phone being taken off the hook. "Elizabeth?"

"Good morning, Charlie. I've been very concerned about you," she announced in her usual energetic way. Charlie had often had frightening daydreams, speculating on what Elizabeth Kendrie must have been like when she was young; in her late sixties, she had more energy than any other two people Charlie knew.

"I'm getting better, thank you. That's why I called you."

"Good gracious, do you mean you're going to ask me a favor after all these years? I don't believe it."

"You've done dozens of favors for me, Elizabeth, and you know it. You're doing one right now, as I recall."

Elizabeth's chuckle was deliciously rich. "If you mean Nico, he's not a favor, he's a delight. Why, half of the women I know are livid. And to make matters worse, I won't show him off to them. I haven't enjoyed myself so much in years."

Charlie accepted this. "Well, if you're inclined to help again, do you happen to have a copy of *Les Contes d'Hoffmann* I could borrow?"

"Of course," she said promptly. "Who would you like to hear? Domingo? Gedda? I've got Feuier's recording, but I think it might disappoint you."

"Whichever one is closest to the production done here. I want to do some timing and figure out what's happening onstage. I won't be able to make much sense out of my talk with the conductor until I've heard the work."

"You need a cross between the one Sills did and the Sutherland. Poor old *Hoffmann's* had a rough time of it. Everyone's always tampering with him. Very well. I'll have Henry bring over the two recordings. You can return them whenever you like."

"Thanks, Elizabeth." He was aware that she was being unusually soft-spoken. "Do you have company, Elizabeth?"

"Other than Nico? No. Why do you ask?"

Charlie didn't quite know how to phrase his question, so he tried a general approach. "You're sounding very mild. I was wondering if it was because there was someone there and you were afraid to be as frank as you often are."

Uncharacteristically Elizabeth did not give a rallying response. "I had a phone call two days ago, Charlie. It was very unexpected. From a troubled young woman whom I happen to like and respect. I gave her some advice then. I hope it was the right thing to do."

"Morgan?" Charlie asked quietly.

"She was very frightened. She cares for you too much for you to use her cynically. I told her I thought you were too humane to compel her or to lie to her. I hope now I said the right thing." There was a stern note in her voice, and Charlie knew that if he abused Morgan, Elizabeth would never forgive him.

"I didn't realize until recently . . ."

"Then you're a blind fool," Elizabeth interrupted with her familiar asperity.

"About myself, Elizabeth. I was reluctant to . . . become involved. But I came so close to losing her. She's the most valuable thing in my life. Nothing else matters as much as she does. Nothing." He heard the vehemence in his voice and was startled.

Apparently it satisfied Elizabeth. "Good. Then I told

her the right thing. You will have to be kind to her, Charlie. She's not used to genuine emotions." She hesitated, then changed the subject once more. "I need your advice myself."

"What is it?" Charlie had learned to be on guard when she spoke this way.

"What if this Feuier thing is truly murder?" Her concern tightened her tone, and she sounded like the old woman she was instead of the cavalry general she usually resembled.

"It's a question of evidence and proof, Elizabeth. Like any other case. I can't tell you any more until I know more myself. I'm having a meeting this afternoon with Inspector McAllister, and when it's over, I should have a little better idea of what's going on. I'll let you know then."

"Very well. I suppose I'll have to wait." She made a resigned noise. "I'll send Henry over in an hour if you'll be in."

"I'll be here. Thanks again, Elizabeth."

"I won't say you're welcome until this matter is concluded," she said, a tartness coming back into her words. "Call me when you know more."

"I will. I promise." He often found Elizabeth's determination admirable. The formidable old woman was worth any three businessmen he knew. Occasionally Charlie took secret delight in knowing that both his partners were afraid of her. But he knew he had to deal with her as squarely as he could at all times, and it was sometimes wearing to do so. "I won't keep you in ignorance any more than I'm kept in ignorance. And that's the best I can do, Elizabeth."

"I trust you, Charlie," she said, and almost meant it.

Owen McAllister was very neat. His shirt was immaculate and without wrinkles. His tie was the proper width. He wore a dark, many-buttoned vest and a tailored, dark suit. His strong features were not quite handsome, but were more attractive for that reason. He was clean-shaven, his brown hair expertly cut and groomed. Only the smudges under his icy eyes betrayed his fatigue. "You're Moon?" he asked, holding out a square, well-manicured hand as Charlie closed the door to the cramped office behind him. "How's the shoulder? I heard you had a lot of stitches."

"Seventeen," Charlie said, returning the pressure of the hand. "It could have been worse."

McAllister nodded, dismissing the subject. "It's good of you to come. I know this is irregular, but the circumstances . . ."

"How are you doing on the investigation? Have you turned up anything useful?" He wanted to be sure that McAllister did not digress from the matter at hand.

"Well," McAllister said as he resumed his seat, "we've got two calls on this drug-dealer business that might be worth something. Most of the calls have been senseless maundering, usually about this guy or that who burned them or gave them bad shit. *All* drugs are bad shit, but you'll never convince them of it."

"Where was Feuier getting it, do you know?" Charlie asked, feeling a certain sympathy toward Owen McAllister.

"It sounds like Feuier had his own supply. The rumor is," McAllister said carefully, avoiding Charlie's eyes and speaking in a flat, almost nonchalant way, "that this Feuier guy was a messenger. Apparently every time he came to America to sing, he brought a little present from Marseilles."

The other chair in McAllister's office was piled high with folders, and Charlie found no other place to sit. He turned rather stiffly toward McAllister. "Can you prove that?"

"Prove it? How?" McAllister shook his head

lugubriously. "I doubt we'll ever get more than rumor. Who'd believe a dealer or a junkie on the stand, even if you could bring them into court? You ever tried to cross-examine a junkie?"

Charlie nodded fatalistically. "It isn't easy."

"Well, that's the rumor. And Feuier had some connections in France who were pretty unsavory types. It *is* possible that he did them occasional favors. Feuier used drugs himself. And he went through women like a guy with a cold goes through Kleenex. I thought you ought to know."

"Damn right I ought to know." Charlie began to tap on the shelves beside him, his fingers marking out an insistent rhythm. "How many other people know this? About Feuier, I mean?"

"Strictly confined to my department and to you. We've got word from the Board of Supervisors that public knowledge of Feuier's dealing would be undesirable. But Feuier was rotten clear through. It's frustrating to protect a man like that. Even if he is dead."

"Do you have anything more than hearsay to go on? Anything at all?" Charlie wanted proof as much as McAllister did.

"Short of a written confession, we aren't likely to get it. Dead men don't write confessions."

"So no proof," Charlie said shortly. "We agree Feuier was a bastard. Is there anything else? Do you know it was aconite for sure?"

"As sure as we'll ever be, which leaves quite a hunk of room for margin. It'll be rough in court. But *if* it was aconite, he must have taken it some twenty to forty minutes before he died. He was in a state of physical stress because of all the singing, which in all probability speeded up the effect of the aconite. If he took another drug, all bets are off." McAllister sagged back in his chair and gestured to the stacks of paper on his desk. "Reports, all of them. Cronin's demanding we come up with something for him, and there's nothing here he can use to make an accusation."

Charlie had stopped drumming with his fingers. "I see. Is there any preferred suspect?"

"Well, that big Italian looks likely. Felicity Cooper dug up some pretty damaging stuff about him."

"Which you can't use in court," Charlie reminded him, "not unless you've got corroboration. That might be hard to come up with." He tried to lean back against the shelves, but the movement hurt his shoulder, and at last, he braced himself against McAllister's desk.

"Sorry I can't offer you a chair. That one"—he gestured toward a folding chair by his desk that was covered with file folders—"can't be used yet. I don't have any place to put the stuff on it." He made a gesture to show his helplessness. "I tried to get another one, but they tell me not until January. We're being economical again. So I can wait for extra file cabinets and more chairs. So that the voters will think we're being careful with their money. God, they skimp on the strangest things."

"I can believe it," Charlie said, but refused to be sidetracked. "How does your investigation stand at the moment?"

"In a mess. I don't know what we're going to do. The best we can come up with is to find for misadventure at this rate, and Cronin doesn't like that. I'll tell you what I think. I think that Feuier was too much of a motherfucker for this not to be murder. Someone with a good motive—and from what I can tell, there are dozens of 'em—got fed up and killed him." He smoothed his vest though there were no wrinkles in it. "It's what I would have done, I think, if he'd messed with my life the way he has with some of them." He put one hand to his head. "I hate the drug dealers. Two weeks ago we had six murders in the Fillmore District, all done by black junkies killing other

blacks for a couple of bucks and change so that they could
get a fix that would keep them going long enough to
commit another murder. Great. Just great. I admit it was
clever to use a singer for a messenger. Who would have
thought it? The guy was a big star, a heavy in the classical
music world. Who'd ever think Enrico Caruso was a
smuggler? Rock musicians, that's one thing, but opera?"

Charlie regarded McAllister evenly. "What are you
trying to tell me?"

McAllister shrugged uncomfortably. "I guess I don't
want to find the murderer, if there is a murderer, all that
badly. People like Feuier . . . It was only a matter of time
before someone got worried about him and dropped him
into the Hudson or the Mediterranean or the Pacific."

"But it doesn't happen that way," Charlie reminded
him, and saw the distress in McAllister's face deepen.
"Gui-Adam Feuier died on the stage of the Opera House,
with half the culture vultures in the city watching."

"I know. I know." McAllister nodded miserably.

"And if he was murdered, the law requires that the
murderer be apprehended and punished. You know
that."

"Don't talk to me about the law, lawyer!" McAllister
burst out. "The law is a crock of shit."

Even a month ago, Charlie would have been angry
enough at that to walk out of McAllister's office and to
refuse to cooperate with him again. But now, with his
shoulder aching and much of his thoughts still in turmoil,
Charlie said, "Sometimes it is. But that's not the fault of
the law."

"All right," McAllister growled, somewhat mollified.
"You're being more cooperative than I have any right to
ask. I won't go off like that again. But it galls me, it really
does, to have to find a killer who did something that
should be called a public service." He held up his hands.
"I know the objection. Once you start that kind of

thinking, those standards, where do you draw the line? That's how Hitler justified the Jews, and as a Jew myself, I do understand." He gave Charlie a quizzical look. "I guess you do, too. Sioux?"

"Ojibwa."

"Part of the Algonquin language group, aren't they?" Charlie nodded, mildly surprised. "That's right."

McAllister gave Charlie a half smile. "There's a very large Indian population in the Bay Area, Mr. Moon. Upwards of thirty thousand." He pushed back from his crowded desk.

But Charlie was not quite ready to bring the interview to a close. He motioned to McAllister. "When are you planning to talk to Solechiaro again?"

"Again?"

"Someone's already talked to him once. Don't deny it. And I should have been there. Don't try that kind of thing again or you'll get no cooperation from me. There's Hendricks and Nørrehavn and Malcomb and Tey and Baumtretter to begin with, and the list is quite long. I've already talked to some of them." Charlie shifted his position again, making a face as he did. His shoulder and back were beginning to hurt in earnest. "We can compare what we're told if you like, but I tell you right now that you'd better have an excellent reason for asking for information. Because I'm retained by a patron of the Opera Company, and not by the company itself, let alone the singers on an individual basis. I can't refuse to answer your questions on the basis of the confidential relationship between attorney and client, but if you start asking gratuitous questions, you might find me very stubborn."

Obviously this had deflated part of McAllister's argument. He gestured his acceptance. "I'll go along with that," he said, resigned. "Anything to clear this up as soon as possible."

"Okay." Inwardly Charlie was relieved. For a little while

longer, he would have a fairly free hand. He knew with a certainty that was frightening that if he did not have the answer in another few days he never would have it. "I'll keep you posted if I learn anything. And you do the same for me."

McAllister got to his feet. "I will." He held out his hand. "I guess we could have done this on the phone, but, well, you can appreciate my position."

"You mean," Charlie said with a wry smile, "that you didn't know whether or not I'd be willing to help you, and you had to be prepared for the worst."

"Something like that." When they had shaken hands, McAllister gestured toward the door. "It's a mess, this case. Thanks for helping me out."

"I'm an officer of the court," Charlie reminded him as he went to let himself out. "I won't forget that. Neither should you." He nodded once to McAllister and went out.

Morgan was waiting when the taxi dropped Charlie back at his house. "Where've you been?" she asked before he had taken more than a few steps toward her.

"Downtown. Police headquarters." He handed the cabbie a tip, then came the rest of the way up the front steps. "Comparing notes on the Feuier case."

"With the cops?"

"Who else?" he asked as he pulled out his keys and opened the door. The house seemed more familiar to him now, and even the boxes stacked in the hall still waiting to be unpacked no longer bothered him.

Morgan followed him into the entryway and turned to close the door. "I was worried. I thought you might be hurt."

"No, I'm okay. But thanks." He turned to look at her and saw that she was frowning. "What is it? Are *you* okay?"

"I don't know." She pushed past him into the living room and sat down on a straight-backed chair, hands in her lap, her spine rigid. "I've been thinking today, a lot. After aikido, I went down to the beach and walked for a couple of hours. It didn't help. I still don't know what to say to you." She turned to him, rather pale, and waited for the rebuke.

He crossed the room and looked down at her. After a while, he said, very tenderly, "I love you with my life, Morgan. You'll need more than honest doubt to alienate me."

"I want to talk," she announced, as if she had not heard him.

"Okay." He went to the sofa and sat facing her. "Talk. I want to listen."

The room was noticeably darker when Morgan stopped and at last met Charlie's eyes. "Well?"

He thought over all he had heard. "You're afraid that we'll be competitors, and that will destroy us?" He had picked her first argument.

"Aren't you?" Her chin had come up to meet this challenge.

"But why should we? If Willis tries to play us off against each other"—and secretly he admitted to himself that this could very easily happen—"then we'll leave and establish our own partnership."

She stared at him. "You'd do that?"

He was tempted to tell her that he had considered just such a move, with or without her, but knew that this was the wrong time. "Yes."

"What about the prestige and the money?"

"What about them?" he asked easily. "Prestige can be earned. And I've been broke before. It doesn't frighten me. I don't particularly enjoy it, but you're worth a few money qualms." He smiled. "You said you had doubts about your own feelings. That concerns me a great deal more."

"I'll bet." Her nastiness was deliberate, and she watched to see what effect it had.

"Morgan," Charlie began, leaning forward, "I know you have doubts. You're afraid I'll want you to throw away everything you've worked for. I won't. I'm proud of you, of your work. You're one hell of a lawyer. You're courageous and tenacious and honest. I don't want you to give that up for anything. I mean it. You said that you want, eventually, to be a judge. Good. Because you'll be good at it. I'm not asking you to choose between me and the law."

"But you said you want . . . a permanent arrangement."

He met her eyes. "That's right. I do."

"And that means all the other things—marriage and kids." She did not doubt for a moment that this would be his requirement.

But Charlie hesitated. "Marriage, yes, if you're willing. Not right now, but when you're sure. But kids." He looked away from her. "If you want kids, we've got problems."

"What do you mean?" She looked startled.

"Lois didn't want kids. Not mine, anyway. We talked about it a lot. We were full of zeal and social conscience and who knows what else? Anyway, I've had a vasectomy. No kids unless they're adopted." It was difficult to say this to Morgan, and he wasn't sure why.

Morgan blushed. "I didn't . . . After we slept together, I wondered if . . ."

With more irritation than he meant to show, Charlie said, "Oh, yes, you were safe."

"Charlie, don't."

"Look, you said you don't like women who trap men. Well, I don't like men who trap women. I wouldn't have done that to you. How could you think I would?" He drew a ragged breath. "Of course," he went on in another voice, "yeah, I know how you think I would. It's all around us, isn't it?" When she didn't speak, he went on. "I'm willing to try to do it another way if you are. We don't have to be anything we don't want to. This is between us, no one else. We can make our own terms, Morgan."

This time she looked up. "You haven't lied so far."

He resisted the urge to argue. "Not so far. I don't want to lie to you." He moved swiftly and crouched down beside her chair. "That ritual I told you about. If you decide you want it. It's not absolutely binding, if that worries you. But it does require honesty. I wouldn't have given you my magician's finger if I was lying to you. I couldn't."

Fleetingly, clumsily, she touched his face. "I want to believe you so much. I want it all to be true. That's why I'm reluctant to do anything. Do you understand at all?"

Charlie put his hand over hers. "Yes. And if I could banish that fright from you, I would." He could sense the pain that lay behind her doubts. He wondered if she would ever tell him who had been cruel enough to betray her and leave her with this fear.

She tried to smile. "I think you would. I think you mean it."

He rose. "We'll do it one thing at a time, Morgan. Okay?"

She stood beside him, in the circle of his arm. "Okay. One thing at a time."

Sunday, November 7

The coroner's office had decided at last that it was aconite, administered in a highly concentrated form, that had killed Gui-Adam Feuier. Charlie listened to Owen McAllister as he read the report over the phone. "Either he was very lucky or he was a very knowledgeable chemist," McAllister concluded. "If Feuier hadn't been on heroin, he would probably have died about an hour after the opera—that's enough time to get out of the Opera House and back to his hotel before the full paralytic effects hit him."

"Then that doesn't eliminate suicide," Charlie said.

"Yes, it does. Feuier knew about the heroin. The murderer didn't."

"But he—or she—knew about aconite." Charlie felt a strange twinge in the back of his mind. The murderer knew about aconite, how to get it, and something about the dosage. That meant luck or a background in chemistry. There had been something in one of Ty's files about chemistry.

"So it seems. Well, that's it. I don't know what else to tell you. At least we know what we're dealing with now." McAllister sighed. "Good luck."

"Thanks. To you, too." Charlie hung up quickly and sat staring across his study. The afternoon sun made the room glow, and he could see out the window the houses across the street and, to the left, the towering greenery of Golden Gate Park. At his feet, Rufus yawned and shifted position to take advantage of the sunlight.

On impulse, he rose again and went downstairs. He stared around the living room, then picked up the two albums of *Les Contes d'Hoffmann* Elizabeth had loaned him. He had already listened to them twice, but he still had the nagging sensation that part of the answer was in the music, in the action of the opera itself. With a sigh, he put the Sutherland-Domingo recording back on the turntable.

The act was roughly thirty minutes long, complete with a duel. Though the recording he was listening to had put the quintet that climaxed the act into the epilogue, the Opera Company production had kept it at the end of the third act, giving the act an extra six minutes. That meant that either Feuier had taken something in his dressing room that poisoned him or he had swallowed the aconite on stage. Logically it would have had to be in the wine he drank in a toast at the beginning of the act.

But no one had gone near the prop table. Domenico Solechiaro had been backstage watching the opera, but on the side opposite the property cases. He had made no attempt to go near it, and the cup Hoffmann drank from was never on the side of the backstage where Solechiaro had stood.

Charlie sat reviewing his notes. Hendricks was on stage with Feuier, always near him, in fact. Later, Nørrehavn entered.

*   *   *

When the records were finished, Charlie got up and put on the Sills recording and sat down to listen again.

Later in the day, about sunset, Charlie called Rufus and took him out for a walk. It was brisk, and a line of fog hung off the coast, glowing in the sunset. Later it would drift inland, wrapping the city in a softening mist. For now, it turned the sunset to glare.

Under the bandages, Charlie's shoulder was itching. He knew this was a sign of healing, but it was infuriating to be unable to scratch. He set his pace, making it as brisk as he could without tiring himself unnecessarily. To his private disgust, he knew he was still weak. Walking was pleasant, and he found that the mechanical act of putting one foot ahead of the other gave him a chance to free his mind.

Rufus romped along beside him, delighted at the unexpected run. Between the move and Charlie's atypical inactivity, he had been quite upset. But now Charlie was more himself, and the house was less strange. He frisked, waving his curled, plumed tail.

They walked for several blocks along the north side of Golden Gate Park. There were leaves on the ground, and the cypress and eucalyptus whispered and rustled in the slow wind. Fulton Street had its share of traffic, which was not unusual for a Sunday evening. The city was starting to glow with light, the dark shapes of the hills defining themselves with points of brightness.

It was very nearly dark when Charlie returned to his house. A thought had been pestering him most of the way back. Cort Nørrehavn had been a chemist once. He had an MS in biochemistry and came from a family of academics and scientists. Gui-Adam Feuier was heavily implicated in the death of Nørrehavn's wife, and Cort had made no attempt to hide his conviction that Feuier was personally responsible for her suicide. That certainly stood the test of method and motive. The only thing that was lacking was opportunity.

Charlie shied away from that. He liked the Dane and respected his emotions. He admitted to himself that he did not want Nørrehavn to have done it, at the same time understanding his probable desire for vengeance.

After feeding Rufus, Charlie made himself a snack of cheese and apples. Food was at last beginning to taste good again, and he enjoyed having his appetite back. He debated with himself for a few minutes, wondering if he should call Morgan and wish her good night, but at last decided against it. She was still unsure of her feelings, and would think such a call too pushy. He wanted to hear the sound of her voice, but there was time enough for that in the morning, at work.

Monday, November 8

Lydia Wong had a wide smile for Charlie as he came in the door. "Glad to have you back," she said from behind her desk. "You've been missed."

"I missed you, too," Charlie said as he pulled off his coat. He struggled to open the coat closet and saw from the other garments there that both his partners were in the office for a change.

"Willis wants to talk to you," Lydia added.

"Of course he does." Charlie felt a kind of oppression. He was not quite up to dealing with Willis Ogilvie yet. "When am I permitted into the presence?"

"First thing." She reached into her desk and pulled out a stack of message slips. "Here. You've got very popular recently."

Charlie took them, but with his left arm still taped to his side to protect his shoulder, he could not leaf through them. "Is there anything important?"

"One or two of them. Particularly the one from Rocco Lemmini. He wants to hear from you as soon as possible."

"Great. Anything else?" The sheaf of memos was quite large, and privately Charlie dreaded having to deal with even half of them.

"Well, the Hawkins matter has been postponed. You don't have to appear in court until the end of the month. But Mr. Hawkins wants to talk to you. Apparently the other side has made a move to settle out of court. And William Patrick wants you to take on his gallery. They're having trouble with certain printmakers."

Charlie nodded. "Nothing like getting shot to improve business, apparently," he said, rather sardonically. "I'll get to these as quickly as possible. Let me know if there are any more calls. Oh, and a Maestro Richard Tey is coming in today. It's important that I speak to him. Do you have the time he's coming?"

Lydia consulted her book. "He was scheduled for afternoon, but he called on Friday and asked if he could make it in the morning. I said I'd call him if there was any trouble."

"What time?" Charlie asked, hearing the door open behind him.

"Quarter till eleven. If that's okay with you."

Charlie had turned, meeting Morgan's eyes as she came into the office. "Yes, Lydia. Fine. Good morning, Morgan."

"Good morning, Charlie," she said bitingly. "Are there any messages for me, Lydia?"

Lydia produced a set of three held together with a paper clip. "Mr. Randolph would appreciate it if you'd call him as soon as convenient."

"Thanks. I will." Morgan refused to look at Charlie. She glanced through the messages, then went down the hall.

Though he had expected something like this from Morgan, he had to stifle the urge to object. Any opportunity to talk with her then was ended as Willis Ogilvie flung open his office door.

"Charles, m'lad!" he cried out, hailing the returning

hero. "I've been waiting for this occasion. Good to have you back with us! You're quite a star of the firm now." He chuckled fulsomely, attempting to clap Charlie on the back, but hesitating because of the wound. "It was a fine thing you did. A fine thing. I was saying to the Governor this last weekend there aren't many lawyers who'd go to such lengths for a client, and a client taken on at less than the usual fees. Jerry was very impressed. He told me how much he respected you." Willis beamed, relishing his political plum. He thrust his hands deep into his coat pockets. "I don't know, Charlie. I doubt I'd have had your courage in the same situation." This humility obviously called for a disclaimer.

"You never know until you're there what you'll do," Charlie said, wishing he could escape.

"That's quite true," Willis said, nodding his large, leonine head sagely. "And you met the challenge and emerged with honor."

Charlie looked at Lydia and came perilously close to making a face. "Well, Willis, it left me with a lot to catch up on. I have a great many calls to make." He held up the sheaf of memos as proof. "I've lost three days already."

"Yes. Well, I won't keep you, but remember, Shannon and I are counting on having you to dinner as soon as you're up to it."

"Fine, Willis. Fine." Charlie turned and all but fled down the hall.

Once in his office, however, he sat with the memos spread out in front of him, his attention directed at the spire of the Transamerica Pyramid. He wanted to talk to Morgan, but knew he could not. He wanted to postpone his interview with Tey, but for no good reason. Most of all, he wanted to tell Willis Ogilvie to leave him alone. But that would come later. He dragged his attention back to the desk, and a few minutes later, began making calls.

*   *   *

Shortly before ten forty-five, Richard Tey walked into Charlie's office. He was dressed casually in dark slacks, a turtleneck sweater, and a rather old tweed jacket. His sandy hair was negligently brushed, but his short beard was meticulously trimmed. He moved decisively, with economy, so that his inner energy was all the more apparent. He met Charlie's dark eyes with his hot blue ones. "Charles Moon? I'm Richard Tey."

They shook hands, and Charlie said, "I'm glad to meet you at last, Mo. Tey."

"Call me Richard." He pulled up the chair nearest the desk and dropped onto it. "Sorry to have taken so long to get together with you. This new recording of the *Le Martyre de Saint Sebastian* is quite a headache. And *teen*-agers! I've got three of them. I swear they must work in relay teams. We went fishing part of the weekend. I thought I'd drop. Hell, I'm forty-six. I'm not up to that kind of nonsense any more." The crinkle around his eyes and the vigor of his movements belied that, but Charlie said nothing. "And this *commuting* to New York. Some-times I wish I had an orchestra of my own and could stop running around this way."

"Why don't you?" Charlie asked, wanting to keep Tey at ease.

"Because there are a lot more conductors than or-chestras in the world, that's why. I like doing opera. I like the Bay Area. But San Francisco and Oakland have their conductors already. So I do a lot of traveling. Last year, I went down to LA and conducted the silliest film score you ever *heard*. It was all watered-down Brahms with a little bit of quasi-Copland thrown in for a modern touch. But, God, they paid me well. I've got a family and a mortgage and all the rest of it. In a way, I'm lucky. I'm doing what I want to do, most of the time. And I have a pretty good reputation. You know, I used to live in New York." He stopped talking for a moment. "I was robbed three times—burgled. And mugged once. And somebody tried to kill my kids. That's when I said *screw* it."

Charlie's face set, memory still raw in him. "I don't blame you for moving."

Richard Tey heard the constraint in Charlie's voice and looked up sharply. "Oh, hey. I'm sorry. I heard about Wednesday. Wednesdays are damned unlucky recently."

"It seems that way, certainly," Charlie agreed at his most neutral.

"Hell, you don't want to hear about this. You want to talk about Feuier's death, don't you? I'm still rattled by it. Sorry for talking all around it this way."

The irritation Charlie had felt disappeared. "I understand."

"I don't know how much I can tell you," Richard Tey said measuringly. "I was in the pit when it happened, and I hadn't seen him backstage." He looked at Charlie squarely. "I avoided him. Because I was ready to slug him."

Everything that Charlie had learned about Feuier robbed this statement of any shock it might have had. "Why? What had he done?"

"He was ruining the production, that's what he'd done. He sang sloppily, he ignored direction, and never so much as glanced at the pit or the monitors. The prompter had given up on him before I did." Tey brought his square, muscular hands down on the desk. "One man was destroying the whole production. The production deserves better than that. The audience deserves better than that. Hell, Offenbach deserves better than that."

"Did he know how you felt?" Charlie asked as he picked up a pencil to take notes. "Had you told him?"

"Damn right he knew. I just about brained him at the final dress rehearsal." He made an exasperated sound in memory of that rehearsal. "Ty talked to me about him. He was very worried. Neither of us had any idea of what could be done to save the work."

"I gather that Feuier wasn't very reasonable," Charlie said calmly, his eyes narrowing as he studied Richard Tey's reaction.

"*Reasonable?* The only thing he thought was reasonable was the praise and aggrandizement of Gui-Adam Feuier. All the rest was inconsequent folly."

Charlie had heard enough of Feuier to find this merely repetitious. So he said, "Mo. Tey . . . Richard. There is reason to believe that Feuier was given the chemical that killed him some time during the last act of the opera."

"During? You mean onstage?"

"Possibly," Charlie said with caution. "Because of that, I'd like to know how well you remember the act."

"As an act or as something I was conducting?" Tey had moved nearer the desk and leaned forward as he asked.

"Is there a difference?"

"Sure." He drew the word out, and Charlie was irresistably reminded of extended notes and musical emphasis. "If you want to know what happened at each moment of the opera, if I was looking at the stage I can tell you."

"If you were looking at the stage? What else would you look at?" Charlie regarded Richard Tey with puzzlement.

"Why, the *orchestra*, man. There were seventy-two musicians in the pit with me, remember. I conducted them as much as the singers onstage. More, maybe." He moved back in the chair. "But, yeah, if I go over it measure by measure I think I can tell you what happened. Do you want me to try?"

This was much more than Charlie had hoped for. "If you're sure you can . . ."

"I have before. It's a technique that keeps my mistakes to a minimum. I do it after every performance—symphonic, operatic, choral, orchestral, anything." He propped his elbows on his knees and took his chin in his hands. "I haven't gone over that performance yet. I didn't want to. It might be difficult. It's been more than a week . . ."

"If you think you can't, you don't have to try. I wasn't expecting anything like this."

"No, no." Richard Tey cut short Charlie's words. "I can do it. It's going to take a little longer, that's all." He frowned into space. "God, there were so many problems with that production. Let's see. You're interested in the third act. Give me a minute." He seemed to withdraw into himself. He nodded and occasionally hummed. "Yeah. I think I can do it. Let me see."

Fascinated, Charlie leaned forward. His face was intent as he watched Richard Tey. "If you can, tell me what was going on onstage. Where people were, what they were doing."

Richard Tey nodded. "Yeah. Okay. Here goes." He closed his eyes and straightened up, his body suddenly alert. "We started out in D in six-eight time. That's the 'Barcarole.' A slow curtain up on the twenty-eighth measure, Nicklausse and Giulietta singing offstage, Nicklausse stage left, Giulietta stage right, in front of the monitors. By the sixtieth measure, the chorus starts drifting onstage. Let's see. Basses behind the sopranos, mostly over to stage right, the tenors and mezzos farther downstage left. Hoffmann enters through the arches overlooking the Grand Canal, stage right, and comes downstage. He's wearing a long cloak and a mask which Feuier always lifted. He didn't like having his face hidden. That night, let's see. He went almost all the way downstage center. I could still see him when I cued the orchestra. At measure eighty-two, Cort enters and moves toward the terrace at stage left."

"Cort? But he's the villain. Doesn't he come on later?" Charlie had remembered making a note of this in his listening.

"Usually, yes, but in this production, he is onstage most of the time. He has a wonderful costume, a black, embroidered Napoleonic coat, almost as if he were going to sing Scarpia. He drifts into the background by the terrace, almost like a shadow. You have to look to see him . . ." Richard Tey stopped and frowned. "No, wait a minute. He didn't do it in that performance. Feuier was masking him, I think. That must have been it." He opened his eyes and looked at Charlie. "He went to the other side of the stage."

"What was there?" Charlie asked, though he had a good idea already.

"Oh, a great big papier-mâché feast. There was an alcove beside it. Cort went and disappeared into it."

"Immediately?" Charlie watched Richard Tey very closely.

"No." Tey said it slowly. "No. He stopped by the table and turned, focusing on Feuier, with the rest of the chorus. He was three-quarters back, facing Feuier. The effect was good, considering. It was better when he could get onto the terrace, but with Feuier taking up center stage . . ."

"How long did he stand there?" Charlie asked.

"Oh, six, seven measures."

"In minutes?" Charlie already had some idea after his numerous listenings to the opera.

"Maybe two." Richard Tey shrugged. "Everyone was looking at Feuier. The 'Barcarole' was coming to an end then. The chorus was getting into position for the 'Couplets Bacchiques.' It's a drinking song. Six-eight time in A flat. There's a brief recitativo before it begins. Hoffmann is brought wine, takes a healthy swig of it, and starts the song."

"Where did the wine come from?" Charlie hated to ask that question and anticipated the answer.

"One of the supers brings it to him." Richard Tey

scowled. "He was a little late with it, because of the repositioning that Cort had to do. Feuier was supposed to have it on *Le rire à la bouche,* and didn't get it until the intro to the 'Couplets.' By that time, Elise was hanging on his arm, glaring at him as if she wanted his balls on a stick. Which she probably did."

"Where did the super get the wine?" Charlie had to drag it out of Tey now, but he knew the answer.

"It was on the supper table—" Quite suddenly Tey stopped. In another, softly horrified voice, he said, "On the supper table."

All Charlie could do was nod.

"Holy shit! But he couldn't have done it."

"Were you watching him every moment?"

"No, of course not. That's a transition, and half my attention was on the orchestra."

"Was anyone watching Cort?" How weary he felt suddenly! Charlie wanted to lean his head on his hand. He thought perhaps he had come back to work too early, that he was still feeling the effects of the flesh wound in his shoulder. But he knew that had nothing to do with it.

"Hell, no. We were all watching Feuier. We had to." Tey got up impulsively and moved restlessly around the room. "This is completely *insane!* It doesn't make any sense. The risks, man, no one would . . ."

"Are you sure?" Charlie forced himself to speak sharply.

"Of course I'm sure. Cort couldn't have. He's a civilized man. I mean, sure, he's got reason to hate Feuier, better reason than most of us. But to do this onstage? In front of everyone? There were over three thousand people in the house. I can't believe *any*one would try . . . something like that."

"But you said yourself you were watching Feuier. And Cort was standing three-quarters back."

"Yeah, but *he* was watching Feuier, too. Everyone

focused on Feuier then. There was no way . . ."

"Do you like magic, Richard?" Charlie asked conversationally.

"Magic? What does that have to do with . . ."

"I go to the Magic Cellar a lot. It's a nightclub. Magicians work there. There's a popular trick called the cut and restored rope, and I know how it's done. I've got the instructions at home. I've tried it a couple of times. But when Martin or Harry or Vic do it, even though I know what they're doing and how they're doing it, I can't see it. It's partly skill, and it's mostly misdirection." He waited while Richard Tey thought this over.

"But he couldn't," Tey said a few moments later. "There was no way. Even standing right there by the table, how could he have done it? Besides, Cort isn't the kind of man to commit murder. It isn't in him."

Charlie nodded heavily. "Don't bet on it. He had a reason. An excellent reason, you said so yourself. The test is method, motive, and opportunity. Cort's a chemist, did you know that? He's got an MS in biochemistry." He felt terrible saying it, but now he could no longer doubt. "If it had been your wife, how would you feel?"

Richard Tey drew his brows together. "I don't know that much about it. I know she killed herself. There were a lot of unpleasant rumors about her and Feuier . . ." He stopped, his voice breaking off like the end of a note. "Feuier took a lot of the wine that night."

Something more occurred to Charlie. "He might not have planned it very long ago. Did he make that compensatory movement in other performances?" He wanted to find some mitigating circumstance for Cort Nørrehavn, while at the same time he felt a sympathy for the man. "Can you remember?"

"Yeah." Richard Tey leaned heavily onto one foot. "Yeah, the first night, Feuier practically *lived* downstage center. Cort made that cross then, too. I remember that he talked briefly to Ty about what Feuier was doing with the blocking but asked him not to make an issue of it. He said he could manage." Richard Tey's eyes grew even more intense. "I thought then about how professional he was being, and what discipline he had."

"You were right about him," Charlie said carefully. "He has professionalism and discipline. You don't know what he might have gone through, just being in the same room with Feuier." He reminded himself that it was not his job to find excuses for Cort Nørrehavn. Then he asked, "Could you say, for sure, under oath, that Cort in any way tampered with the wine?"

Richard Tey blanched. "What do you mean?"

"I mean, did you actually see him do anything to the wine? Anything at all. Did he touch it? Pick up the glass?"

"Hell, no." Richard Tey began to stride the width of the office, his hands moving as if he were conducting his own conflicting emotions. "I told you, everyone was watching Feuier. All I can say for sure is that Cort stood near it. So did half the chorus. Jocelynne even handled the glass once, when Feuier started the second verse of the 'Couplets.' *She* might have done something to it, herself." His expression darkened. "Maybe she did."

"Do you really think so?" Charlie knew the answer but waited while Richard Tey considered it.

"No," he admitted. "I don't think she did anything to it. But I don't think Cort did anything, either." He stood still for a moment. "Christ, man, we're talking about deliberate murder, not some kind of prank! Cort Nørrehavn isn't the type . . ."

"Is there a type? I've met murders who were meek, mild sorts, as well as raving lunatics. Besides, whether it's deliberate murder or not, do you like Ty Malcomb or Domenico Solechiaro any better in the role?"

"Ty?" Richard scoffed. "He's got reason to want

Feuier out of the way, but he'd never do something that
would harm the Opera Company."

"Make the cops believe that," Charlie interpolated.

"And Nico. *Nico?*"

"He's the other one the police are most interested in.
Solechiaro, Ty Malcomb, and Cort. "Well?" Charlie began
to drum his fingers on the desk.

"But that's ridiculous! Nico wouldn't harm anyone."

"Nevertheless," Charlie said quietly, "he's one of the
most likely suspects. He was backstage. He had access to
Feuier. There was serious trouble between them, over
Solechiaro's sister. It seems plausible enough for the
cops."

"It's *preposterous!*" Richard Tey declared emphatically.

"More so than Nørrehavn or Malcomb?"

"Absolut . . ." Tey stopped. "Oh God; oh, God; oh,
God." He sank into the nearest chair and clapped his
hands over his eyes. "Cort." He muttered something to his
hands, then looked up at Charlie once more. "But he's the
best of the lot of them."

Charlie nodded, feeling desolate. "I know. I know."

Like all grand Nob Hill hotels, this one had an inescap-
able, subdued richness. At the end of the hall, a large vase
was filled with fresh flowers, and the table it stood on was
genuine Empire. This particular floor was made up
entirely of suites, and on each door there was a discreet
brass fitting in which the name and apartment number of
the occupant was inserted. Charlie stopped at the one that
said NØRREHAVN, NUMBER 458.

From inside, there was the sound of a piano and
singing. The phrase was a long one and building. *"Gli
uomini in dii mutare/e in un sol bacio e abbraccio/tutte le genti
amar!/e in un sol bacio e abbraccio/tutte le genti amar!"*

Charlie was about to knock when the music changed and continued. *"Or io rinnego il santo grido!/ Io d'odio ho colmo il core . . ."*

"No," Cort Nørrehavn said impatiently as the music struggled to a stop. "No, that is not the way. You see, here there is this idealism, pure, he says he was, wanting to make men gods with a single kiss. But then, you see, the change. It must sting. It must reveal how utterly he had fallen away from his ideal. See how the phrasing goes . . ." He started to sing again, without accompaniment.

As much as he wanted to wait, listening, Charlie knew that he had to knock, to stop the singing. He raised his hand and rapped gently, just enough to be heard.

Once again the singing broke off, and Charlie heard steps approaching. The door was opened by Cort Nørrehavn, who gave Charlie a quizzical look. "Ty called and said you wanted to speak to me?" This ended like a question, on an upward reflection.

"Yes."

"I see. This is my practice time. Will you be long?" He nodded toward the living room of the suite. "My accompanist can only stay another ten minutes."

"Whatever you wish," Charlie said, stepping inside as Cort motioned for him to enter.

"It's important?" Cort did not wait for an answer. "Yes, of course it is. You would not be here if it were trivial. Very well. I'll ask Mr. Dunne to come back this evening." He returned to the living room as he spoke and nodded to the young man seated at the piano. "Mr. Moon, this is Mr. Dunne. The University of California has been kind enough to lend him to me for my stay here."

The pianist was very young, certainly no more than twenty-one or twenty-two. He was obviously very much in awe of the Danish baritone. Rather bewildered, he rose and took Charlie's outstretched hand. "Mr. Moon? Glad to meet you."

Cort nodded and turned his attention to Dunne. "I'd like you to work some more on the *Chénier*. I'm not wholly prepared, and I must sing it in seven weeks. Remember, Gérard must change completely from one line to the next. Put the sting into the music, as Giordano wanted you to." He put one hand on the young man's shoulder. "You are doing very well. But I, I fear, am a perfectionist. Even my wife, when she accompanied me . . ." He looked away. "Tonight, then. Shall we say around seven?"

"Seven. I'll be here." Dunne was already gathering up his music and stuffing it into a small attaché case. "Thanks a lot for everything, Mr. Nørrehavn." He snapped the case shut and all but bolted for the door.

When he had gone, Cort shrugged eloquently. "He's so very earnest. Cooperative to a fault. Yet I can hardly endure him. The years with Linnet . . ." A fleeting look of pain crossed his face and was gone again. "Well, Charlie, what do you want to say to me?"

Now that he faced Cort, Charlie found he could not speak in the way he had intended at first. He went to the window and turned so that his face would be in shadow. "About Feuier."

"Ah. I guessed as much. What about him?" Cort came leisurely across to the elegant little sofa beside the piano. He sat down, waiting for Charlie to go on.

"He was on heroin, you know."

"So I understand."

For a moment, Charlie considered simply leaving. It was contrary to everything he believed in as an attorney, but his humanity bothered him. "I've done some more investigating, as I told Ty I would. The police are investigating as well, now that they're certain a crime has, in fact, been committed."

"I'm aware of that. An Inspector McAllister called me yesterday. His questions were most polite and very general in nature." Nothing in Cort's contained, intelligent face revealed alarm, but Charlie sensed that he was very much troubled.

"Cort," Charlie said, quite suddenly, "no matter what, there's no evidence strong enough to convict . . . anyone. There are too many variables. A good lawyer could tear the case to pieces in a few minutes. Without a confession, there's nothing that can convince anyone beyond a reasonable doubt. There's not even enough evidence to bring the case to trial. All anyone can do is guess, and guesses are not admissible as evidence." He realized that he was pleading with Cort, and the slightly withdrawn expression in the Dane's serious eyes worried him.

Cort nodded, touching his lower lip thoughtfully. "I see. You are telling me that perhaps there will be no trial?"

"Perhaps. There are suspicions, of course."

"Naturally," Cort agreed. "Given a man like Feuier."

"And you're a likely target for some of those suspicions," Charlie continued, wishing it were easier to explain.

"Of course," Cort agreed, watching Charlie.

"There are questions revolving around Ty Malcomb, too. He and Feuier did not get along well."

Cort made a terse gesture of scorn. "Ty? Never. He's an honorable man, and he has too much at stake here to risk it on such scum as Feuier." There was very little emotion in Cort's face, and only the crispness of his speech suggested his feeling.

"The other questions concern Solechiaro."

At that Cort sat upright. "Nico? Impossible!"

"The police don't think so, Any more than they think Ty is blameless. Their suspicions could hurt both of them . . . and you, very much. If Feuier's death remains a mystery, there will be questions following you and Solechiaro and Ty Malcomb for many years. Those questions will affect the Opera, too. Matters are difficult enough without that." He saw a strange look flicker across Cort's face.

"*Jeg har gjort en farfærdelig fejl*," Cort said softly. Then he looked up at Charlie. "Feuier was a monster." He said this in a tone so cold that Charlie almost flinched. "He ruined everything he touched."

"It doesn't matter to the law," Charlie murmured, his chest tight with sorrow.

"Linnet was the light of my soul. Without her, even this, my music, is . . . stale." Cort got up then and walked to the piano. He touched the keys with his right hand, and fragments of melody, hesitantly played, sounded in the room. "Do you know *Boccanegra*? It is a gem for baritone. Simon dies of poison, very slowly, even by operatic standards." The remnant of a smile pulled at his mouth. "In the end, he sings of his dear mistress, that he'll be with her once more. I don't believe in heaven, Charlie. Or in hell." He changed the melody again, somber chords announcing a formal doom. "In *Don Giovanni*, I've been dragged to hell innumerable times. It's ceased to be real."

"It might never come to trial, Cort. You know that no one will be arraigned unless there's a very convincing case against him. The way things stand now, that's impossible." Charlie clenched his free hand at his side.

Cort seemed not to have heard him. "None of it is real any more."

"Was Feuier supposed to die slowly?" Charlie had not moved from his place before the window and was grateful for the light at his back. He wondered if Cort could see his face at all, and if he could, what he read there.

"I didn't know about the heroin until later. But it makes sense. Something Linnet said, the last time she called me." He put his hand flat, discordantly on the keys. "Vengeance is a very empty thing, did you know that?"

Charlie cleared his throat. "Not that way, perhaps. But I know why you might want it."

"Do you? Well, I suppose you're fortunate. They say it's rare to love deeply." He moved away from the piano. "I had forgotten how much I could hate. And now that, too, is gone." He looked down at his hands. "When I was very young, not quite sixteen, I killed two Gestapo officers. One was very high-ranking. I used a garrote on one of them, and on the other a knife. Afterward, I felt completely numb, as if the soul had gone out of me. I was unable to sing for more than a year."

"Cort, you . . . the murderer . . . of Feuier, there's no way now that he could be punished. It would be very easy for him to get away with the crime."

As he glanced again at the piano, Cort said, "I suppose I ought to thank you for this. You could have done this another way. Am I wrong in suspecting that this is not entirely legal?"

"I know more than one code of laws, and I have no proof, only a guess and a certain amount of circumstantial evidence. Certainly not enough to make an arrest possible, not in a case like this with so many possible suspects involved." Charlie stepped nearer to Cort. "I thought you should know. It's your choice, after all."

"So it is," Cort said lightly. "My choice."

Charlie had rarely seen such loneliness as there was in Cort's face then. "Is there anything you want me to do? Would you like to retain me? You should have help. If you'd rather talk to some other attorney, I'll recommend one. Ty can get you help, too. He'll do anything he can for you."

"Indeed," Cort said, looking away.

"For God's sake, decide quickly. I'm an officer of the court. I have certain obligations in this matter. I can't keep what I know to myself, even though it might make no difference. My knowledge can't count as evidence. Unless there is a signed confession or something tangible I know nothing about."

Cort spoke dreamily. "I won't ask that of you."

Feeling very helpless, Charlie closed his hand again. "Don't try to deal with this alone, Cort. Please."

"But it's my choice." Cort looked at Charlie then, a sad twist to his mouth. "I need some time to myself, Charlie. As you have made so clear, there are decisions to be made." He indicated the door. "You have done all you could, and more. There is nothing left for you to do." He was moving toward the door, gently signaling Charlie to leave.

But Charlie hesitated a moment longer, searching for something to say to Cort that might rouse him from this terrifying quiet. "I know I can help you."

"Perhaps. Later. But now I need time to myself." He opened the door. "You need not fear for me, Charlie. I understand what you have told me. I should have expected it. No, I'm not frightened. Don't concern yourself. I'm not . . . anything."

Charlie paused in the door. "Look, give me a call when you've thought this over, will you? There are special circumstances . . ."

"Of course," Cort said urbanely, smoothly polite. Then he met Charlie's eyes for an instant. "I would never have let Nico hang, or Ty."

As the door closed behind him, Charlie felt a tide of despair run through him. He knew he had failed. How would he tell Ty of this? he asked himself as he started down the hall. He had an oath to honor, an oath to uphold the law. But how would he explain that to

Elizabeth, or to Domenico? He pushed the button and waited for the elevator, trying not to think at all. Murder was never justified. If it was, then the law was a travesty, and Charlie believed in the law. The devastation of Cort Nørrehavn's life rose around him like quicksand as the elevator doors opened. The law had not saved Cort. It had not saved Linnet. He stepped into the cage.

The elevator doors closed as Charlie touched a button, and the questions followed him down. What would he tell Ty? What would he tell McAllister? What would he tell Solechiaro, Tey, Morgan? When the elevator stopped at the ground floor, Charlie lingered inside, faced with the most difficult question of all—what would he tell himself?